Mia focused on the Levines' Santa's workshop display across the street, now lit up as if it were the middle of a sunny day. A gingerbread-style house the size of a child's playhouse represented the workshop. A half-dozen smiling elves stood sentry around it. A pair of feet stuck out from the workshop's front door. This puzzled Mia. "Nonna," she yelled, "did you add something to the Levines' display?"

"Huh?" Elisabetta blinked a few times.

Mia put her hands on her grandmother's shoulder and turned her toward the Levines' house. "There. In the workshop. Did you add elf feet?"

"What? No. Why would we do that? It doesn't look like Christmas. It looks like a house fell on a witch."

Mia got a sinking feeling in the pit of her stomach. She took her mother's hand. "Come. We need to get a closer look at whatever's going on over there."

Mia and Gia hurried across the street. Mia opened the gate of the chain-link fence that surrounded the Levines' front yard. "Careful, Mom. Don't disturb anything."

"Why?"

Mia peered inside the house. Her stomach churned as her worst fears were confirmed. "Because," she said to her mother, "this is a crime scene . . ."

Books by Maria DiRico

HERE COMES THE BODY

LONG ISLAND ICED TINA

IT'S BEGINNING TO LOOK A LOT LIKE MURDER

Published by Kensington Publishing Corp.

A CATERING HALL MYSTERY

It's Beginning to Look a Lot Like Murder

Maria DiRico

KENSINGTON
PUBLISHING CORP.

www.kensingtonbooks.com

This book is dedicated to
Elisabetta DiVirgilio Seideman. *Mia madre*.

CHAPTER 1

"How can you type with those nails?" Mia wondered.

The nails in question belonged to her Belle View Banquet Manor coworker, Cammie Dianopolis. 'Twas the season and Cammie's nails reflected this. Each was a true work of holiday art, extending off a finger by a full inch or more and sporting a design celebrating one of the twelve days of Christmas, with the thumbnails doing double duty to meet the required twelve days. Glitter and appliquéd rhinestones added a festive sparkle.

"You think I type. That's adorable." Cammie held up her cell phone. "I'm recording our business conversations—i.e., this one. I have an app that'll transcribe it and turn it into a doc I can print out and read while I'm getting my pedicure." She checked her phone. "Which reminds me, I gotta leave for my appointment in fifteen."

"Is it too much to ask that you at least put in a full morning here?"

"Yes." Cammie wagged a finger at Mia. Sunlight glinted off a ruby-red rhinestone. "Must I constantly remind you of our deal?"

"You will continue to work here if by *work*, we mean coasting." Mia recited this by rote. She and her father, banquet hall owner Ravello Carina, put up with Cammie's absenteeism for several reasons: despite her lax office hours, she always delivered; she was a close friend; and her ex-husband was Detective Pete Dianopolis. Pete wrote self-published thrillers under the pen name Steve Stianopolis. Assuming he would be the next Lee Child or James Patterson and being a cheapskate, Pete begged out of his twenty-five-year marriage before the money he envisioned poured in and made him a chick magnet. When the pour turned out to not even be a trickle, he skulked back to his ex. Pete would do anything to win back Cammie, which included providing the occasional stealth info on a couple of murder investigations that had dogged Belle View and the Carinas.

Mia glanced out the small window behind her. It was December and snow blanketed the banquet hall parking lot, which it shared with the Flushing Bay Marina. In the distance lay the bay—and the LaGuardia Airport runway. As if on cue, a plane roared above them, on its final approach to the airport. The room's furnishings vibrated for a moment, then stopped. "Getting a pedicure in the winter seems like a waste of money," Mia said.

"Oh, for sure. But it's a waste of Pete's money, not mine. Plus, going over the notes from this morning as someone pampers my tootsies is my idea of multitasking."

The women heard a light rap on the doorframe and looked up to see Shane Gambrazzo, former male model and current Belle View employee, standing there, his six-three perfect physique filling the doorframe. With his chiseled features, windswept, naturally blond hair, and pale green eyes that provided a perfect contrast to his tawny complexion, Shane was an easy candidate for handsomest man alive—which he absolutely hated. He was determined to live down his magazine cover-boy past and prove his worth in the event industry. As far as Mia was concerned, Shane was doing exactly that and then some. In the mere few months he'd worked at Belle View, bookings had increased exponentially. She was convinced some women—and a few men—invented events simply to breathe the same air as Shane. If he noticed, Shane chose to ignore it, instead focusing on negotiating great deals on everything from rentals to bulk toilet paper. Shane was proving to be a dreamy-come-true employee.

"Just wanted to let you know that I got the signed contract for the Adrianakis-Mahmoud wedding."

"They were talking about a guest list of four hundred," Mia said. "That's major coin. Great work." She avoided eye contact and delivered the compliment to a spot above Shane's shoulder, which was the best way to dodge getting sucked into his vortex of gorgeousness. "I don't know if you saw it, but I emailed a list of prospective clients who specifically asked for you to lead their tour of the facilities."

"Oh." Shane didn't seem happy about this. "Are you sure you're okay with that? Me giving all these tours instead of you? I feel like that's happening more and more."

Mia, remaining focused on the spot, waved a hand to dismiss his fears. "I could not be more okay with it. I've got plenty on my plate and welcome the extra time."

"If you say so." Shane didn't sound remotely convinced.

"Hey Shane, you got any special Christmas plans? Like, with *someone* special?" Cammie was fascinated by the newest staff member. Using her endless hours of free time to Google him, it was she who discovered the cover boy–playboy past he seemed determined to put behind him. Cammie was equally determined to match him with Mia, which entailed sussing out the competition.

Mia shot Cammie a warning look to back off. But Shane, who was on to Cammie's attempts at data retrieval, simply shrugged. "Probably just stay home and recover from all our holiday parties."

Mia applauded Shane's efforts to keep his relationships at Belle View purely professional, even passing up the boozy party postmortems the staff occasionally indulged in. The downside of this was Shane coming across as "a stiff," as Mia's frenemy Teri Fuoco bluntly put it. Teri, a nosy reporter with the local e-paper, the *Triborough Tribune*, had finagled a few dates with Mia's sous and dessert chef, Evans, giving her more opportunities than Mia liked to hang out at Belle View.

There was a pause in the conversation. Considering Shane's past wild exploits, Mia thought he exuded a surprising awkwardness when it came to social interaction at Belle View. She worried he might not feel like a fit with her and her coworkers and vowed to do whatever it took to make him happy. She even managed to convince herself this was for purely professional reasons.

"Do you have plans?" Shane asked the women, succumbing to the pressure of engaging with her and Cammie.

"There's the party here for everyone Christmas Eve," Mia said, "which I hope you'll come to. Christmas Day, I'm gonna visit Posi in jail"—Mia's older brother, unable to break his habit of stealing sports cars and selling them to rich Eastern Europeans, was finishing a sentence at a nearby minimum-security facility—"and then I'll probably have a quiet dinner with my dad and *nonna*. You're welcome to join us."

"Thank you," Shane said, his tone polite. Mia tamped down her disappointment at the pro forma non-response.

"My plan is to milk Pete for all the gifts I can get out of him," Cammie said, her tone bright.

"Mmm-hmm," Shane said, unsure of how to respond. "Well . . . I'll check out the list you sent me, Mia, and start booking the tours."

Shane left for his own office. Mia released a breath and deflated. Cammie eyed her. "You're gonna have to make eye contact someday."

"Not if I can help it."

Cammie gave an irritated grunt. "*Peismatáris os moulári.* Stubborn as a mule." She made a face at Mia and picked up the bottle of circa-1980s mauve nail polish she'd bought from a site that sold discontinued cosmetics. Cammie had landed on a style during that flashy decade and still swore by it, down to a wardrobe and makeup built around the period's signature colors of peach, turquoise, and the aforementioned mauve.

Cammie headed off for her winter pedicure. Mia's cell rang. She checked the caller ID and bit her lower lip. Kaitlyn Venere's super sweet sixteen was the current bane of Mia's existence—that and the Bianchis, new parents who insisted on what Mia considered a wildly inappropriate Nativity theme for their baby's first birthday, with the family in the roles of Joseph, Mary, and baby Jesus. But teen Kaitlyn's effort to keep up with or even, God willing, outdo her uber-competitive classmates with her celebration, made her a hormonal roller coaster of emotions and drama. Mia dreaded Kaitlyn's calls but also felt for the girl, whose parents had basically given their daughter a blank check, then cut and run from the planning.

Mia steeled herself, then pressed the green button on her cell phone. "Hi, Kaitlyn."

"Daniella Di Nunzio stole my Tiffany's theme!" The news was accompanied by histrionic sobs. "I thought Grace Haddad was my friend, but she wants to get in Daniella's group, so she told her my theme and now she's friends with her and not with me and Daniella's doing my theme and I hate her, and I hate Grace!"

Mia fumed on Kaitlyn's behalf. High school was no picnic for anyone, but social media, reality shows, and influencers seemed to have turned it into a cutthroat hellscape for the current generation, where no secret was safe, and no friend could be trusted. "I'm so sorry. But let her have the Tiffany's theme. We can do better."

"We can?" Kaitlyn sniffled but sounded hopeful. "How?"

Caught, Mia tap-danced. "I've got a bunch of ideas floating around in my brain," she lied. "Let me narrow it down to the best of them and get back to you."

"Okay. Thanks, Mia."

"Of course. That's what I'm here for. Don't worry about a thing. You're gonna have the best party ever."

"I have to, or my life is *over!*"

Kaitlyn delivered this with the force of a Greek tragedian and signed off. Mia groaned and shook a fist at the heavens. Then she texted Shane: **We need a new theme for Kaitlyn.**

Another one?! he texted back.

Yup. Mia accompanied this with a line of crying emojis, which Shane responded to with a bitmoji of himself with his head exploding. *Even his avatar is gorgeous*, Mia thought. She followed this with some internal scolding. Shane shot her another text, this one about the first birthday revolving around a manger: **The Bianchis want camels for their wise men.**

Of course they do she wrote back. A minute later, Shane sent her a cartoon of a camel dancing, set to the Bangles' "Walk Like an Egyptian." Mia chortled. Her personal interactions with Shane might border on robotic, but they enjoyed a warm, jokey camaraderie through technology.

Her cell rang again. Mia looked at it askance. She relaxed when she saw the caller wasn't Kaitlyn. She didn't recognize the number and decided to let it go to voicemail, in case the call was spam. Mia opened her internet browser and tapped in *unique sweet sixteen themes*. A list popped up that proved to be no help at all, being that she and Shane had already burned through most of them with Kaitlyn. She debated better wording and went with *over-the-top sweet sixteen parties.* Her cell rang again. The screen showed the same number as before. *Whoever it is really wants to talk to me.* Mia took the call.

"Mia, *bella*, hello. It's Donny."

She sat up straight, the sweet sixteen forgotten. Donny was Donny Boldano, head of the Boldano crime family. Her father Ravello had been a lieutenant in the organization, but now ran Belle View as a legitimate business for them, much to Mia's relief, as well as her father's, who had burned out on running the family's illegal gambling enterprises. "Mr. B, hi. How are you?"

"Good. Good. I'm calling from a burner phone."

"Yeah, I wondered. I didn't recognize the number." Mia's heart thumped like a bass drum. Why was Donny Boldano calling her instead of Ravello? And from a burner phone? She panicked for a moment, thinking it might be bad news about her beloved father, but calmed down when she reminded herself that she'd seen him leave his office for the men's room only ten minutes earlier. He was still in the building. And probably still in the men's room. Which made Donny's call all the more curious.

"You're probably wondering why I'm calling you. Especially from a burner phone."

Donny wasn't exactly reading her mind. These were obvious questions under the circumstances. "Yes. Exactly."

"Uh . . ." There was a long pause. Whatever Donny had to say wasn't coming easy. Mia's heart thumped again. "Mrs. B and I would like to talk to you about something. Don't worry, it's not business," he hastened to add. "Everything's good with Belle View. You're not in trouble."

"Oh, thank God," Mia couldn't help saying.

"It's . . . um . . . a personal matter. Do you happen to be free tonight?"

Mia, whose social life over the past few months had consisted of feeding her cat and bird, then falling asleep in front of the TV or her laptop screen, said, "Yes. I am free."

"Wonderful. I don't want you getting stuck in rush hour traffic, so let's say eight. We'll have cake and coffee. Oh, and sweetheart—please don't mention this to Jamie."

"No worries. He's been so busy with school and Madison, I haven't seen or spoken to him in weeks."

Donny signed off. Mia leaned back in her chair and considered the odd conversation. Jamie Boldano was the youngest of the *capo di capo*'s two sons. He eschewed the family business to become a teacher and was now working toward a master's degree that would allow him to transition into a career as a family therapist. When Mia returned to New York after her adulterous husband was presumed dead in a boating accident, she and Jamie had danced around the possibility of picking up a relationship that had petered out in high school. But they soon came to realize their lives were headed in different directions. Jamie was planning to move into his girlfriend Madison's apartment in Manhattan, but his eventual goal was a therapy practice and white picket fence home in Connecticut. Mia was a proud outer boroughs girl whose dream was eventually owning her own Astoria two-family home, preferably right next door to the one she currently shared with her *nonna*, Elisabetta.

She heard lumbering footsteps coming down the hall, indicating her father's approach. A minute later, Ravello appeared at her door. He looked perturbed. "*Bambina*, I'm lost."

"You don't mean that literally, I hope," a nervous Mia said. At a recent Belle View birthday party for a centenarian with a touch of dementia, the guest of honor had been found wandering the parking lot coatless in twenty-degree weather after getting off-track on his way back to the Marina Ballroom from the bathroom. Fortunately, Mia had discovered the elderly man before frostbite set in and steered him back to the ballroom in time to blow out two of the one hundred candles on his birthday cake.

"No, thank God." Ravello, reliving that frightening moment, crossed himself.

"Lin's present?" Mia guessed. Her father had a girl-friend for the first time since his marriage to her mother Gia had been annulled almost six years prior. Lin Yueng was an elegant former attorney who owned a florist's shop in the East Village. Ravello was smitten when he took her flower-arranging class on a cruise and had pur-sued the relationship from the sea onto dry land. Mia wasn't ashamed to admit she'd take the lovely Lin over her own mother Gia, a beautiful narcissist now living in Italy with her second husband, a low-level crook who'd been deported after serving a sentence for a variety of petty crimes. If threatened with waterboarding, Mia wouldn't be able to recall her last conversation with Gia.

Ravello parked himself on one of the two folding chairs in Mia's office. He ran a hand through his thick thatch of hair, which remained dark brown without a speck of gray despite his fifty-plus years. "Lin's so . . . classy. I don't know from classy. With your mother, it was all about the bling. Lin doesn't even wear jewelry ex-cept tiny little gold stuff. And clothes? Fuhgeddaboudit."

"Let me talk to Madison. She might have some inter-esting ideas. And deals." Mia had come to like Jamie's girlfriend. They'd bonded the way women who'd dated the same man often did—by making good-natured fun of his quirks behind his back. Madison, a blogger at a popu-lar fashion website, had also endeared herself to Mia with her connections and discounts. "But here's an interesting development, Dad. Donny Boldano called. He wants me to meet with him and Aurora tonight. Just us. And not tell Jamie."

Ravello stared at his daughter. "Just you?" he repeated.

Mia nodded. "Any idea what it might be about?"

Her father shook his head. "Not a clue." Ravello crossed his arms in front of his chest. His face darkened. "And I don't like that. I don't like that one bit."

CHAPTER 2

Being that it was early December, night had already fallen when Mia left Belle View to run home and grab a quick dinner before the drive to the Boldanos. She'd calmed her father down, reassuring him that there was no menace in Donny's tone. Over the past few months, Donny had expressed pleasure multiple times about the uptick in business at Belle View. Mia's only concern was a fear that Donny and Aurora had hatched a plan to try and reunite her with Jamie. Mia knew Jamie's father hadn't been happy when his son fell in love with a non-Italian girl. But as far as she knew, Donny had come around. She'd even heard him brag about Madison's *Mayflower* passenger ancestors. Personally, Mia thought that if everyone who claimed they had *Mayflower* ancestors actually had them, the boat would have sunk leaving its British harbor. But there was no denying blond, blue-eyed Madison's Waspy origin story.

Mia drove her pre-owned Honda Civic through Astoria, past street after street gussied up to the nth degree for the holidays. The neighborhood observed the old-fashioned tradition of decorating the weekend after Thanksgiving, and the decorations went up with blinding, blinking lights, an exorbitant-electric-bill extravagance that made sunglasses at night not a song but a necessity. Lawns and roofs featured a rainbow of lights and blow-up figures. Every door and window frame glowed. The displays were shameless in their gaudy abandon. A entire home on Forty-first Place was dressed up as a gingerbread house. Even the home's roof featured an arrangement of lights designed to look like tiles made of candy. On Forty-second Place, a sign in the yard shared the call letters of a radio station where anyone could tune in for holiday songs timed to the house's light display. *It's like every Target in America emptied its holiday displays here*, Mia thought as she drove by a house programmed to cast laser snowflakes on itself.

There was a method to the decorating madness. Each year, one block won a cheesy gnome Santa Claus trophy for best decorations. More importantly, every home's front yard featured a box mounted on a pole to collect donations for charity. A second trophy went to the block that raised the most money for their chosen nonprofit. Mia and Elisabetta's block, Forty-sixth Place, was raising money for the local animal rescue.

Mia stopped for a red light. While she waited for the light to change, her attention wandered over to the two-family house on the corner. Known locally as the Miracle on Forty-fifth Place, the home belonged to Jacinta Benedetto, contemporary to Mia's grandmother and Christmas display archrival. For the most part, Jacinta's decorations were on a par with her neighbors. But one item set her apart from all others. In the dead center of her small yard stood a four-foot animatronic of adored Astoria native son Tony Bennett, dressed as Santa Claus. And Tony Benne-Santa not only moved, he sang, crooning "Have Yourself a Merry Little Christmas" in his famed mellow tones. Mia's grandmother Elisabetta, a lifelong Tony Bennett fan, coveted the one-of-a-kind treasure. The fact haughty Jacinta could claim the crooner as a distant cousin on her husband's side—the legendary singer's birth name was Benedetto—only fueled Elisabetta's competitive streak.

The light changed and Mia continued on her way, passing her own home. The Carinas might not have Tony Benne-Santa, but their display stood up to the rest of the neighborhood's outdoor décor. The tiny front yard was a forest of fake trees, decorated within an inch of their artificial life with lights in all sizes and a rainbow of colors. The front door was wrapped like a gift in red satin with a giant green bow in the middle of it. The door and every window were outlined with more lights. Elisabetta had wanted every light in the tableau on chaser mode but Mia, fearful the visual fracas might trigger a seizure in an observer, managed to talk her out of it.

Since she only planned on a brief stop, Mia parked in the alley behind her house and traipsed through the snow to the storm cellar door. She pulled it open and scurried down a short flight of stairs into the home's finished basement. With its dark wood paneling and reproductions of paintings featuring children with giant doe eyes, the space was a throwback to the early 1960s. The basement included a second kitchen, a time capsule of white tin cabinets and a stove that was pushing seventy but still worked. A vintage wringer washer usually draped with Elisabetta's drying homemade pasta sat squat in the kitchen's far corner.

A long table took up the entire center of the room. Usually the site of Sunday dinners with the extended family, this night it was covered with strands of Christmas lights, which were being untangled by Elisabetta, Mia's peppery octogenarian grandmother, and a few of the Italian and Greek grandmothers who'd lived on the block for fifty, sixty, even seventy years and were affectionately dubbed "Nonna's Army" by her amused granddaughter. Philip Barnes-Webster, younger than the rest of the army by decades, was the latest addition to the posse. He'd moved to the block in the spring with his husband Finn, toddler Eliza, and baby Justin. Once Philip proved he wanted to fit in with the neighborhood, not gentrify it, he and his family had been warmly welcomed into the generally Mediterranean fold.

Elisabetta, whose wardrobe was mostly a selection of velour tracksuits, was clad in a red-and-green holiday number that featured a heavily sequined reindeer on the back of the hoodie. "*Ciao, Mia bella*," she greeted her granddaughter without glancing up from her task.

"*Ciao*, Nonna. Hi, everyone." The others returned her greeting in a variety of Italian, Greek, and English responses. Mia took in the crowded tabletop as she shed her winter coat, a black woolen designer number Madison had scored for her at an unbelievably good price. "More lights? Nonna, we have nowhere to put them. The house already looks like it could be on one of those extreme holiday decorations shows."

"These aren't for us. I reached the Levines. They're in Florida for the winter but gave me the okay to decorate their yard, as long as it's not religious. We're going with a Santa's workshop theme with a cute little elves' house and lots of toys, which will go to needy children on Christmas Day."

"That should work."

"We need all the help we can get if we wanna beat that Jacinta Benedetto." Elisabetta curled her lip. According to Carina family lore, Elisabetta's enmity with her neighbor dated back to her teens, when Jacinta moved into the neighborhood and promptly elbowed Elisabetta out of the way to claim the title of local alpha girl.

"She's always bragging, 'My husband's Tony's cousin.'" Andrea Skarpello, who happened to be the landlord of Mia's sous-chef, Evans Tucker, said this in a derisive, singsongy tone. "Like she'd ever be on a first-name basis with Mr. Bennett. I bet she never even met him."

"She met him long enough for Mr. Bennett to give her Tony Benne-Santa," Elisabetta muttered. "The rest of her block's only okay, so if we do a good job with the Levines' yard, we might got an edge." Elisabetta gestured to Philip with her head. "Now if I could just get this one to . . . *come si dice*? How do you say?" Elisabetta had lived in America since she was a child but still spoke with an accent and preferred her native tongue. ". . . Up his game."

Unseen by Elisabetta, Mia and Philip exchanged an amused look. The Barnes-Webster décor consisted of two rows of perfectly placed white poinsettias lining the steps of their stoop and a beautiful, three-dimensional crystal snowflake dangling above their front door. The decorations couldn't be more elegant—or more out of place, given their neighbors' decorations-on-steroids. "Our snowflake is an exact replica of the UNICEF snowflake hanging over Fifth Avenue," Philip said in defense of his tableau.

Elisabetta was unimpressed. "Feh. If we're gonna win the trophy, you better . . . how do you say? Go big or go home."

Mia couldn't resist teasing her grandmother. "For someone who keeps asking, 'how do you say,' you seem to know exactly what to say."

Elisabetta ignored her. "Philip, if there's extra lights here, they're all yours."

Philip managed a strangled "thank you," then whispered to Mia, "T-a-c-k-y."

Mia felt for the poor, tasteful man. "I like an all-white theme. I even suggested it to you once, Nonna. Remember?"

Elisabetta made a face. "*Si.*"

"You almost gave your grandmother a heart attack when you brought that up," Phyllis Carullo said, her tone reproachful. The other members of the army seconded this with vigorous nods.

"It would certainly be different for the neighborhood, and make our block stand out," Mia continued, undaunted. "Maybe you could keep with white and just ratchet it up a little, Philip."

"Maybe." Philip sounded thoughtful, not doubtful, which Mia took as a good sign.

Elisabetta tossed Mia a strand of lights. "Instead of giving me grief, *rendite utile*. Make yourself useful."

Mia began unknotting the strand. "I have time to do this one and that's it. I need to scarf down something and then head out to Donny and Aurora's."

Elisabetta dropped the strand she'd picked up and stared at her granddaughter. "You're going to the Boldanos? *Ma perche?*"

"I don't know. Donny asked me to come over. He says it's personal, not business, so relax. Donny loves me. I just hope he's not trying to manipulate Jamie and me back into a relationship."

Her grandmother returned to unknotting a strand. "You need a boyfriend."

This statement engendered even more vigorous nods from Elisabetta's crew. Mia gave an annoyed grunt. "Wrong. I'm doing a whole lot better now than I was when that loser Adam was in my life. Not that I would wish death on anyone, but I am so much happier as an almost widow." Given that her husband's body had yet to turn up, Mia felt a constant need to qualify her status.

"What about that hunkadoodle-do who works with you?" Philip wiggled his eyebrows suggestively.

"*Si.* Shane." Elisabetta mimed a beating heart. All the ladies giggled.

"Argh, Nonna, I love you, but you are the *worst*. Here . . ." Mia tossed her light strand on the pile of unknotted ones. "I gotta go."

Mia hurried upstairs to her own apartment. Nonna's terrier mutt Hero barked a hello as Mia passed. She stepped over Doorstop, her beloved, but lazy ginger Abyssinian cat who lay splayed out at the apartment portal, and headed to the kitchen, where she wolfed down a serving of leftover lasagna she retrieved from one of the ancient ricotta containers her grandmother insisted on reusing until they crumbled into plastic shards. Mia debated changing into more casual clothes, then opted to stay in her work attire of low-heeled, black boots, black wool pants, and aqua turtleneck sweater that complemented her bright blue eyes. She fed her pet parakeet, Pizzazz, then heaped cat food into Doorstop's bowl. She gave him a quick pet on her way out the door, and he responded with a languid meow.

It had stopped snowing, which would make for a much better drive to the Boldano compound in Stony Harbor, an upscale town on Long Island's South Shore. As Mia slipped into the driver's seat, her phone pinged a text. A message reading **Got 'em** was accompanied by a photoshopped image of Shane as a wise man giving her a thumbs-up from atop a camel. Mia guffawed and "laughed" the image. *He even makes great memes*, she thought as she pulled out of the alley and headed toward the Island.

Given the hour and the weather, traffic was light, and Mia reached the Boldano home in record time. Casa di Boldano was a traditional, white-columned house that would have completely blended in with the neighborhood except for its surfeit of security cameras. Mia punched a code Donny had given her into the front gate, which slowly swung open. She parked in the circular front driveway. Donny, alerted to her arrival, stood waiting at the front door. Like her grandmother, Donny tended toward tracksuits for everyday wear, but tonight his short, wiry frame was clad in brown corduroy slacks and a beige V-neck sweater. *If Donny's wearing real pants and not tracksuit pants, this must be serious*, Mia thought. A wave of anxiety washed over her.

"Mia, *bella, ciao*." Donny greeted her with a kiss on

each cheek. "Aurora's waiting for us in the office." He ushered her into the foyer, then led her to his office through a series of immaculately decorated rooms that made Aurora a source of gracious inspiration for Family wives.

Mia was surprised to see that Aurora wasn't alone in the room, whose wood-paneled walls were padded for sound retention, a necessity for a "businessman" like Donny. Stefano and Vera Boldano, Donny's retired brother and sister-in-law, sat next to Aurora on the room's large sofa, sumptuously upholstered in a tweedy brown. The three rose to greet Mia with more cheek kisses. "It's great to see you," Mia said to Stefano and Vera. "I didn't know you were in town."

"Very, very briefly," Stefano said. "A quick stop on our way up from Florida to a Bermuda cruise."

"Nice."

Everyone reseated themselves, Mia and Donny opting for wingback chairs facing the sofa. Aurora lifted a tray of delectable pastries off the coffee table and offered it to Mia. "Cookie?"

"No, thank you. Well, maybe a mini-cannoli." Despite her nerves, Mia couldn't resist the treat. She also accepted a demitasse of espresso from Donny. "So . . ." Mia prompted, trying to move things along. The long day was beginning to catch up with her.

"So . . ." Donny glanced at his wife, who responded with an infinitesimal nod. "I'll get right to it. A young man has shown up on Jamie's doorstep claiming to be his long-lost brother."

"That's all this is about?" Mia said, surprised. "It's obviously a scam. And if anyone knows how to take care of a scam artist, it's you, Donny."

"The thing is . . ." Donny hesitated. "We can't be sure it is a scam."

Donny paused again. Finally, Aurora said what he didn't seem able to. "Jamie is adopted."

Mia's mouth dropped open. Since it was filled with half a mini-cannoli, she quickly shut it. She digested this stunning revelation. "Wow. Jamie never told me. We've known each other since birth. I mean, it's not like he *had* to tell me or anything, it's just—" Part two of the revelation, even more shocking, dawned on her. "He doesn't know." The room buzzed with tension. "Am I right?" She pressed. "Does Jamie know he's adopted?"

"No." Aurora dropped her head in her hands and began to weep. Her husband helplessly muttered reassurances.

A sympathetic Vera rubbed her back. "There, there, sweetie. You did what ya had to do." Vera honked this out with the New York accent she would never shed no matter how long she lived in Florida.

Aurora took a napkin from the coffee table and wiped her eyes. "I experienced complications after giving birth to Donny Junior that made another pregnancy impossible, so we adopted a second baby—James Henry Boldano. We were living in Italy at the time—"

"We all were," Stefano said. "Things were . . . a little tense in the States."

Mia knew by *tense*, he meant the heat was on the Family, hence a break in activity. "How long were you there?"

"About a year, maybe a little more," Aurora said. "We came back with Jamie. For all anyone knew here, I'd had a baby while we were there, so we kept it that way. I fell in love with Jamie the second he was placed in my arms. I knew God had a plan for him and I was that plan."

Aurora began weeping again. Stefano and Vera joined

her with sympathy tears. Mia even heard Donny sniffling. "I have to be honest," she said. "I don't know why you didn't tell Jamie. It would have explained so much to him about why he felt different from the family. And the Family. About why he always felt like he didn't fit in."

"We went old school," Donny said. "Like in the old days, when people kept news like this to themselves and a person could go to their grave without ever knowing where they really came from." The tone in Donny's voice indicated he regretted those days were long gone.

"I wanted to, but it was a hard subject to bring up," Aurora said. "And the older Jamie got, the harder it got."

Donny, angry, threw his hands up in the air. "But with all this DNA all over the place, you can't keep anything to yourself. And now this con man, this *stronzo*, shows up."

"Has Jamie's supposed brother produced any DNA evidence?"

"He showed us some vial he spit into, but I didn't look too closely." Donny said this with distaste.

Mia noted this as a sign of fraud. "The guy wouldn't be carrying around a vial. It would have been submitted to a company for testing. What's his name? And how did he glom on to Jamie? How does he even know about the adoption?"

Donny gave a helpless shrug. "His name is Lorenzo Puglia. He told us he was raised by a single mother in Sunnyside who broke the news to him that he had a brother, our Jamie, with her dying words. I smelled BS, believe me. The guy obviously thought we'd be all, *'Marone, e un miracolo!* Welcome to the family!'" Donny didn't need to spell out that would never, ever happen.

"We're bringing you into this, Mia," Aurora said, "because it's time for us to tell Jamie the truth. We have to, to save him from whatever game this Puglia character is playing. We figured it would be easier on everyone if a third party were present, someone special and close to all of us, especially Jamie. That's you. If you'll do it."

"Of course I will. Jamie's one of my best friends on earth. I can't imagine not being there for him when he finds out." Mia fought, then gave into the urge for a second mini-cannoli. "I'm not gonna lie, Mr. and Mrs. B. This is gonna be hard on him."

"We know."

Aurora's voice was strained. Her lower lip quick quivered. Vera patted her on the shoulder, then poured Aurora a finger of a bright yellow liqueur. "Nothing like a shot of Strega to take the edge off." Jamie's mother grabbed the glass and downed it.

Donny took Mia's hands in his and squeezed them. "*Mille grazie*, Mia. All we ask is that you keep this news to yourself until we meet together to tell Jamie. You can share it with your father. I trust him with my life. But no one else."

Mia nodded her agreement. A thought occurred to her. "Does Donny Junior know?" Jamie's older brother, a textbook goombah who barely made it out of high school, lived to tease his more cerebral little brother and give him grief.

Donny Senior shook his head. "We're not saying a word to Little Donny until we talk to Jamie."

"Good. I'm worried he might throw this in Jamie's face."

A bookcase suddenly rotated out of place and Donny Junior burst into the room from a secret location, eliciting startled screams from the office occupants. "I would never do that," Donny Junior declared with passion.

"Donny, what were you thinking?" his angry mother scolded. "You know your father has high blood pressure. You could have given him a stroke."

"Or me," Mia said, pouring herself a small shot of Strega. "I know you have a hidden bar, but what the hell is *that*?" She pointed to a small room behind the faux bookcase.

"It's a panic room," Donny Senior said. "We've got a few around the place. This one was a birthday present from Aurora." He glared at his son. "You got a lot of nerve, sneaking up on your family like that."

Donny Junior returned his father's glare. Even though he had half a foot on his father, he was often referred to as Little Donny by friends and family. He and "Big Donny" shared the same coloring, muddy brown eyes, and fleshy facial features, making it impossible for anyone to deny that Little Donny was a biological Boldano. "I've seen how you all been whispering to each other and shutting up the minute I came into the room. When I heard Mia was coming over by herself, I knew something was up and if you weren't gonna tell me, I was gonna do whatever it took to find out what was going on." His expression softened. "Jamie is my brother. I know we're always on each other, but I love him. And I should be part of this conversation."

His father began to protest, but Aurora cut him off. "You're right, son," she said. "You should be. We'll tell Jamie tomorrow night. At Piero's restaurant. Jamie loves Piero's mushroom pasta alla carbonara. It'll make the news go down easier."

That's so typically Italian, Mia thought. *If there's a*

problem, a dish of homemade pasta will solve it. But as far as she was concerned, there wasn't a pasta dish in the world that would ease Jamie into this revelation.

After confirming a time for Operation Come Clean with Jamie and stuffing down a few more mini-cannoli to counteract the shot of Strega, Mia left Stony Harbor for Queens. Her anxiety level roof-bound, she slept badly that night. It didn't help that Doorstop decided to snooze horizontally, reducing her bed space to around ten inches. In the morning she opted for a cold shower to shock her system awake, despite the chilly early winter weather. Mia shivered as she dressed. Since she planned to go to Piero's straight from work, she opted for an all-black ensemble that could transition from day to night.

Mercifully, Mia's roster of duties at Belle View kept her busy enough to shelve her worry about the hammer that was about to drop on her friend Jamie. But the day held a new surprise for her . . . one more ominous and fraught with complex emotions if that was possible. Mia was absorbed in tracking down a location that would rent her a donkey for the Bianchis' manger first-birthday party when someone gave her door a gentle tap. "Enter," she called, still focused on her computer screen.

"*Ciao, bambina mia,*" the visitor said, her voice soft and melodic.

Mia froze. *No. It can't be.*

But it was. Mia slowly turned her attention away from the computer to the doorway. Standing there was her black sheep of a mother: the infamous Gia Carina Gabinetti.

CHAPTER 3

Mia gaped at Gia. She tried to remember exactly how long it had been since she'd laid eyes on the woman who'd birthed her and then lost progressive interest in mothering as the years went on. Gia had remarried and moved to Italy a mere few weeks after her marriage to Ravello was annulled. Which would make it about five years since mother and daughter had been in contact, except for the occasional card or desultory short phone call.

Mia found her voice. "Gia . . ." Going with a first name instead of a mother-related moniker felt appropriately distancing.

Gia came into the tiny office and negotiated her way around the desk to Mia. She bent down and enveloped her daughter in her arms. "*Bellissima*, I've missed you so much."

"You have?" Mia said this with genuine surprise.

Gia, her arms still around Mia, nodded with vigor. "You have no idea."

"You got that right." Mia didn't bother to mask the acidity in her response.

Gia released her. She hung her head. "I deserve that slam. I'm sorry. For . . . I dunno . . . everything."

Mia inhaled a deep breath and slowly exhaled. She didn't have the time or energy for a fight with her mother. She'd accepted long ago that Gia was what she was. If Gia had an ulterior motive for her sudden visit—which Mia was sure she did—it would come out eventually. In the meantime, Mia would choose to play nice. It was the holiday season, after all. "So . . . welcome home. I have to say, I'm surprised to see you."

A relieved smile lit up Gia's lovely face. She hadn't aged during her five-year absence. She was still every bit the Italian beauty who captured Ravello's heart and swanned through life on her looks and charm. Mia searched her mother's face for signs of cosmetic procedures and saw none. *I'm not sorry I inherited those genes*, she grudgingly admitted to herself.

"I missed my babies and just decided to hop on a plane. Especially with Christmas coming. Brought back so many memories."

Mia forced a smile. Unable to let Santa or even the Easter Bunny get credit for the gifts she picked out, Gia had dispelled those myths early on. Mia's memories of holidays past always included heavy doses of stroking her mother's ego.

"Look at you, running this fantastic establishment." Gia swept the room with her hand. "I'm so proud. And working with your father. He's not here, is he?"

Mia didn't buy her mother's forced casual tone for a

second. Gia knew exactly where Ravello was—having lunch at Roberto's Trattoria, like he'd been doing every day at this hour for years. Her mother had obviously timed her visit to Ravello's absence. Mia debated whether to call her mother on this, then went with a simple, "No. He's at lunch."

"Ah."

"So . . . how's Angelo?" Mia couldn't stand her mother's obnoxious, deported jailbird of a second husband, but felt compelled to ask out of politeness.

"He's good. Very good."

"Good."

Finished with niceties, Mia waited for her mother to make the next move.

"Well . . ." Gia worried the handle of her leather purse. Mia noticed several spots on the purse where the leather was faded. She gave her mother a surreptitious once-over. The hem and sleeves of her camel wool coat were slightly frayed. Mia could tell Gia had taken a Sharpie to a few scuffs on her once-stylish black boots. She'd used the trick herself a few times when she was low on funds. Maybe it was age, maybe it was having to admit she'd made a few bad choices in her own life, but Mia felt an unexpected wave of compassion for her mother. "Would you like a tour of Belle View?"

Gia beamed. "I would love that."

The women began in the downstairs Marina Ballroom, the smaller of the two event spaces. Gia oohed and aahed over the view of the Flushing Marina. Her response to the wide vista framed by floor-to-ceiling glass windows in the upstairs Bay Ballroom was even more effusive. "It's gorgeous. Look at those boats bobbing out there. Ooh, a plane just landed at LaGuardia. How romantic."

"We've been doing okay lately, so I got to spruce the place up a little," Mia said, thawed by her mother's enthusiasm. "I went with very neutral colors. Beige walls, beige carpet with enough of a design to hide messes, but not enough to take away from the view, which is our big selling point."

"Listen to you. Such a businesswoman." Her mother's gaze was filled with pride, and Mia couldn't help preening.

Mia led her mother down the glass-paneled circular staircase to the banquet hall's main kitchen, where they found Guadalupe Cruz, Belle View's giantess of a chef, stirring something in a giant pot. A former army cook in Iraq, Guadalupe reveled in the challenge of preparing food for large gatherings, the more massive the better. Evans, Belle View's sous-chef who was also the facility's dessert maven, was sipping soup from a bowl. Mia glanced in the bowl and saw miniature meatballs floating in a pale broth loaded with carrots, celery, onions, spinach, and tiny balls of pasta. "Wedding soup?"

Evans nodded, but Guadalupe spoke. "It's for the DiVirgilio family reunion. Take a sniff."

Mia bent over the pot and inhaled the rich scent of broth, meat, and vegetables. "Mmmm. Smells *deliciozo*." She raised her head. "We've got a special visitor today. Guadalupe, Evans—this is my mother, Gia."

Both coworkers reacted with raised eyebrows. They knew how the Carinas felt about Gia. But Guadalupe and Evans responded with polite greetings, and Gia returned them with enough warmth to win herself a tad of acceptance. Not wanting to push her luck, Mia quickly steered her mother out of the kitchen.

"It's a wonderful facility, sweetie," Gia said. "I think it—and you—have a bright future." She sighed. "Which I look forward to saying someday to your brother. I better get going if I'm gonna to make it to the correctional facility before visiting hours are over."

"How long are you in town?" Mia asked, stopping before the rest of the sentence—"Will I see you again?"—came out.

"Not sure. I'm keeping things open-ended." She kissed her daughter on both cheeks. "I'm at the La-Guardia Marriott. I'll call you."

Mia watched her mother go, then turned and saw Shane standing in the hallway. "Loop and Evs texted me your mother was here," he said. "You okay?"

Mia was simultaneously gratified to hear that her newest employee was on a nickname basis with "Loop" and "Evs," and miffed they were gossiping about her personal life. "I'm fine. Just kind of surprised my mother suddenly popped up. I would have been happy with at least an 'I'm on a plane, see you in eight hours.' But that's not her style."

"Loop and Evs told me a little about her. They were worried. Hope that doesn't bother you."

Shane's brow creased with extremely handsome concern. Mia felt slightly woozy, then pulled herself together. "No, I think it's sweet of all of you," she said, and meant it. She gave a mirthless laugh. "The thing is, by the time I clock in tonight, I can pretty well guarantee you that having my mother suddenly show up out of nowhere after basically being out of my life for five years, won't be the worst part of my day."

*   *   *

"The breadsticks here are delicious, aren't they? So crisp. All breadsticks are crisp, that's why they're called *sticks*, not *bread*, but Piero's have a special crunch, if you ask me. An extra something. More crunch than your average breadstick. Did you know he makes them himself?"

Aurora Boldano babbled this nervous monologue as she passed around a breadbasket at Piero's, a phenomenal restaurant hiding behind a 1960s-era hole-in-the-wall exterior. The place was empty except for the Boldano family and Mia, which she knew was intentional on Donny Senior's part. It was critical that the conversation about to take place be private.

Jamie Boldano took a breadstick and handed the basket to Mia, who passed it on without looking at him. Jamie had been trying to get her attention since he'd arrived in the tension-filled dining room twenty minutes earlier. Frustrated, he broke his breadstick, which snapped in half with a sound so sharp it startled the others. "You're right, *cara*," Donny Senior said to his wife. "These are very crispy breadsticks."

Jamie tossed his breadstick on the table. "All right, that's it. Someone needs to tell me what the flipping flip is going on here. Everyone's acting weird, Mia won't even look at me, and we just spent five minutes talking about breadsticks. Which, by the way, no one is eating, and that is a waste of the best breadsticks in Astoria, and maybe the whole city."

Aurora opened her mouth to speak but no sound came out. Agonized, she shot a pleading glance at her husband.

"Jamie . . ." Donny Senior began. He faltered.

Jamie's freckled face paled with alarm. "Oh my God. You're dying."

"No, no, no," Donny hastened to assure his son. "I'm

in great shape. I mean, I could drop a few pounds. Who among us couldn't? But . . ."

"We're all healthy," Donny Junior said. "It's not about that. It's . . ."

He trailed off. He and his parents gave Mia a beseeching look. She shot one back that telegraphed *Really?* then faced Jamie straight-on. "Jamie . . . you know how much your parents love you—"

"So, so much," Aurora jumped in. Her husband nodded agreement so hard he almost threw out his neck.

"Well . . . out of love, sometimes parents do things that seem right to them at the time, but looking back, not so much," Mia continued. "Like, with the best of intentions, they might not tell a child something they're afraid would hurt them. Again, it's all above love—"

"Mia, what are you trying to say?" Jamie interrupted, impatient. "Get to it already."

"Fine." She sucked in a breath, blew it out, and got down to it. "It appears," she said, "you're adopted."

A pall of silence descended on the room. Jamie stared at her. He worked his jaw. "What—what do you mean? It 'appears'? What *is* that? Am I adopted or not?"

"You are," Donny Senior said in a tone pained and somber.

"And we couldn't have asked for a better son," Aurora said, weepy. "We love you so much, Jamie, so—"

Jamie held up a hand and she shut up. He stared down at the table. "All these years," he muttered, "all these years I felt like I was different. Like I didn't belong. And I didn't."

"No, bro, buddy, that's not true." Donny Junior delivered this with a serious intensity Mia had never seen the Boldanos' shallow, cocky offspring exhibit.

"Shut up, you know it is," Jamie snapped at him. He focused his ire on his parents. "How could you never tell me this? What were you thinking?"

"That you were our son," Aurora said. She leaned into him. "From the second, the very second, you were placed in my arms," she said with a fierce passion, "you were my beloved baby boy. It's who you were and who you'll always be."

"You hear that, buddy?" Donny Junior said, aiming for jocular. "You didn't even come outta her and you were her favorite."

Ay yi yi, Mia thought, cringing at his ham-fisted attempt to lighten the mood.

"Junior, *idiota*!" his father yelled at him.

"I'm trying to make him feel better!" Donny Junior yelled back.

"It's not working!" Jamie yelled at both of them.

"*Stai zitto, tutti quanti!*" Aurora yelled at all of them. Then she burst into tears.

Jamie, unmoved by his mother's sobs, glowered at his family. Mia felt compelled to step in. "I know this is a huge, huge thing to find out—"

"Ya *think*?" he said with a bitter laugh.

"But your parents are old school."

"Very, very old," the elder Donny said. He pointed to his head. "Like, maybe we're not even all there up here." Jamie turned away from him. "*Giacamo*, bello, your mother and I made a mistake. A terrible one. We know that now. But like Mia said, we did it out of love. We thought we were protecting you. I know you need time to be okay with this. But we'll get through it. We're family."

"No, we're not." Jamie delivered this with venom. "But you know who is? Lorenzo. My *real* brother."

"Hey," Donny Junior protested, wounded.

"That's what brought this out in the open, Jamie," Mia said. "We all have a bad feeling about this Lorenzo guy."

"That's a nice thing to say when you haven't even met him. Remind me why we're friends again?"

Mia wasn't used to being an object of Jamie's sarcastic wrath. It hurt, but she persisted. "I'm sorry, but a guy suddenly appears out of nowhere, says he's your brother, and wants in with the family? It's hinky."

"Really? Because the way I see it, he's the only one around here who's telling the truth." Jamie jumped to his feet. "I'm done with the Boldano family. Every single one of you can go straight to hell. I'm going with the family that hasn't been keeping secrets from me since I was born." Piero appeared from the kitchen with a tray holding the family's entrees. He set it down on a stand. Jamie grabbed a plate from the tray. "And I'm taking my pasta alla carbonara with me!"

He stormed toward the exit. "You want me to put that in a to-go container?" Piero, clueless about the night's drama, called to him.

"No! And I'm keeping the plate!"

The restaurant door slammed shut. Jamie was gone. The only sound in the room came from Piero, who had a habit of clicking his partial denture in and out of place. "He took his pasta alla carbonara," Donny Junior finally said, sounding hopeful. "That's a good sign."

"I wish," Donny Senior spoke in a voice laced with sadness, "but I don't think even Piero's pasta alla carbonara can save us here. Piero, *mio amico*, pack up our dinners. None of us feel like eating right now."

"*Si,* boss," Piero said. He placed a compassionate hand

on the glum man's shoulder. "I got a fresh tiramisu in the fridge. I'll throw that in too."

He picked up the tray and returned to the kitchen. "Mia, *cara*, I'm so sorry about dragging you into this," Aurora said. "Jamie has no right to be mad at you. You were just the messenger."

"Please, don't worry about it. He'll figure that out once he calms down." Mia, thoughtful, tapped a finger against her lip. "I gotta ask . . . Are you sure Lorenzo isn't Jamie's birth brother?"

"A bazillion percent sure."

Mia was struck by the force of Donny Senior's decisive response. But she tabled that to focus on another issue. "If he's not . . . then how did he know about Jamie being adopted?"

The head of the family's face darkened. "That's the question we've been asking ourselves ever since the mook came into the picture."

It's a question that someone needs to answer, Mia thought as Piero came back from the kitchen with plastic bags filled with to-go containers. *And given I'm the only person here who has a shot at a relationship with Jamie right now, that someone is me.*

CHAPTER 4

Mia placed her to-go bag on the passenger's seat and got into the car. Shaken by the Boldanos' crisis, she took a minute to center herself before starting the engine. An image of an odd-looking animal, half zebra, half donkey, popped up on her phone screen, followed by a message from Shane: **Found a donkey for Bianchis. Place also had a zonkey. Now that I know what they are, I want one.**

Mia relaxed. She sent back a string of laugh emojis and received a quick response. A thumbs-up and then Shane wrote back: **U okay? How'd it go?** Mia texted a teary, sad face. A second later, her phone rang. "Hey."

The sound of Shane's deep voice with only a hint of a Queens accent gave Mia heart palpitations. She cursed them and forced a nonchalant, "Hey."

"If you need a drink, which I'm guessing you do, we're at Singles."

"We?"

"The gang. You know—me, Loop, Evs, Cammie, Teri."

Oh, so now you're a gang? And Teri's part of it? Mia pulled a face. Pesky reporter Teri Fuoco had found a way to infiltrate the Carinas' turf. Since it was genuinely inspired by her massive crush on the amused Evans, Mia cut her a little slack—but just a little. "I wouldn't mind a glass of something," she said to Shane. "I'm parked on Steinway. I can walk over."

Mia got out of the car. Her stomach rumbled. She grabbed her to-go bag and tromped down Steinway Street in her heavy winter boots, careful to avoid patches of ice. Two blocks later, she reached Ditmars Boulevard, Astoria's main thoroughfare. With its on-the-nose name, low-key interior, and dim lighting, Singles was all in on attracting the local unmarrieds, and the occasional married on the make. Mia went inside, stopping to hang her coat over another coat on a row of packed hooks. She saw her friends at one of the bar's perfunctory trestle tables and headed to them. They exchanged greetings. "I'm glad you came," Cammie said. "Now I can write this off as work and deduct the hours from my schedule tomorrow."

"You were coming in tomorrow?" Mia asked.

"Not anymore, thanks to this 'business meeting.'"

Mia rolled her eyes. "Now I really need a belt."

"I ordered you a chardonnay," Shane said.

He knows my drink! Mia scolded herself for being delighted by this and simply said, "Thanks."

Shane moved over to make room for her on the end of the wooden bench. Given the tight space, their legs couldn't help touching, which sent a frisson coursing through Mia. Shane clenched and unclenched his fists, and she couldn't help wondering if he felt the same spark. *Wishful thinking*, she thought, and then instantly scolded herself for the thought. A waiter delivered her drink. Mia thanked him and took a big gulp of wine, which soothed her. "It's been . . . a night. Anyone mind if I eat?" There was a chorus of noes, so she pulled out her tin of pasta alla carbonara and went at it.

"So, what's up with the Boldanos?" Teri asked.

Mia saw right through Teri's lame attempt to sound like she was making small talk. "Nothing I'll ever tell you."

"Tell her whatever you want," Evans said. "She knows I'm history if it goes public. Right, Teresa?"

The besotted Teri replied by batting her eyes at Evans like an old-timey cartoon vamp, which provided an odd contrast to her rumpled-reporter look of chinos and rugby-style thermal pullover. She mimed zipping her lips. Despite their generally adversarial relationship, Teri had helped Mia out on a few occasions, creating a grudging trust between the two women.

Mia needed to talk, so she decided to open up, albeit with vague, carefully chosen wording. "Someone's appeared on the Boldano scene with a story we find very sketchy. He's managed to suck in one family member, though, which is creating a huge problem. One that could tear the family apart."

"If anyone knows about sketchy, it's the Boldanos," Teri said. "They haven't been able to suss out the guy's real story? That surprises me. They've got boots on the ground all over the city."

"I know. It's complicated. Donny Senior can't afford

to take a heavy hand with this one. He's too close to it. And . . ." Mia took a break to ingest a forkful of pasta. "I get the feeling he might be hiding something."

"A guy like Donny with a secret? NG. Not good." Shane, who hailed from the Gambrazzos, a now-defunct former rival Family, knew whereof he spoke.

"You got a name for your mystery man?" Teri asked. "I can see what I can dig up on him."

Mia debated whether to share specifics with the reporter. On the one hand, she was exactly that: a reporter. On the other, she was great at her job and might be able to uncover useful information. "Lorenzo Puglia," she said.

Teri tapped the name into her phone. "I'll do a search first thing in the a.m."

"Thanks." Mia held up her tin container. "Anyone want to finish this? Piero's mushroom pasta alla carbonara."

The others, except for Cammie, gave enthusiastic yeses, and Mia handed off the tin. "I gotta save my appetite," Cammie said. "Pete's waiting for me outside. He got a reservation at Park One, that hot new place in Manhattan."

"Now?" Mia said. "It's almost ten o'clock."

"It's the only opening they had. Pete really had to pony up for it." Cammie couldn't have sounded more pleased about this. "I'm doing their ten-course tasting menu. God knows when we'll be done."

"Or how Pete'll pay for it on a detective's salary." Even Mia had to laugh at Teri's wisecrack.

"Anyhoo," Cammie continued, ignoring her, "it's a good thing I don't have to work tomorrow."

"About that—" Mia began.

"Bye-yee. Love you—mean it."

Cammie blew a kiss as she raced away before Mia could finish her sentence. Mia shook her head at her incorrigible employee's back. She yawned. "I better take off too. No idea what tomorrow will bring, but if it's anything like today, I'll need my strength. I'll kick in for my wine."

Mia reached for her purse, but Shane put a hand on hers. "I got this." He quickly pulled his hand away but not before another jolt of desire rocketed through Mia.

Guadalupe held up Mia's almost-empty leftover container. "You mind if I hold onto this? I wanna break down the ingredients. Best carbonara I ever tasted."

"Sure. I could put you in touch with Piero. I'm sure he'd give you the recipe. He's a great guy."

"Nah." The chef rubbed her hands together with gusto. "I like a challenge."

Mia smiled at the Belle View chef. "Go for it, Loop."

The former soldier stiffened at the sound of a nickname her boss had never used before. "Ma'am," she said with a slight nod, her response stilted and formal.

Mia got the feeling Guadalupe was fighting back an urge to salute and made a mental note to skip the nicknames with her employees. Her phone pinged a text. She looked down and saw Shane's avatar winking at her. Despite her best efforts, her heart fluttered.

Mia gave Jamie a few days to come to terms with the curveball life had thrown him. In the meantime, there was her mother's sudden reappearance to deal with. Not wanting to keep Gia's presence a secret from Ravello, she was relieved when her father seemed more curious than perturbed by the news his ex was in town. Mia credited this to Ravello's current romance and vowed to buy his girlfriend, the lovely Lin, a whopper of a holiday gift.

"Could it be," Mia mused to Ravello over early-morning coffee at Belle View, "that Mom simply missed her children?"

She and her father considered this, then simultaneously said, "Nah."

Ravello stroked his chin. "I wonder what she wants. Because you know she wants something."

"Oh, yeah. She keeps sending me texts to get together and I'm so conflicted about seeing her, I keep dodging them."

"You can't dodge her forever, *bella bambina.* Better to get it over with."

"I guess. I know one thing. We can't meet at my place. Nonna would kill her."

Ravello chortled, choking on a slug of coffee. He coughed and wiped his eyes. Elizabetta's hatred of her former daughter-in-law was legendary in the family. She laid the breakup of her beloved son's marriage solely at Gia's feet and vowed with the histrionics of a jilted Puccini heroine to throttle the woman if she ever darkened a Carina door again. "Ha," he said. "I recommend meeting your mother in a neutral location. Under assumed names. Wearing wigs."

Mia grinned at her father. "And maybe fake mustaches."

He returned her grin. "Sounds like a plan."

Still, Mia hesitated about scheduling a meetup with her mother. Instead, she checked in with the Boldanos. "Jamie cut us off," a distraught Aurora told her. "Blocked our calls, our emails. He's spooked us."

"I think you mean he ghosted you, Mrs. B." Mia

checked her phone. During a previous adventure that almost ended up with Mia taking a deadly dip in the Long
Island Sound, she and Jamie had installed an app that allowed them to track each other. She saw that the app was
still active. "Give me a little time. I'll see if I can talk to
him."

Aurora signed off with profuse thanks. It occurred to
Mia that she hadn't heard back from Teri regarding her
promised investigation into Lorenzo Puglia, so she gave
the journalist a call. "Sorry I haven't been in touch," Teri
said. "I've been scrounging around for intel on your guy,
and I've come up with nothing."

"Hmmm . . ."

"You bet 'hmmm . . .' If both me and the Boldanos
can't dig up anything on him, I have to believe that's no
accident. Everybody's got an internet fingerprint, unless
they hire someone to scrub the web clean."

"You think that's the case here," Mia said.

"Yup."

Mia pondered this. "Thanks, Teri. I appreciate the
help. It looks like I'm gonna have to engineer a face-to-
face with Mr. Puglia."

"Be careful. And tell Evans I'll see him tonight."

Teri giggled. Mia winced. "Don't do that," she
scolded. "You know, go all *tee-hee-hee*. It's disturbing."

"Oh, really?" Teri unleashed a stream of girly giggles
just to annoy Mia, then disconnected the call.

Mia tossed a couple of expletives at the phone, then
got back to work. By the time she finished checking the
items off her to-do list, it was seven p.m., and she was the
only employee left at Belle View. She made a pit stop in
the kitchen for a bite. Guadalupe's attempt at re-creating
Piero's signature mushroom pasta alla carbonara, while

not completely on a par with his, was delicious, so Mia enjoyed the bacon and cheese–enhanced dish for the second night in a row. Hunger assuaged, she looked up Jamie's location. "Uh-oh," she murmured. He was at Hot Bods, a cheesy club housed in a former warehouse a block from the bridge that led to the city's notorious Rikers Island jail. Mia couldn't imagine what straitlaced Jamie would be doing there. A panicked thought occurred to her. *He's been kidnapped!* Heart racing, she ran to her office, grabbed her coat, and dashed out of the building to save her friend.

Dumpy as Hot Bods was, it had valet parking. Mia jumped out of her car and threw her keys to the startled valet. She rushed into the building. Unlike the amiable chill décor of Singles, Hot Bods was aggressively low-end. Long bars sat at opposite ends of the space from each other. A stage area featuring dancers in skimpy outfits sat between them, high above a dance floor packed with patrons. Heavy metal music blasted from huge speakers on either side of the stage. Mia, anxious, searched the crowd for her friend. Someone tapped her on the shoulder. She turned, ready to swat a drunken lothario, and found herself face-to-face with Jamie.

"Hey, Mia," he said, sounding puzzled. "What are you doing here?"

"I could ask you the same question," she shot back. "In fact, I'm gonna. Jamie, what are you doing at Hot Bods? This place is so . . . not you."

A slight, relatively attractive guy materialized at Jamie's side. He was close to Mia and Jamie's age, but had the shaved head of a man who had gone bald way too early. He sported an attempt at a hipster goatee and wore a brand of jeans and T-shirt Mia recognized as expensive.

The same went with his designer sneakers. It was a high-end outfit for someone Mia immediately pegged as low-rent. He addressed Jamie. "Bro, they're taking our food orders."

"Be there in a minute. Enzo, I want you to meet one of my closest friends, Mia."

"*The* Mia Carina? It's an honor."

How does he know who I am? Mia, suspicious, wondered. The obvious explanation was that Jamie had talked about her to him. But Mia's instincts told her that like any good grifter, "Enzo" had done his homework.

"Mia," Jamie said with pride, "this is my brother Lorenzo."

"Hello." Mia response was polite but cool.

She lifted her arm to offer an elbow bump, but Lorenzo grabbed her hand in both of his and squeezed it. "Any friend of my brother's is a friend of mine. We're getting something to eat. You should join us."

"Sure," Mia said, extricating her hand from Lorenzo's. She pulled a vial of hand sanitizer from her purse and discreetly sanitized. Lorenzo started off. Mia grabbed Jamie's sleeve and held him back. "If you wanted to come to Hot Bods, why didn't you come here with your real brother? Little Donny's been trying to get you to skeevy places like this for years."

Jamie pulled his arm away from Mia. "I am here with my real brother," he said in an icy tone. "You can stay if you accept that. If not, don't bother."

Left with no choice, Mia followed him to a table where three people besides Lorenzo sat. Lorenzo handled the introductions. "This is my girlfriend, Renata Esposito; her brother Santino, and their mother Aida."

Everyone exchanged greetings. Lorenzo pulled out a

chair for her next to Santino, who'd included a very un-subtle leer with his hello. She leaned away from him as he leaned toward her. His breath smelled like cigarettes, alcohol, and a mint that failed to mask the less-savory scents. "Jamie should've warned us a model was coming for dinner," Santino said in a salacious tone.

Mia didn't have to groan. Santino's sister and mother did it for her. Aida swatted her son's arm. "Dummy, leave her alone."

"Yeah, Santi," his sister parroted, her arm entwined in Lorenzo's.

A waiter approached to take their orders, saving Mia from Santino's further advance. She passed on ordering, instead taking the time to evaluate her dining compan-ions, beginning with Renata. With her thick, chestnut hair, almond-shaped gray eyes, and full lips, Lorenzo's girlfriend was pretty in a way that would have held up without the mask of makeup she wore, which screamed of YouTube influencer videos. Her brother sported simi-lar features, but the early lines on his face and puffy bags under his eyes indicated hard living. Mia guessed the sib-lings to be in their mid-twenties, although Santino's life choices were already taking their toll and prematurely aging him. Mother Aida was a zaftig woman in her late forties with a hefty bosom she didn't mind showing off in a low-cut hot pink slinky top over too-tight shiny leg-gings in a pink-and-black cheetah print. She had sturdy hands devoid of nail polish, as did her daughter. Mia learned why after a polite inquiry into their jobs. "I'm a masseuse at Rejuve," Aida said. "The new spa on Stein-way."

"And I'm an aestha—essata—"

"Aesthetician," Mia said, helping Renata out.

"Yeah. I do facials. Why can't they just call it that?" The aesthetician crooked her lip, annoyed.

Mia conceded she had a point. "What about you?" she asked Lorenzo. She avoided putting the question to the amorous Santino, not wanting to encourage him.

"I'm between careers," Lorenzo said, "so right now I'm doing deliveries for Sorrento Deli and Pasticceria in Long Island City."

"Ahh." Mia kept her response neutral. She'd seen enough entry-level hoods spend a fortune on designer wear they hoped would impress their higher-ups to know that there was no way driving a delivery truck paid for Lorenzo's expensive togs.

The waiter delivered an assortment of greasy fried food and Mia concentrated on peeling the coating off a mozzarella stick Aida offered her in an attempt to discourage Santino's come-ons. A pretty girl who was barely out of her teens passed their table. She caught Lorenzo's eye and smirked at him. He quickly looked away but not before Renata noticed the interaction. She glowered at him and shot daggers at the young girl's back.

Dinner conversation proved innocuous, but Mia remained on guard for any signs confirming her negative instincts about Lorenzo. The waiter delivered another round of drinks, followed by dessert. "Mia, have you talked to Jamie's family about our situation?"

Lorenzo put this question to her so unexpectedly a forkful of Black Forest cake went down the wrong pipe and she gagged on it. Santino grabbed the chance to pat her back and then rub it suggestively. Mia leaned so far away from him she came close to ending up in Aida's lap. "Yes. As a matter of fact, I have." She addressed Jamie. "Your parents made a mistake not being honest with you from the beginning. They know that now. But that doesn't cancel out their love for you. This is killing your mom and dad. You gotta talk to them."

"She's right," Aida declared, to Mia's surprise. Even more surprising were the vigorous nods of agreement from her children. "At the end of the day, nothing means more than family. Not career, not money, not nothing. Let your parents make it right with you, Jamie. Before it's too late."

"Jamie, I love you with all I got in me. But I'm with Aida on this." Lorenzo released a strangled sob. "I'm sorry. I was just thinking of my poor, late mother. I thank God above that she told me about you, my brother. To think if she'd gone to her grave with that secret . . ."

Overcome, he dropped his head in his hands. Mia gritted her teeth when Jamie put a reassuring hand on his shoulder and Lorenzo lifted his head and managed a wan, grateful smile. Having had enough of Lorenzo's theatrics, Mia rose to her feet. "It's been nice meeting you all, but I need to go."

"I should go too," Jamie said. "I have a paper due in the morning for my early childhood psych class."

Jamie went to stand up, but Lorenzo pulled him back into his seat. "Dude, it's still early. The live band doesn't even come on for an hour." He hailed the waiter. "Another round, bud."

"My shift is ending," the waiter said. "I'll let my replacement know. He'll start a new bill." He held up a check. "Who gets this one?"

"He does." The Espositos and Lorenzo all pointed at Jamie, and the waiter dropped the check in front of him.

Mia steamed but said nothing. She threaded her way through the incoming crowds to retrieve her coat. She lifted it from the coat hook and when she lowered it, Lorenzo was standing in front of her. "Don't worry, Mia. I'm working on Jamie."

"Working on him or working him?" she couldn't stop herself from snapping.

"I respect you for being so protective of your friend." Lorenzo placed a hand on his heart. "But know that all I want is for Jamie to make good with his parents so we can all be one big, happy family." A bass line thumped over the speaker system. "Oooh, 'Livin' on a Prayer.' This song never gets old." He yelled to his girlfriend, "Hey, Renata, get your fat butt outta the chair, we gotta dance to this song."

He hurried away, leaving Mia glowering after him. Trying to ingratiate himself with the Boldano family, sticking Jamie with the check—even worse, distracting Jamie from his studies and off-track from his path toward a graduate degree. Lorenzo Puglia was more than an obnoxious, opportunistic sleazeball. He was a terrible and perhaps dangerous influence on his "brother," Jamie.

CHAPTER 5

The dinner left Mia feeling discomfited. When her mother texted her to see if she might want to meet for a nightcap, she texted back an impulsive "sure," which is how she came to be sitting across from Gia at a wine bar on Astoria Boulevard. "You look upset," her mother said. "What's wrong?"

Mia was taken aback by Gia's perceptiveness. Usually her mother was blind to anyone's concerns but her own. *Maybe she is changing.* "It's a thing going on with the Boldanos." She shared the family's drama, once again sticking to the vaguest of facts.

"So," Gia said. "Someone wants to get in with the Boldanos. That's usually law enforcement trying to place an undercover agent."

"I hadn't thought of that, but I can pretty much say it's not the case here."

"Then it's someone playing the long-lost relative card."

"More like that."

Gia sipped her Bellini. "The cure for that is DNA."

"You mean scoring some off of Lorenzo? He tried faking it already. If I could get the real thing, it could give Donny and Aurora what they need to shut the whole thing down. Thanks, Mom."

"Of course." Gia gave a hesitant smile. "You haven't called me 'Mom' in a while. I like it better than 'Gia.'"

"It was an accident."

"I'll take it as a sign of progress. Like you meeting me tonight. It means a lot to me, Mia *bambina*."

She sang the name. Mia grinned. "That's what you used to do when I was little."

"So I wasn't all bad, huh?"

"You had your moments." Mia delivered this with a guarded edge but felt a warmth for her mother she hadn't felt in years. And for first time in longer than she could remember, Mia allowed herself the hope of having a true relationship with her mother.

Mia came up with the perfect way to collect a DNA sample from Jamie's purported brother. She and her father were throwing a tree-lighting ceremony to celebrate their first Christmas as proprietors of Belle View. Amid a profusion of holiday decorations, a giant Scotch pine tree festooned with unlit lights sat center stage on the outdoor patio where many a couple had posed for wedding photos with the lovely-despite-its-name Flushing Bay in the background. She let the Boldanos know she had a plan and then went to work on convincing Jamie that his parents, eager to reconcile with him, were willing to meet Lorenzo with the goal of accepting him into the family. Not wanting to be distracted by the shade her grandmother would throw at her mother, Mia didn't invite Gia to the party, but she summoned the courage to alert Elisabetta to her nemesis's presence in town. Elisabetta responded with the expected histrionics and a threat to put *una maledizione*—a curse—on her son's ex-wife. "I thought you already put a curse on her," Mia said.

"*Si*, but according to you she seems fine, so I gotta come up with a new one." Elisabetta's dark tone was a reminder not to get on the octogenarian's bad side, and Mia found herself feeling sorry for her mother.

The evening of the tree-lighting ceremony, the Carinas and their guests mingled in the Marina Ballroom, enjoying drinks and a dessert bar featuring cannoli cake, a variety of cookies and pastries, and *struffoli*, a traditional Italian holiday dessert made of small, fried dough balls coated with honey and sprinkles. Mia and Ravello used an outside caterer to free up her staff. Guadalupe, uninterested in being freed up, busied herself intimidating the poor, hapless woman she perceived as a competitor. Evans brought Teri as his date, which Mia didn't love but couldn't say no to for fear of offending the brilliant, if odd, assistant chef. Cammie, never one to miss a party she could clock off as work hours, showed up with her ex-husband, Detective Pete Dianopolis, who had reluctantly hired a limo on Cammie's behest to chauffeur them to the event. Only Shane passed, having come down with a cold that did nothing to detract from his looks, despite bleary eyes and a red nose.

"Are you sure Jamie's coming?" Aurora asked Mia. She clutched her wineglass so hard Mia feared it would break in the woman's hand.

Mia checked Jamie's location on her phone. "He just parked."

"Ah, *va bene.*" A nervous Aurora passed the wineglass back and forth from one hand to the other. "Boys, did you hear that?" she said to her husband and son. "Jamie's on his way."

Donny Senior acknowledged this with an anxious head bob. His son gave a grunt loaded with resentment. Little Donny, still hurt by his brother's rejection, had to be strong-armed into Mia's plan by his parents. He was the evening's wild card.

A minute later, Jamie came into the ballroom. He'd brought his girlfriend Madison, who didn't seem too happy about being relegated to the sidelines by Lorenzo and his coterie of Renata, Santino, and Aida, who surrounded Jamie like bodyguards protecting royalty. Renata and Aida were dressed like royalty themselves, Renata in a green velvet full-length dress heavy on sequins, her mother in a poufy red satin number. Aida even wore a tiara. Mia and Madison exchanged a hug. "How are you holding up?" Mia asked Jamie's girlfriend. She knew Lorenzo's insertion into their lives had created tension for the couple.

Madison made a face. "Between us? I *hate* him." She hissed this into Mia's ear, venom in her voice.

Jamie tapped on a glass with a knife. "Excuse me, everyone." The room fell quiet. "I want you all to meet a few special friends of mine." He gestured to the Espositos. "This is Renata, Santino, and Aida."

"I know I speak for my family when I say it's a pleasure and honor to be here," Santi said, holding his wine-glass up as if to toast.

"And . . ." Jamie clapped a hand on Lorenzo's shoulder. "This is my brother, Lorenzo. Yes"—he shot a warning glance at the Boldanos—"My brother."

Lorenzo took a step forward, the step accompanied by a jingling sound. Mia glanced down at his feet and saw he was wearing green high-tops with red jingle bells attached. There was a beat of suspense. Then Donny Senior stepped forward. "A toast to your brother." He raised his glass, clinked with Lorenzo, and the two men drank. The room released a collective sigh of relief. "*Grazie a Dio*," Mia murmured. Then she announced to her guests: "*Mangiamo*. Let's eat."

Mia skipped food, preferring to keep an eye out for trouble, which looked like it might be coming from Donny Junior's direction. His mood grew increasingly sour with each drink he knocked back, despite Mia giving the bartender instructions to water down his drinks. After an hour or so, Ravello instructed everyone to put on their jackets and join him on the patio. As festive music sang out from speakers, he flipped a switch, illuminating the tree. Guests clapped at the sight. A few burst into a slightly inebriated, off-key version of "Jingle Bells." Lorenzo threw an arm around Jamie's shoulder. "I love the holidays. Especially Christmas. This is what it's all about. Celebrating with friends. And family."

"You're not neither." Donny Junior didn't bother to say this under his breath.

Lorenzo faced him. "Excuse me?"

Donny Junior took the challenge. "You're not a friend. And you're sure as hell not family."

"Donald, *stai zito*," his father warned.

Jamie pushed his brother away from Lorenzo. "Back off."

Donny the younger pushed Jamie off. "Tell us who you really are, you lowlife," he hollered at Lorenzo.

"Who are you calling a lowlife, you lowlife?" Renata yelled this at Donny Junior in defense of her boyfriend.

"Him. And you!"

That's all it took for the altercation to devolve into a melee. Jamie, Donny Junior, Lorenzo, and Santino traded punches while the women in their lives cried and shouted helplessly for their menfolk to stop. "The tree!" someone screamed as the ball of testosterone collided with the Belle View Christmas tree. There was a loud *thud* as the tree trashed onto the patio. The fighting foursome landed on top of it. Ravello, Pete, and Evans pulled the four to their feet. "Get in the car," Donny Senior yelled at his oldest son. "*Adesso.* Now."

Donny Junior stomped off. "You're dead to me," Jamie yelled after him.

"If anyone's gonna be dead around here, it's him," Donny Junior yelled back while shooting Lorenzo the bird.

"Here's hoping," Mia heard the usually reserved Madison mutter.

The debacle brought the party to a close. Jamie and his cohorts helped Ravello and a few other guests right the tree. He left without exchanging a word to his parents. "I'm sorry about all this," he said to Mia on his way out the door. "Mia, I know you mean well. But do me a favor and stop trying to fix things for me. They are what they are. And I'm good with that. Okay?"

"Okay." Mia crossed her fingers behind her back.

Aurora and Donny Senior were the last to leave, the

strain of the evening evident on both their faces. But Mia hoped to soon have good news for them. She held up two wineglasses. "I got what I need. DNA samples from Jamie and Lorenzo."

"If you need any help getting the results fast-tracked," Donny Senior said, "Let me know."

The mere mention of the Boldano name insured Mia received the test results in a lightning-fast three days. The news came as no surprise to her. "They're not related," she told Mr. and Mrs. Boldano over the phone. "This Lorenzo scam artist isn't even a hundred percent Italian. He's big mutt mix of everything from Italian to Irish to Eastern European."

"His mother and me will have to break the news."

"With all due respect, I worry Jamie won't believe it coming from you. He knows how much you don't want Lorenzo in the picture and might accuse you of doctoring the results. I'm not saying he won't be mad at me—" her cell alerted her to an incoming call. She checked and saw Madison's name. "I'm getting another call I should probably take."

"No problem. And yes, you break the news to Jamie. We owe you, Mia. Big-time."

The Boldanos signed off and Mia took Madison's call. "Jamie broke up with me," his girlfriend sobbed.

"Oh, Madison, I'm so sorry."

"We had a fight because he wants to drop out of grad school. It's that SOB Lorenzo's fault," Madison wailed. "Why is he still around? What's the point of dating a mobster's son if they won't whack someone when they need to?"

"Whoa," Mia cautioned. "Madison, I know you're upset, but please don't go there. I need to talk to Jamie. Let me track him down and get back to you."

"'Kay." Madison sniffled. "Thank you so much, Mia. I'm really, really glad we're friends."

"Me too," Mia said, meaning it.

The two agreed to let each other know if either of them heard from Jamie. Madison showed her gratitude by forwarding a 50 percent–off coupon to a high-end Tribeca shoe store. Mia checked Jamie's location on her phone and saw he was at his apartment. They hadn't spoken since the fateful tree-lighting ceremony, so Mia felt it was safe to assume he'd ignore her call. She saved the shoe coupon to an e-file labeled *Madison's Awesome Deals*. Then she threw on her winter coat, wrapped her neck in the multicolored scarf Elisabetta had crocheted for her using a riot of mismatched thread ends, and left Belle View for Jamie's place.

Jamie lived in a one-bedroom apartment on the top floor of a brick-fronted postwar five-story walkup on Thirty-second Street. As usual in Astoria, parking was a nightmare, but Mia managed to squeeze her Honda between two SUVs, whose snow-covered roofs indicated they hadn't been moved in a week. The lock on the building's front door was desultory at best and it was no match for the trick Mia's brother Posi had taught her for jimmying a door latch open with a credit card. Mia tromped up the stairs. By the time she reached Jamie's door, she was perspiring and out of breath. *I gotta lay off Nonna's leftovers*, she thought as she rapped on Jamie's door. She saw his hazel eye in the peephole.

"What?" he said from behind the door.

"We need to talk."

"So talk."

"From out here? Sure." Mia spoke in a loud voice. "Hey, Jamie, remember that time in high school when you decided it would be cool to look like one of the guys in NSYNC, so you got a super-tight perm and dyed your hair blond and I still have the pictures of it on my phone?"

"Shut up!" Jamie opened the door and pulled her inside. "What do you want?"

"To show you this." Mia took a business envelope out of her purse and handed it to him. Jamie extracted a letter from the envelope and examined its contacts. "Lorenzo isn't related. He's barely Italian." Jamie ripped up the letter. "You can do that, but I've got a copy. Several."

"I ripped it up because I know."

Mia stared at him. "What? What do you mean, you know?"

"You think I'm naïve? Like, I'd just let some guy show up and claim to be my brother without checking him out? I snuck a DNA sample from Lorenzo myself."

Mia creased her forehead, trying to process the twist. "Then why—but why—I don't understand why you made such a big deal about him to your parents."

"I wasn't going to. I was actually going to call Lorenzo on his BS. Maybe even have him busted for fraud. But when Mom and Dad told me what they told me . . ." Jamie paced his small, neat living room, decorated in castoffs from Aurora's Colonial furniture phase. "They've been lying to me since I was born. About who I am. Where I come from."

"So you did all this to get back at them?"

"Yes." Jamie took a heavy seat on his couch and dropped his head in his hands.

"You broke up with Madison over this."

"Not over this, just . . . I'm confused right now, okay?" Annoyed, he jumped up and began pacing again.

"I'd like to say you're exactly who you were before all this went down. But I get that you need to—what's the word? Rejigger. Re-something."

"Recalibrate."

"Yeah, that." A thought dawned on Mia. "What do you know about this Lorenzo character? And the Espositos? You're hanging around with people who want to take advantage of you, Jamie. They could be dangerous."

"You think I don't know how to take care of myself?" Jamie said, affronted. "I may not be a Boldano by birth, but I was raised like one. So back off. You and everyone. How do you keep finding me, anyway?"

Mia held up her phone. "The app. Remember?"

"Right." Jamie picked up his own cell phone and futzed with it. "Deleted. Now go. I don't want anyone around right now."

Mia opened her mouth to argue. Then realizing it was pointless at the moment, she said, "Okay. But when you want someone around, I'll be here for you. As will your parents and hopefully Madison. I'm not giving up her deep discounts without a fight."

When she got to her car, Mia let the engine run until it was warm enough to produce heat. While waiting, she texted Donny and Aurora that she'd delivered the DNA news to Jamie, who would need time to process it. She'd let Jamie tell them he already knew Lorenzo was a fraud—or not. That was his call to make. After sending the message to the Boldanos, she texted Madison a message of hope. Yes, Jamie was going through a rough patch, but Mia was confident he'd emerge from it more committed to his girlfriend than ever. Mia included a few possible dates for the two women to go shoe shopping before the 50-percent coupon Madison sent her expired.

Given the demands of Belle View's holiday season schedule, worrying about Jamie's estrangement dropped down on Mia's list of priorities. Number one was talking teen Kaitlyn off the ledge when she called in hysterics because the queen bee in her grade said she "might or might not" come to Kaitlyn's birthday party. "I ran all those themes you sent me by Daniella," the sixteen-year-old sobbed.

Daniella, Daniella . . . Mia flipped through her mental note file on Kaitlyn's looming nightmare. *Right, the alpha Mean Girl.*

"And she was like, meh. If she doesn't come, my life is OVER!"

Mia rubbed her eyes. "This Daniella's been a problem for a while now. Let me ask you this: Has anything changed around school recently?"

"We got a new girl in our grade. She's really pretty. And has an accent. Like from England or London. You know, one of those countries. Sounds all fancy when she talks."

"Ahhh. I got it now. Daniella's threatened. She's using you for a power play that'll pull the attention back to her. Here's what you do. What's the new girl's name?"

"Juliet. Even her name is like, pretty."

"Invite Juliet to your party. She'll be thrilled to be included. Once Daniella hears Juliet's coming, she'll be at your party in a heartbeat. Trust me on this."

"Okay." Kaitlyn sounded doubtful. "But I still need a theme."

An invoice for the Bianchi camel rental popped up on

Mia's screen. She had a brainstorm. "How's this? A literal 'party animal' theme. We're having a manger first-birthday party the afternoon before yours. I can have the animals stay and we'll set them up as a petting zoo for your party. It'll be like a throwback to when you all were kids, which will make your friends feel all grownup and meta. I think. I'm never sure if I'm using that right. Anyway, I bet no one else is doing that theme. We can put together an awesome Evite for you to send out. And maybe give out huge stuffed animals as favors. You know, the kind you win at carnivals." *Please oh please let her say yes because I don't have another idea in me*, Mia prayed.

Fortunately, Kaitlyn screamed an enthusiastic "Yes!" to the theme. "Everyone loves stuffed animals. Even the boys, though they'll never say so. I'll invite Juliet right now. Love you."

"Love you too," Mia, who'd grown used to the teen's effusive sign-off, responded. She emailed Shane with an update and asked him to come up with a cute design for Kaitlyn's Evite. Within minutes he sent her a party animal graphic featuring a mix of cuddly creatures and celebratory teens. Mia texted the image to Kaitlyn, receiving a string of happy emojis in return, plus the message **Juliet AND Daniella coming 2 party!!!!!** Mia gave herself a smug pat on the back.

Her calendar dinged an alert. Egged on by Elisabetta, Philip was kicking up his holiday decorations a notch—or more. He'd blocked off the front of his house with the giant screens used on TV for home makeover reveals and was planning his own reveal that evening, complete with a coffee truck. Mia hesitated, then typed a message to Shane: **Fun holiday street party on my block tonight, if**

you're not doing anything. She tried to ignore her pounding heart as she waited for his response, which came quickly: **Sorry, can't. Thanks though.**

The pounding stopped, replaced by mortification. Mia kicked herself for extending the invitation. "Don't dip your pen in company ink." She said this out loud to scold herself. Her phone pinged a text. Mia checked and saw it was from her mother: **Busy tonight? Would love to see you.** Suddenly feeling vulnerable, Mia texted back the same invitation she'd sent to Shane. She was comforted when her mother wrote back, **Love 2 come. See you there.** *There are times*, Mia concluded, *when no matter how old you are, you need your mommy*.

Mia wrapped up work for the day. On her way home, she called Elisabetta to warn her Gia would be Mia's guest at Philip and Finn's decoration unveiling. "I'm expecting you to play nice, Nonna."

Her grandmother reacted with a stream of foul language in a combination of Italian and English, but ended with a reluctant, "Fine. But *per te*. For you."

Forty-sixth Place looked magical, with every house festooned in a sparkling array of red, green, gold, and silver lights and decorations. The life-size Nativity scene in Phyllis Carullo's house reminded Mia she needed to order costumes for the Bianchis' first-birthday party. She snapped a photo and sent it to herself as a note. The night was clear and cold, but not unbearably so, the air pungent with the scent of roasted chestnuts from a local vendor, and hot chocolate along with coffee emanating from the coffee truck. Mia, bundled up in a gray mid-calf puffer coat, watched a group of tweens try to prove how cool they were by ordering coffee she knew they'd take two sips of and throw away. Her mother and grandmother stood stiffly on either side of her, pretending to be absorbed in the espressos Mia had fetched for them. "Nonna's being good," Mia whispered to her mother, "but there was a threat of putting a curse on you."

"Another one?" Gia cast a glance at Elisabetta. "I have to say, she's good at them."

The melancholy in her mother's voice caught Mia by surprise. She was about to question her when she saw Elisabetta narrow her eyes and start muttering under her breath in Italian. Mia caught the words for *witch*, *hag*, and a few that translated into more scatological expressions. She followed her grandmother's eyeline to see Jacinta Benedetto marching their way, followed by her Forty-fifth Place geriatric entourage. The crowd instinctively parted to make way for the related-only-by-marriage-to-Tony-Bennett neighbor. According to local reports, Jacinta had once been a hottie. But with her dyed orange hair, arched, penciled-on eyebrows and slash of red lipstick, she'd come to resemble the psychotic clown from a horror movie. This didn't affect the intimidating aura of arrogance and superiority she projected.

Jacinta crossed her arms in front of her chest and smirked at Mia's grandmother. "*Buona sera*, Elisabetta."

As if on cue, Elisabetta's friends grouped behind her. Elisabetta mimicked her enemy's stance and expression. "*Buona sera,* Jacinta." She had to look up to deliver the cold greeting to the woman, who towered over her. Unlike Elisabetta, Jacinta's close to six-foot height hadn't been reduced by osteoporosis, something else that riled Mia's grandmother.

Jacinta gave the Carinas' front yard a once-over, followed by a derisive sniff. She whispered to a woman standing next to her, who passed it down the line to the tune of a group snicker. Jacinta gave her straw-like hair a toss. "*Andiamo*," she told her followers. "*Questo è* boring."

The group turned and paraded off to their home turf of Forty-fifth Place. Elisabetta chucked her thumb under her chin in a nasty gesture. "*Ragazze cattive*," she yelled after them.

"Did Elisabetta just call them mean girls?" Gia asked, bemused.

Mia nodded. "Whoever said high school never ends was right."

"That's a depressing thought." Gia's phone beeped an alert. She pulled it out of her coat pocket. "Angelo. I missed his call."

Mia glanced over. Seeing her stepfather Angelo's image on the screen, she grimaced. "Ugh."

"You always make that face about him," Gia said, noticing. "And that sound."

Mia shrugged. "Just because you love him doesn't mean I have to. Or even like him."

Before Gia could respond, Philip bounded out in front of the screens hiding his home, his husband Finn on his heels. "It's time," Philip announced.

"That Jacinta is giving me *agita*." This came from Elisabetta, who had joined her granddaughter and former daughter-in-law. She gestured to the screens. "Philip better, how you say? Knock it out of the park."

"Once again, Nonna, that's exactly how you say it."

Philip and Finn each took a screen and rolled it back as if drawing a curtain. The onlookers gasped with delight and applauded. The men had transformed their small front yard into a snowy winter wonderland, complete with a sledding hill placed over their front stoop. "There's more," Philip told the crowd as Finn organized eager children into a line for sledding. He held up his cell phone and gave it a few taps. His home lit up with an array of white lights so bright Mia feared it might sear her retina. She wasn't alone. "I'm blind!" Elisabetta screamed, so discombobulated she clutched Gia's arm instead of Mia's.

"You're all right," said her former daughter-in-law in a voice soothing but loud enough to be heard over speakers blasting "Rockin' Around the Christmas Tree." "Your eyes will adjust."

To give her own eyes a break, Mia focused on the Levines' Santa's workshop display across the street, now lit up as if it were the middle of a sunny day. A gingerbread-style house the size of a child's playhouse represented the workshop. A half-dozen smiling elves stood sentry around it. A pair of feet stuck out from the workshop's front door. This puzzled Mia. "Nonna," she yelled, "did you add something to the Levines' display?"

"Huh?" Elisabetta blinked a few times.

Mia put her hands on her grandmother's shoulder and turned her toward the Levines' house. "There. In the workshop. Did you add elf feet?"

"What? No. Why would we do that? It doesn't look like Christmas. It looks like a house fell on a witch."

Mia got a sinking feeling in the pit of her stomach. She took her mother's hand. "Come. We need to get a closer look at whatever's going on over there."

Mia and Gia hurried across the street. Mia opened the

gate of the chain-link fence that surrounded the Levines' front yard. "Careful, Mom. Don't disturb anything."

"Why?"

Mia peered inside the house. Her stomach churned as her worst fears were confirmed. She stood up and pointed to the green high-tops with jingle bells on the feet of a dead Lorenzo Puglia. "Because," she said to her mother, "this is a crime scene."

CHAPTER 6

Word quickly spread that there had been an "incident." The police arrived and taped off the yard, which drew more looky-loos. After crossing herself and muttering a prayer that Lorenzo find eternal rest, Elisabetta finagled a bullhorn from a neighbor and exhorted the curious crowd to drop generous donations into the block's donation boxes. "Out of tragedy comes something good," Elisabetta said in a solemn tone, which she followed with protests when Mia removed the bullhorn from her possession.

Mia saw an unmarked car pull up in front of the crime scene. Detective Pete Dianopolis got out of the driver's side of the car. His ex-wife Cammie, clad in gold spike heels and holding a doggy bag, exited from the passenger's side. Mia went to them. "We were having dinner at

Park One again when the call came in," Cammie said. "We were only up to the fourth course, so this better be good."

Mia pointed to the feet sticking out of the workshop. "That's Lorenzo Puglia. Jamie Boldano's fake brother."

Cammie eyed the scene. "Is he dead?"

"Very."

"Okay, then. I feel a little better about missing the last six courses. Tell Pete I'll be in the car."

Cammie tottered back to the unmarked cruiser and got inside. Mia sidled up to the chain-link fence and watched the police work the area. Pete conferred with a younger man, his partner Ryan Hinkle, who stifled a yawn. The detective, father to a rambunctious infant, always seemed sleep-deprived. A motorcycle roar clashed with the cheery holiday tunes still singing from Philip's outdoor speakers. Evans, who lived down the block from Mia, pulled up on his Harley-Davidson. Teri, who was riding shotgun, hopped off. She removed her helmet and handed it to Evans, then extracted a notebook from the inside pocket of her leather bomber jacket. She strode up to Mia's side. "I got a heads-up from my editor there was a police action on the block. What've we got here?"

Mia, always wary of giving the nosy reporter too much information, kept her answer short. "There's a body in the workshop."

Teri leaned in and studied the scene. "Not just any body. The guy who claimed he was Jamie Boldano's brother. I remember those sneakers from your tree-lighting party. Thanks for inviting me to that, by the way."

"That was on Evans, not me."

A flash of rotating red lights colored the area. Mia and

Teri turned to see that a van from the coroner's office pulled up. "I'm gonna see if anyone will talk to me. See if I can get any deets on how he was killed."

"You don't know that. Maybe he died a natural death."

Teri cast Mia a skeptical look she knew she deserved. "Right. He felt a natural death coming on and made sure to position himself inside a Santa's workshop with his feet sticking out."

She took off to dig up dirt for the *Tri Trib*, leaving a glum Mia to her thoughts, all of which were troubling. By masquerading as Jamie's long-lost relative, Lorenzo Puglia had earned himself some powerful enemies. No one, especially the police, would consider labeling all the Boldanos suspects a rush to judgment. Even Jamie could wind up categorized as a suspect. For all Mia knew, her friend might have confronted Puglia about the deception and snapped. But she also considered it safe to assume that the past of a grifter like Puglia was littered with angry, vengeful marks.

A couple of TV news vans pulled up to the scene. Pete Dianopolis looked up to see them and Mia waved to catch his attention. The detective rolled his eyes but came toward her. "This would make a great opening scene for a Steve Stianopolis thriller," Dianopolis said.

"It would make a fantastic book," Mia said, sucking up to him. "It's such a mystery. Who is this guy? Who would want him dead, and then plant him in this lovely holiday display?"

Pete gave her the side-eye. "We know who he is. And who would want him dead. And so do you."

Curse those stupid sneakers. "Fine. It's Lorenzo Puglia. But don't assume this has anything to do with the Boldanos."

Pete gave a dismissive snort. "Seriously? Mia, come on."

"No, *you* come on. Can you imagine any of them leaving a body in such a public place?"

"Yes. Donny Junior. He's an idiot."

"He's . . . got issues," Mia acknowledged. "But even he isn't this stupid."

"So *you* think. But me? I can see it."

"Pete, you're a good detective. A great one, really." Mia was happy to see Cammie's ex couldn't help being flattered by the compliment. "I don't have to tell you that a guy like Puglia has a past. I do understand why you need to consider the Boldanos suspects. But I hope—no, I know—you'll dig deeper."

"Well, yeah," Pete said. "That's my job." He smoothed his black hair, once salt-and-pepper. The glare from Philip and Finn's lights highlighted a patch of black on Pete's hand from whatever hair color he was using to hide the salt. "About me being a great detective . . . you ever mention that to Cammie?"

"Many times," Mia said with a wink. "Many, *many* times."

"Good to know." He looked to the car where Cammie was cooling her heels. "I better wrap up this investigation. Cammie will kill me if I keep her waiting too long." He blinked. "Your neighbor's display is so bright we didn't even have to set up our floodlights. Tell them I appreciate the assist."

Pete returned to work. The onlookers, bored and cold, began to disperse. Mia suddenly remembered her grandmother and mother. She found her mother, pale and shaking, huddling near the coffee cart for warmth. "Mom, are you okay?" Mia asked, concerned.

"That boy in there," she said, teeth chattering. "He was somebody's son."

Having discovered a few bodies in the recent past, Mia considered herself something of a murder veteran. She placed a comforting arm around her mother. "I'm sorry you had to be here for this. I know this is no excuse for murder—if it was that—but if it makes you feel any better, he was a very bad person, someone's son or not." Gia didn't seem convinced. She shrunk further into the confines of her down jacket. "You need a belt of something. Let's get you back to my place."

"I don't think Elisabetta would appreciate that."

"Too bad." Mia scanned the crowd. "Where is she, anyway?"

"She went home. I heard her mutter something about Christmas bling."

"Meaning she's in the basement hunting down more decorations for our already-way-too-much front yard. She won't even know you're there."

Gia shook her head. "Thanks, but I'm a little worn out by the whole night. I'll grab a cab to my hotel."

Mia subtly examined her mother. Her lovely face with the high cheekbones and dark almond eyes Mia regretted not inheriting, looked drawn. Something was definitely going on with Gia, but rather than press her, Mia chose to let time tell her what it was. "I'll get you a cab," she said.

Mia walked her mother to the corner, where as luck would have it, a cab was discharging occupants. Mia's heart jumped into her throat when she saw who they were: Lorenzo's girlfriend Renata, her brother Santino . . . and Jamie. Renata was a weeping hot mess. "Where is he?" she screamed. "Where's my boyfriend?"

She raced down the street to the scene of the crime,

Jamie and Santino close behind her. Mia placed her mother in the cab. "I'll keep you posted."

She slammed the door shut and took off after the others. Renata, who had devolved into full-on hysterics, was being tended to by an EMT medic while her brother, who looked like he could use some medical attention himself, watched helplessly. Jamie stood by the chain-link fencing, staring at the police activity. Mia joined him. "Santi and Renata saw it on TV," Jamie said dully. "They recognized his sneakers. Santi called me right away. It's awful."

"I know," Mia said, feeling sympathy for her friend. "I'm sorry."

"Do they think he was . . . ?"

Jamie couldn't finish the sentence, but he didn't have to. "Yes," Mia said.

He flinched. "Could it be . . ."

"Your father? Your brother? Your mother?"

"My girlfriend."

"Right," Mia said, recalling Madison's venomous hatred of the scam artist upending her romantic life. "She was not a fan, as they say. But like I told Peter, can you imagine any of them dumping a bod—leaving someone"—she motioned to the workshop—"here?"

"So, Pete already suspects them."

"I guess it's kind of hard not to," Mia had to admit.

The coroner pushed a gurney through the gate into the front yard, knocking over several elves. Jamie turned away. "This is my fault. If I hadn't acted out to get back at my parents, Lorenzo would still be alive."

"You can't blame yourself, Jamie. Not to speak ill of the dead . . ." Mia crossed herself to make up for the fact she was about to speak extremely ill of this particular dead person. "But Lorenzo was pond scum. A shyster. I'm guessing that when it came to people wishing him from this earth, your family would have to get in line and take a number. And it would be a high one."

"Could be. I don't know." Jamie shoved his hands deep into the pockets of his old peacoat. "I'm done punishing my family. It's immature and stupid. I'm gonna call Madison and apologize to her for what I put her through. Hopefully, she'll take me back."

"If you need my help on that score—"

"Right." Jamie said this with a glimmer of a smile. "The discounts."

Mia quirked her head and held up her hands. "As the Levines would say, I'm a schnorrer."

"You're also an amazing friend. One I don't appreciate enough." Jamie removed his cell phone from an inside pocket of his coat. He tapped on the phone for a minute, and then returned it to the pocket. "I reinstalled the location app and accepted your request. You're always there for me. Now I'll always be there for you. That is," he added, insecure, "if you can forgive me for being a jerk."

Mia placed her hands together as if praying and made a small bow. "You are forgiven, my friend."

The coroner's gurney, loaded up with its late charge, began its journey to the department van. As it wheeled past Renata, she let out a piercing scream and then fainted. "Uh-oh," Jamie said. "I better go see if I can do anything."

He started toward the Espositos. Out of the corner of her eye, Mia saw Pete glance toward Jamie. The detective's eyes lit up like the elves in the Levines' yard had delivered him a present. Mia grabbed Jamie and flipped him around in the opposite direction. "Pete alert." She pushed him toward a knot of people traipsing toward Twenty-first Avenue. "Go. *Now*."

Jamie braked. "You don't think he—"

"Suspects you? Yes. As long as he's got a jones to collar any Boldano, why leave you off the list? Lorenzo almost destroyed your relationship with your family, thanks to his BS. Sounds like a motive to me."

Fear colored Jamie's face. "Sonuva . . . You're right." He took a step, then stopped. "Mia . . . you don't think . . ."

"You killed him? Of course not." She saw Pete making purposeful progress toward them. "But I'm super-worried he might. So *go*."

Jamie needed no additional convincing to make a speedy exit. He disappeared into the crowd. Before Pete could corner her, Mia raced up the front steps of her house. She locked the front door and extinguished the outside lights. The bling blaze of the Carina holiday decorations went to black as Mia climbed the stairs to her apartment, knowing a restless night awaited her.

CHAPTER 7

Since NYPD's hands were tied until Lorenzo's death was officially ruled a homicide, the Boldanos earned a brief respite from being in Pete's crosshairs. Mia hoped he was using the time to ID other potential suspects. Given how much trouble Teri encountered trying to research the con artist, she knew it was no easy task, but Mia assumed NYPD had better access to criminal records than a Queens beat reporter.

In the meantime, Mia paid a long-overdue to her brother Positano at the Triborough Correctional Facility. She greeted guard Henry Marcus like the old friend he was, given the number of sentences various friends and family members had served at the institution. While waiting for her brother to join her in the visiting room, she gazed out a small, barred window, where fat snowflakes drifted lazily toward the street. *We might have a white*

Christmas this year, she thought. She recalled Lorenzo sharing at the Belle View tree-lighting party how much he loved the holidays. *His Christmas sneakers will never jingle again*, she thought with a sudden pang of sadness.

"Well, will you look at who decided to honor me with a visit."

The acerbic comment came from her brother. Mia tore herself away from her wintry musings. Posi folded his arms in front of a chest pumped up from prison gym workouts and gazed at her with a reproachful expression. In the league of handsome men, he ranked only slightly under Shane. Inspired by an ex-con who had gone viral with the hashtag *#anotherhotconvict*, Posi hoped to translate his good looks into a post-prison modeling career and billionaire heiress girlfriend like his idol, but so far nothing had come of it.

"Hi, Po." Not allowed physical contact, Mia blew him a kiss. "Sorry I haven't been by in a while. Things have been a *little* crazy."

"Yeah, I heard about that Lorenzo character." Posi parked himself across the table from her in a beat-up plastic chair. "Mom came by this morning and filled me in. Gotta love that *Daily News* headline: Dead Elf on the Shelf."

"Mom was here?"

"Yeah. Today and yesterday. I'm seeing her more than you these days."

"She's making up for lost time," Mia said, "which I don't have to do, since up until the holiday season, I'm here a couple of times a week."

"Noted."

The siblings became quiet. "Any idea why she's in town all of a sudden?" Mia asked her brother. "I know something's up. I'm sure of it. But I can't get a read on what it is."

"Me neither." Posi frowned.

"You think it could just be because she misses us?" Mia asked, her tone tentative.

Posi cocked his head, his expression cynical. "Do you? Don't bother answering. That's what they call a . . ." He creased his brow and snapped his fingers, searching for a word. "Henry, what am I looking for here? I got an 'r' but that's it."

"Rhetorical," the guard offered.

Posi's brow cleaned. "Yeah, that's it. When you ask something as a question, but it's not a question because you already know the answer."

"That was a long way to go to get to 'no, she's not here because she misses us,'" Mia said, annoyed.

"My bad."

"And I think you're wrong. She's changed. I don't know what happened to her, but she's like . . . human. You should have seen how upset she was about Lorenzo. She said"—Mia choked up—"he was 'somebody's son.'"

"Uh-oh. She's sucking you in. Don't go there, little sis. Do. Not. Go. There." Posi drummed his fingers on the table. "Has she said anything about Angelo?"

"Nothing, except that he's good."

"She said the same thing to me when I asked after him. Which means he's not. Or they're not. Sniff around there for some intel."

"I'll try, but I'm super-busy at Belle View."

"Glad to hear," her brother said with a broad smile. "I can't wait to get outta this dump and start working with you. No offense, Henry."

"None taken," the burly African-American guard said. "You'd be lying if you spoke otherwise."

"You wouldn't believe how much business Shane's brought in," Mia said, her voice filled with enthusiasm. "It's insane. Plus, he's amazing with memes and computer stuff, so it's like we have an in-house graphics guy."

"Whoopee." Posi glowered as he said this.

"You've frowned a lot today. You're gonna get wrinkles."

"So?" The glower turned into a pout.

"'So?' From the guy who taught himself how to laugh in a way that wouldn't give him laugh lines? What's your problem? You sound like a five-year-old."

"Hate to interrupt, but"—Henry indicated his watch—"tick tock."

"Thanks for the alert." Mia stood up. "Po, do me a favor. Check with your fellow miscreants here and see if you come up with anything on Lorenzo Puglia. Teri and I think he cleaned himself off the internet. Which means he's got something to hide." Posi grunted a sulky response. "Fine," Mia said. "Be that way."

She went to Henry to retrieve her purse. "Cut him some slack," the guard said in a low voice. "Being here at the holidays is tough on the boys."

"You're right," Mia said, feeling contrite. "Posi, I'm—"
She pivoted back to him, but her brother was gone.

The lull in Lorenzo's case disappeared the minute the news broke that according to the police, he died under "suspicious circumstances." "He took a blow to the head that resulted in a deadly cerebral hemorrhage," revealed Cammie, who finagled the details out of Pete in exchange for what she referred to as "nooky lite." "But what's weird is that he also had cyanide in his system. Not enough to kill him, but enough to make him pretty sick."

"Hmm." Maggie digested this, along with a forkful of leftover moussaka from a big fat Greek wedding. She and Cammie were taking their lunch break in the Belle View kitchen, although "break" was euphemism in Cammie's case, considering she'd only shown up to deliver the report on Lorenzo's demise and snag to-go containers of Greek food for her evening dinner. "Maybe the cyanide made Lorenzo disoriented, and he hit his head when he fell," Mia posited. "The police haven't gone all the way to calling his death *murder*. Do you know if they're exploring the accidental-death angle?"

"Doubtful. There were other injuries on the vic's body consistent with a fight. Oooh, listen to me. I sound like such a pro." Cammie spooned moussaka into a large plastic container. "You don't mind, do you? I promised Pete I'd 'make him dinner' tonight."

"There's ingredients for a Greek salad too. And cookies. Help yourself." Mia hopped off the barstool she'd been sitting on. She rinsed her plate and placed it in one of the kitchen's two industrial dishwashers. "Lorenzo's funeral is tomorrow morning. To make nice with Jamie, Donny and Aurora are paying for everything, including a luncheon here after. Teri got word out through the *Trib*. It'll be interesting to see who shows up."

"I can tell you two people who'll be at the funeral: Pete and Ryan."

"No surprise there. But I hope they eyeball other suspects besides the Boldanos."

"I'll drop a lot of hints with Pete at dinner tonight."

Cammie removed a tin tray from the refrigerator. "But to seal the deal, I'm taking the rest of the baklava."

Conveniently for Mia, the Boldanos had booked her neighborhood church, Our Lady of Perpetual Anguish, for Lorenzo's funeral service. Showing up merely required crossing the street from her home, which Mia did shortly before ten a.m. the next morning. She nodded to Pete and Ryan, who sat in the last pew, the better to suss out the mourners. Mia joined her father and grandmother, who were already there, in a front pew behind Donny Senior, Junior, and Aurora. Jamie was serving as a pallbearer. She was happy to see his girlfriend Madison sitting next to Aurora. It indicated the couple had reconciled.

Mia scanned the small turnout. There were a couple of elderly women dressed all in black whose hobby was showing up and keening at local funerals. Elisabetta and her fellow senior parishioners called them "the weepers." Of more interest to Mia were three men sitting together in a middle pew, ranging from middle age to mid-twenties. The two older men seemed appropriately sad while the younger, a scrawny guy whose sandy hair was already thinning, gave off the vibe of wanting to be anywhere but at this funeral Mass. Mia could relate. She generally found them both depressing and boring. But she wondered if his reluctance stemmed from a more personal grievance. "Be right back," she whispered to her father and grandmother.

"*Va bene, ma* make it quick. The Mass is gonna start any minute." Elisabetta took a pair of earplugs from her purse and stuffed them in her ears. "The weepers haven't been to a funeral in a while. They could get loud today."

Mia approached the three men. She spoke in a low

voice. "Hello, I'm Mia Carina. A close friend of the Boldano family." She name-dropped on purpose to get the men's attention and was two-thirds successful. The older men sat up straight and faced her, but their younger companion slouched and scrolled through an app on his phone. "Were you friends of the deceased?"

"Coworkers," the beefier of the two older men said.

"And friends," the other added.

The young man gave a derisive snort, which earned him an elbow in the ribs from the second man, who barked, "Bradley, show some respect."

"Ow." Bradley rubbed his side and glared at him.

"I wanted to let you know that the Boldanos are hosting a luncheon at Belle View Banquet Manor after we depart from the cemetery. I hope you'll join us."

"Thank you," the first man said. "That's kind of the Boldanos. I'm Ralph Mastacciolo and this is Pauly D'Annunzio. We own the Sorrento Deli and Pasticceria in Long Island City. Lorenzo worked for us as a deliveryman, along with Brad here."

"I'm sorry for your loss."

Brad rolled his eyes, making sure Pauly didn't notice to spare himself another painful rib poke.

Somber music wafted down from the organist in the balcony. Mia scurried toward her pew. She stopped short when she passed a woman in a black leather trench coat, her black hair looped into a tight bun. She clutched a rosary in one hand. "Mom?" Mia whispered. "What are you doing here?"

"Paying my respects," Gia said. "I feel terrible for the young man."

She turned away from her daughter, knelt, and started running the rosary beads through her fingers, indicating the conversation was over. The heavy church doors swung open. Mia made it to her spot just as the pallbearers, who included Santino as well as Jamie, wheeled in an ornate casket. Father Dominic followed, swinging a thurible containing incense above the casket as a sign of honor to the deceased. Aida walked slowly behind him, supporting her sobbing daughter Renata. Pauly blew Aida a kiss. She used her free hand to blow one back. *That's interesting*, Mia thought. She craned her neck to see if detectives Pete and Ryan noticed the interaction and was happy to see their eyes were on the deli employees.

The weepers burst into a show of grief so dramatic and loud that Mia wished she'd brought her own earplugs. They instantly quieted when Father Dominic began to speak. The priest, who was a stranger to Lorenzo, kept the remarks about the deceased generic. Within an hour, the mourners were on their way to Lorenzo's final resting place at one of Queens' many cemeteries. "No wonder they say there are more people who are dead than alive in this borough," Mia commented as Ravello followed the small funeral cortege on the Horace Harding Expressway in his circa–mid-2000s Lincoln.

"Eh?" Elisabetta removed her earplugs. "*Mi dispiace*, I forgot to take these out."

"Mama, you don't have to come to the burial site," her son said. "You can wait in the car if you want."

"Nah, it'd be good for me to take a *passagiata* before lunch." Elisabetta patted her stomach under her heavy black woolen coat, which was older than Mia. "Make room for a second helping of *struffoli*."

"Have either of you ever been to Sorrento Deli and Pasticceria in Long Island City?"

Her father and grandmother answered in the negative.

"Why do you ask?" Ravello's tone was wary. He had an uncanny ability to sense when Mia was up to something.

"It's where Lorenzo worked. His bosses and coworker were the three guys at Mass today. I invited them to the luncheon. I thought maybe we could order from them sometime."

Her father muttered something in Italian that loosely translated to "here we go again." "You think they know something about Lorenzo?"

"I'm thinking if anyone does, it's them. So it wouldn't hurt to get to know the Sorrento staff better."

The cortege exited the expressway and drove through local streets until it reached the somber stone gates marking the entrance to St. Charles Borromeo Cemetery. The chain of cars, led by the hearse, traveled up the cemetery's center road until finally pulling over and parking. The mourners left their cars and tromped through piles of snow to the burial site. The temperature had dropped from cold to bone-chilling. As Father Dominic sprinkled holy water over the interment site, Mia, who regretted wearing stylish instead of warm boots, hopped from foot to foot to keep frostbite at bay. The priest, whose bulbous nose was turning scarlet, raced through the Rite of Committal to get to the closing prayer. Mia was blowing on her hands, clad in decorative but useless leather gloves, when she saw two couples who appeared to be in their late thirties, accompanied by an older woman whose eyes were hidden behind sunglasses. "Excuse me," the woman said to Mia, her voice low. "Is this the service for Lorenzo Puglia?"

"Yes," Mia said. "Are you a friend of his?"

"No." The woman took off her sunglasses, revealing red-rimmed eyelids. "I'm his mother."

CHAPTER 8

Mia's mouth dropped open. Father Dominic launched into the fastest rest-in-peace prayer she'd ever heard, then darted back to a limo that would ferry him home to the warmth of his rectory. The small group began to disperse. Mia held up a hand to stop them. "Everybody, this is Lorenzo Puglia's mother."

"Joan," the woman said. "Joan Puglia."

The group stared at her. Gia gasped and turned so pale Mia feared she might pass out. Even Renata, who knew Lorenzo biblically, seemed stunned to learn he had a mother.

Joan gestured with a gloved hand to the couples standing with her. "This is Lorenzo's big brother Drew and his wife Bridget." Drew and Bridget, who exuded the confidence and well-maintained good looks of a power couple, said brief hellos. "And this is his sister Chrissy and her husband Kevin."

Kevin gave Mia's hand a hearty shake. "Kevin Turman. Nice to meet you, despite the circumstances."

Chrissy, cheerful and doughy, beamed a smile that her mate, who also exuded affability, mirrored. "I'm the middle kid," she said, offering a piece of information that didn't seem remotely relevant.

"We heard about Lorenzo on the news," her husband said.

"I saw a few pictures," Lorenzo's mother Joan said, "and recognized his jingle sneakers." She choked up and put her sunglasses back on.

"Yeah." Chrissy gave her mother a comforting pat on the back. "He drove us crazy with those things." Lorenzo's middle sister tried and failed to imbue the sentence with a modicum of affection.

"We were disappointed to miss the funeral," Bridget said without sounding remotely disappointed. "But Drew had to put out a fire. Not a literal one. One of his constituents needed help getting an eviction served. Drew is a council member in Hempstead."

Mia doubted anyone ever sounded prouder dropping a Long Island town political position.

Aurora found her voice. "We're so sorry for your loss. We're having a luncheon at the Belle View Banquet Manor in honor of Lorenzo. You must come."

"Thank you," Joan said. It was hard to believe that the dignified woman, who seemed a match for Aurora in stature and grace, had birthed a lowlife like Lorenzo.

Mia and Ravello hurried back to Belle View to host the luncheon and found Detectives Dianopolis and Hinkle had beat them there. Dianopolis was writing in his notepad as Hinkle eyed the lunch buffet with hungry eyes. "We're gonna mingle with the mourners and see if we can dig up any new clues," Pete informed Mia.

"It's a small crew," Mia said. "If you're going for subtle, good luck. But . . ." Mia grabbed the chance to shift the detectives' attention away from the Boldanos. "I know you and Pete were doing a little surveillance at the cemetery. I'm sure you saw the new mourners show up, but you were too far away to get the details on who they were—Lorenzo Puglia's mother, along with a sister and brother and their spouses."

Pete raised an eyebrow. "Interesting."

"They're coming to the luncheon." Mia spoke in a conspiratorial tone, hoping Pete would spark to a new cast of potential suspects.

"Hinkle, I want you all over Puglia's immediate relatives," the detective said to his partner, rewarding her efforts. "Hinkle. Hey!"

Hinkle tore himself away from the buffet. "Sorry. The baby was fussy this morning. All I had time to eat for breakfast was a teething biscuit. I'm starving."

Mia handed each man a plate. "You should eat before the guests come so you can focus all your attention on them. Especially those mysterious Puglias."

She left the two men piling their plates with food. She tracked down Cammie, who was in her office holding a hand under a nail dryer. "Cam, can you keep an eye on Pete and Ryan for me? Relatives of Lorenzo's showed up at the interment. I'm trying to make sure the investigation focuses on them and not the Boldanos."

"You're in luck. I just finished my new manicure, so I have some free time."

"All you ever have here is free time. With the occasional side of work."

"Which is why I love my 'job' so much." Cammie held up her hand. "Look. Little Christmas trees. You have to admit I have a talent for this."

A murmur of voices alerted Mia to the mourners' arrival. When she returned to the Marina Ballroom, she found the Boldanos, Espositos, and Lorenzo's Sorrento Deli coworkers milling around. A few made their way to the buffet line. Renata, clad in a snug, low-neck black dress better suited to a nightclub than a funeral, threw herself into Jamie's arms. "I can't believe Lorenzo's gone," she sobbed.

Jamie, looking acutely uncomfortable, muttered a few sympathetic clichés, and she rested her head on his shoulder. Madison materialized at her boyfriend's side and yanked Renata off Jamie with a force Mia didn't expect from the wispy blonde. *Nice*, she thought, impressed. Renata got the message and moved on. Unfortunately, she moved on to Shane, who was supervising the waitstaff manning the buffet station. "We haven't met," she said, dabbing at her eyes while making sure to push out her ample chest. "I'm the almost-widow."

She gave a dramatic sob and flung herself at him. He froze and shot Mia a helpless glance. Mia marched over and peeled Renata off him. "Renata, you poor thing, you could use a drink. We have an open bar today. Knock yourself out." She pushed her toward the bar, muttering, "literally." She saw Shane was still rooted to his spot. "Go to your office and lock the door," she said under breath. "I'll handle things here."

Shane nodded and made a run for it, which turned out to be unnecessary. Renata had glommed on to a receptive

Donny Junior, ignoring his mother's obvious displeasure. Mia went behind the bar and poured a large glass of red wine. She brought it to Aurora. "*Grazie*," the matriarch said without taking a break from the daggers she was shooting at her older son with her eyes.

"You looked like you could use it," Mia replied.

Aurora nodded. "That one, with his flirting all the time. And with girls like that." She exhaled a disappointed sigh. "I have to be the only Italian woman on the planet with two straight sons in their thirties who have yet to marry and give me grandbabies."

Mia saw Jamie deliver a glass of wine to Madison, along with a light kiss she happily returned. "I think there's a strong chance you'll be down to one single son in the near future."

The Puglia contingent appeared in the ballroom entry and gave a tentative glance inside. Mia went to welcome them. "I'm so glad you came. Please, help yourself to the buffet. I'll bring wine to your table."

Mia led the group to the buffet line. She then went behind the bar and retrieved four bottles of wine. She opened all four. Two were for the Puglia table, the other two for refilling empty glasses, which would hopefully loosen some lips. She aimed a bottle at her first target, Pauly, one of Lorenzo's two bosses. "It must be hard to lose a valuable employee like Lorenzo," she said, mustering up a sympathetic tone as she freshened his glass with a hefty pour of Montepulciano red wine from the Boldanos' own Abruzzo vineyard and winery.

Pauly took a swig of wine and crooked his lip. "He was . . . an employee."

Mia replaced the swig with more wine. "Not so valuable, huh?"

Pauly stole a furtive look at Aida, who was busy heap-
ing cookies and pastries from the dessert table onto a
plate. "Between us? He was a favor hire. For my girlfriend Aida."

Ah-ha, his girlfriend, Mia thought. The kiss Pauly
blew to the older Esposito woman in the church suddenly
made sense.

"She wasn't happy her precious princess Renata had
hooked up with an unemployed loser," Pauly continued.
"So, I made him employed."

Mia, eager to uncover more insight into the links between Lorenzo, the Espositos, and the Sorrento staff,
filled Pauly's glass to the brim. "Sounds like he was not-
so hot-so," she said, adding a wink to send the message
that the conversation was just between the two of them.

"Ha. That was him on a good day. The kid was lazy
and—what do they say about this generation? Entitled,
that's it. Thought he was too good to be delivering deli
and cookie trays. He really worked poor Brad over there.
Made like he was his boss. Nothing I could do about if I
wanted to keep my side of my lady's bed warm."

Ugh, Mia thought. She suppressed an image of Pauly
and Aida sharing a bed, gave Pauly another wink, and
made her escape. She headed toward Brad with her wine
bottle target, but saw he was busy trying to ingratiate
himself with an annoyed Renata, who batted him off like
a skinny black fly. Mia was glad to see that Donny Junior
seemed to have lost interest in her and relocated to his
family's table. Mia rejiggered her game plan and homed
in on Hempstead political operative Drew Puglia and his
mate. She sauntered over to them and held up her bottle.
"Can I top you off?"

Husband and wife each put a hand over their glass and replied in unison, "No, thank you."

Mia knew a couple of control freaks when she saw them. *This ain't gonna be easy*, she thought, but plunged ahead anyway. "I have a brother I'm very close to. I don't know what I'd do if anything happened to him. You must be devastated to lose Lorenzo."

"Yes," Drew said with less emotion than a still life painting.

"I only met him once, but he seemed like a good guy," Mia lied.

"Yes." Bridget alternated with her husband in giving monosyllabic responses.

Mia refused to give up. "I didn't know much about him. I met his bosses at Sorrento. They said he was a deliveryman for them."

"Yes." The nonanswers ping-ponged back to Drew.

"What did he do before then?" Mia asked.

There was a pause. A long one. Drew obviously expected his wife to field the question. When she remained mute, he gallantly stepped in for her. "Lorenzo was an adventurous soul who was beloved by all who knew him, and he will be greatly missed."

He put a hand under Bridget's elbow and steered her away from Mia. *Talk about lip flap*, Mia thought, turned off by the undynamic duo. She scoured the room and landed on Chrissy, sister to the late "adventurous soul" Lorenzo. Chrissy favored her with a warm smile, which Mia took as an opening. She crossed the room and held up her bottle of white wine to match what was lurking at the bottom of Chrissy's glass. "Refill?"

"You know it." Chrissy held out her glass and Mia

gave it a nine-ounce pour. "I'm an hour away from drinking straight from the bottle."

Mia chuckled. She appreciated that the middle sibling seemed completely comfortable with who she was. Chrissy wore a black turtleneck and her feet, clad in utilitarian sheepskin boots, peeked out from under unstylish black polyester pants with an elastic waist she didn't bother to hide with a belt. Sensing a straight shooter, Mia opted for a direct approach. "I've heard mixed things about your brother."

Chrissy inhaled a good ounce of wine and chortled. "Mixed? He should be so lucky. We're only here out of respect for my mother. Even if Dad weren't laid up, he wouldn't be here today."

"Dad?" Mia repeated, confused. "Lorenzo told us he was the only child of a single mother." Still wary about who to trust, she kept the Boldano angle he'd tried to play to herself.

Chrissy guffawed. "He wished. Dad is in the hospital recovering from gallbladder surgery. Mom drove him crazy with the way she babied Lorenzo. And look how it turned out."

Her husband Kevin approached, holding two plates of desserts. "I made you a plate, sweetie. Hello," he greeted Mia with a grin that matched his wife's for warmth. "Great place you got here. Chrisselah, we should think about this for our anniversary party."

"We're coming up on ten years." Chrissy blew an affectionate kiss at her husband and he blew one back. Mia began to wonder if they were for real, then castigated herself for the skeptical thought. "Mia was asking about Lorenzo."

Kevin pulled a face. "That snake. Don't tell me not to

talk ill of the dead. In this case, the guy earned it. You know what he did? Tried to get me to embezzle from my clients. 'You're their accountant,' he said. 'The one doing their books. How are they gonna know?' Like being caught was the problem and not doing something that would take advantage of people who put their trust in me *and* could get me sent to prison. Lorenzo was born bad." Kevin put a hand on his wife's arm. "And I love your mother like she's my own, but Joan didn't help with all her babying."

"I know, I know." Chrissy sighed and shook her head. "She still doesn't believe me about the stealing."

"Stealing?" *Ooh, this is such good stuff. I love these two.*

Kevin pursed his lips. "We realized that after a Lorenzo 'visit,' things in the house went missing. It took a while because we've got three kids under eight, so the place is always a mess. No offense to you, sweetie," he hastened to add. His wife flapped a hand to indicate he needn't worry about it. "Silver and crystal we got as wedding pres- ents, stuff like that. When I caught him dropping a couple of spoons down his pants, that was it. I banned him from the house. Joan insisted there must be a logical explana- tion. You tell me a good reason why a guy needs spoons in his pants." To Mia's ears, Kevin sounded as aggrieved as the day he caught Lorenzo with his pants down figura- tively and filled with valuable silverware literally.

"I'm gonna see if Mom wants to go," Chrissy said. "This has been a hard day for her."

"I'll come with," Kevin said. "Nice talking to you, Mia. We appreciate all you and the Boldanos have done for Lorenzo. You gave him better than he deserved."

They walked away. Mia studied the gathering to see

who she might ply with wine next. She landed on Ralph Mastacciolo but got a nasty feeling in the pit of her stomach when she saw who he was talking to. Her mother Gia held one of his big paws between her delicate hands, listening intently as he appeared to be pouring his heart out. *So much for coming to town because she missed her kids*, Mia thought with a combination of disappointment and fury. *She and Angelo must be on the outs and she's already trolling for stooge husband number three.*

Feeling burned, Mia started toward Gia, determined to confront her. She was waylaid by Cammie, who grabbed her arm and pulled her into a corner. "We're gonna be short two wineglasses going back with the rentals. Pete and Ryan pulled them to match DNA against samples they found on Lorenzo."

Mia sussed out the guests. They'd broken into their clans. The Boldanos laid claim to one table while the Espositos huddled at the next table over. The Puglias were having a family conference at a table far away from the others, but near where the Sorrento deli crew was camped out. Pauly said something to Ralph, who was still being comforted by Gia, then left to join his girlfriend Aida and the Espositos. "Do you know who was using the glasses Pete and Ryan took?"

Cammie gave a grim nod. "Donny Junior. And Jamie."

CHAPTER 9

Mia cursed under her breath. "This room is full of suspects and they *still* have the Boldanos in their crosshairs?"

"Apparently."

Mia deliberated for a minute. "Hmm. I wonder . . . I'm gonna do some sleuthing. Don't leave when this is over. I want to run a few thoughts about this whole thing by you."

"No problem, as long as I can count it as billable hours."

Mia faked a casual stroll over to the Espositos. "Hi, you guys. I wanted to see how you're doing. I know how tough this whole thing has been on you."

She sat down before anyone could chase her off, but the Espositos didn't seem inclined to dismiss her. "A nightmare," Santino concurred. "A flippin' nightmare. Your sympathy is greatly appreciated."

Santino moved his chair closer to Mia's. She subtly inched away from him. "It was really nice of the Boldanos to host this luncheon," she said, "especially considering Lorenzo was trying to scam them into thinking he was Jamie's long-lost brother."

She dropped the last statement like it was a lit M80. But it didn't evoke the response she expected. "It's so generous and kind of them," Aida agreed. "I've been afraid the Boldanos would think we were in on the scam with that idio—Lorenzo. You don't want to tick off a family like them. We even thought they might have been the ones who . . ."

"Eighty-sixed him," Santi said, trying to be helpful.

His sister shuddered. "But you can see they had nothing to do with it. He was too small-time for them to bother with. Which is kinda sad."

Mia had to agree with the late loser's girlfriend. Santi pushed his chair closer. Having run out of room to scoot away from his advances, Mia stood up. "I have to get back to work. If I can help in any way, please let me know."

"You got it," Santino said with a leer.

Gross! Mia thought as she smiled at him.

The luncheon ended shortly afterwards. When the last guest left, Mia texted Cammie to meet in her office. Cammie showed up carrying a caddy filled with manicure supplies. "Can I do a practice mani on you? I watched a tutorial on how to paint little Rudolphs and use red rhinestones as his nose. It's adorbs."

"Why not? I can think out loud while you paint."

Cammie assembled her tools. She picked up one of

Mia's hands and carefully examined it. "I never noticed you were a nail-biter. You're not giving me much to work with here. I'll have to improvise." She began filing Mia's nails.

"Let's talk suspects," Mia said. "Starting with the Espositos. I tried to shock them by revealing I knew Lorenzo was faking his relationship to Jamie, but they didn't react in a guilty way. I believed Aida when she said she was worried her family might get sucked into the scheme and face retribution from the Boldanos."

"That's her, but what about her spawn?" Cammie finished filing the nails on Mia's left hand and picked up her right one. "The daughter's looking to harpoon a whale. Once the Boldano connection didn't pan out, she would've dropped Lorenzo like a Hot Pocket straight outta the toaster. I don't know what the deal is with the brother. My guess is he'd easy hop on to an easy ride. He wants to get with you, by the way."

Mia wrinkled her nose, repelled by the thought. "I know. I may have to play the sexually-transmitted disease card to lose him. But that's for down the road. I may need to work him for more information first."

"I'm skipping your cuticles since you pretty much chewed them down to nothing." Cammie applied a base coat to hand one. "What's your take on Lorenzo's birth family?"

"Yeah, them. Quite a bunch. I think Joan, the mom, is genuinely grieving. I got the impression from his sibs that she spoiled him rotten. Older brother Drew is a career politician, and you can put money on him wanting to trade up from Hempstead councilman. And if you think he's ambitious, his wife makes him look like an underachiever. A con man brother trying to pull one over on a famous mobster like Donny Boldano is a nightmare scenario for them. Drew didn't strike me as the type to get his hands dirty, but I have no problem seeing his missus doing whatever it takes to ensure her family's success and prosperity."

"Other hand."

Mia offered her left hand back to Cammie. "Lorenzo's sister Chrissy and her husband were super-honest about how much they couldn't stand Lorenzo. Honestly, it was almost to the point where I could see either one of them snapping and giving him a hard bonk on the head. Then there's the Sorrento deli group. Pauly only hired him as a favor to his girlfriend. I wonder if Lorenzo was playing them too. You know, the occasional delivery gone 'missing.' Sold on the sly, the money pocketed. Once a grifter, always a grifter."

"You're letting your personal feelings get in the way, ya know."

"What?" Annoyed, Mia pulled her hand away from Cammie. "No, I'm not."

Cammie retrieved Mia's hand. "Yes, you are. You haven't brought up the Boldanos as suspects. Or Jamie's girlfriend, the sorority chick with the first name that's a last name."

"Madison?"

"Right. Like the president. With the wife they named the bakery after. Remember Dolly Madison chocolate and raspberry zingers? *Yum.*"

"Thanks a lot. Now I want one. Of each."

"Back to suspects."

"Fine. The *Boldanos*." Still feeling defensive, Mia emphasized the name. "All Donny Senior and Aurora want is for Jamie to love them again, and they would not accomplish this by offing Lorenzo. If Jamie was gonna kill anyone, which he never would, it'd be his parents for lying to him all these years. As for Donny Junior, I gotta say, it's not impossible. He's not a guy who puts a lot of thought into what he does. I could see him going postal on Lorenzo. Not to intentionally murder him. More like a fight that went wrong. And you're right. I can't rule out Jamie's girlfriend. We were once at a sample sale where a woman went for a purse Madison already had her hand on. It got ugly. The girl can be vicious." Mia furrowed her brow. "Still . . . I'm gonna start elsewhere." She switched hands again with Cammie. "I've got a plan."

Cammie shot Mia a look. "You do know that Pete is good at his job, don't you? Yeah, he took the glasses for Boldano DNA samples, but that doesn't mean he's gonna rule out everyone else. He knows there's a fifty-fifty chance he won't find a match."

"Yes," Mia acknowledged. "I've butted heads with Pete enough to have some respect for him. But I also know that there's a lot going on in Queens and this isn't Pete's only case. All I want is to move things along if I can."

"I can accept that. So, what's your plan?"

"It's a good one."

Mia, excited, instinctively moved to rub her hands together. "Stop that," Cammie scolded.

"Sorry." Mia began detailing her idea. "Lorenzo was living with the Espositos. I'm going to tell them the Puglias would like some of his belongings and snag a few things. Then I'll tell Drew Puglia the Espositos thought his family would want them, which will give me an excuse to visit him and ask a few questions. In a subtle way, of course."

"Of course."

"Then," Mia continued, her enthusiasm growing with each element of subterfuge, "I connect with Chrissy and Kevin by saying that Belle View is looking for a new accountant. Considering the guy who does our books works out of a supply closet in the back of his father's hardware store, this isn't a complete lie. Same with how I get an in at Sorrento Deli. We're always looking for partnerships with stores that can save us the trouble of doing deli spreads or cookie platters. But here's the best part of my plan and it involves you."

Cammie stopped painting mid-antler. "It does?" She sounded wary.

"I want to pay a visit to the salon where Renata and Aida work. I can never get them alone, so I thought we'd each get a facial with Renata and a massage with Aida. We could each ask a few questions and share whatever we come up with. I'll count it as company hours."

"To confirm, you're asking to pay me to get a facial and a message."

"Yes."

Cammie cast her eyes heavenward. "Thank you."

"As soon as we're done here and my nails dry, I'll book us appointments at Rejuve."

"I've been wanting to try them. I was gonna book their 'Day of Beauty' package for my birthday. You just saved Pete a fortune." Cammie glued down a final rhinestone. "There. All done."

Mia held up her hands. Ten reindeer faces beamed at

her, each with a shiny red nose. "Cammie, I love it. You did an amazing job."

Her friend accepted the compliment with a small bow. "Consider it a thank you for our spa daycation. I'm not even gonna charge Belle View for the time it took for the manicure."

Cammie set a timer on Mia's phone and left her with her drying nails. While she sat there, hands splayed out on the desk, Mia replayed Gia's behavior with Ralph at the funeral luncheon, her anger increasing with each passing second. When the timer finally dinged, she went to the Rejuve website and booked hers and Cammie's appointments for the following day, then marched to her father's office. "Mom was all over Ralph today at the funeral luncheon," she declared with no preamble. "She's trolling for a new husband."

Ravello pushed aside his computer mouse, which looked tiny in his large hand. He sighed. "I wasn't going to say anything, but she came by my house the day she arrived. She admitted leaving me was a mistake."

"Did she want to get back together with you?"

"She didn't come out and say so, but she gave me that impression." Mia released a stream of foul language. Her father winced. "*Bambina, marone.* That language would shock a Marine."

"I'm sorry, but I'm so mad at Mom." Mia collapsed onto one of the two utilitarian folding metal chairs that sat opposite her father's desk. "Why can't she ever be honest with us? Or with anyone? All that crap about missing me and Posi."

"I don't think it's crap, *bella*." Ravello leaned back in his office chair, his large body dwarfing the chair. "I think she meant it. There's something different about her. It's like she aged. Not on the outside but on the inside. She used to be light and gay and self-confident. All that seems gone. Instead, she seems weighted down by life. You must have noticed."

Unwilling to cut her mother any slack, Mia chose not to agree with her father. "No." He threw her a reproachful glance. "Fine, she does seem a little down. Payback for all the grief she caused us."

Ravello rolled back to his desk. He leaned in toward his daughter. "*Bellissima*, I understand why you're angry at her. I spent years feeling the same way. And then I met Lin."

"What are you trying to say? That I'd feel better if I had a boyfriend?" Tears stung Mia's eyes, but she fought them back. She knew she sounded childish but didn't care.

This drew another look of reproach from her father. "You didn't let me finish. I met Lin and realized that if I brought my anger into a relationship with her, it would doom it. So I forced myself to let go. And I'm the happiest I've ever been except for the births of my two beautiful children." The tears Mia had managed to control spilled over her eyelids. "Talk to your mother. Find out what's going on with her. Have the adult conversation you've never had before."

"Maybe." Mia swiped at her eyes with the sleeve of her top. "Right now I have more important things to do, like get Belle View through holidays season and keep the Boldano brothers out of jail."

"Uh-huh," Ravello said, distracted. "What did you do to your hands?"

"Oh, Cammie gave me a Rudolph mani." Mia held up her hands and wiggled her fingers. "Cute, huh?"

"Yes." Ravello pondered her nails. "Do you think a manicure would be a good Christmas present for Lin?"

Mia imagined the elegant prosecutor-turned-florist with a set of decorated fingernails and shook her head. "I don't think Lin is the mani-pedi type."

"No," Ravello said, deflated. "Back to square one."

Mia left her father searching the internet for the elusive perfect Lin present. She passed Shane, who was giving a tour to a small group of giggling women in their forties who were elbowing each other out of the way to claim a spot next to him. One woman batted her eyes with such intensity she knocked a false eyelash out of place. Mia plopped down into her office chair and was about to comb through the day's invoices when her cell rang with a call from teen drama queen, Kaitlyn. *Please don't let this be a problem with the sweet sixteen theme. If it is, I swear I'll chop a hole in the Flushing Bay ice and jump in.* "Kaitlyn, hi." Mia loaded her voice with false cheer. "Whassup?"

"Everything's okay with the party." Kaitlyn's voice quivered. "It's other stuff. I just needed . . . I don't know . . . someone to talk to."

Mia felt for the insecure girl. Kaitlyn's parents seemed at a loss when it came to dealing with her teen mood swings, opting to throw money at their daughter in the vain hope it would solve her problems. Mia thought of her relationship with her own parents. A father who tried to be there but often wasn't, emotionally or physically, given his occasional jail stints. A mother who was so wrapped up in her own disasters that she didn't have the bandwidth or interest in dealing with her kid's traumas. At least Mia always had her brother Posi. Kaitlyn was an only child. "Talk to me," Mia told the girl.

Twenty minutes later, Mia had helped Kaitlyn pick out two party dresses online, brainstormed a way the teen could let Dylan Schiff know she *like*-liked him, and helped her come up with a theme for an English paper on *The Great Gatsby*, which as luck would have it, was a favorite of Mia's and one of the few books she remembered reading in high school. "Love you," Kaitlyn said. This time the sign-off was more than words.

"Love you too," Mia replied, meaning it.

Shane appeared in her doorway. "I overheard a little of your conversation with Kaitlyn when I was leading the League ladies out."

"Did they ask for autographs?"

"No. Well . . ." Shane blushed. "One had a copy of an Italian *Vogue* I was in. I wish I could burn all those old magazines."

He delivered this with such bitterness that Mia felt bad for teasing him. "I was kidding. I think it's sweet. And doesn't hurt business, that's for sure."

"Back to Kaitlyn," Shane said, obviously eager to change the subject. "If you want me to, I'm happy to manage her. I got experience doing that with my kid sister."

Shane was so circumspect about his personal life that Mia forgot he had a little sister. But she responded, "No worries. I'm okay with handling Kaitlyn. She's a sweet kid and could use a friendly ear, as opposed to that viper's nest of a high school social scene."

Shane laughed a laugh of recognition. He squinted.

"Why do I see little rainbows every time you move your hands?"

"Oh. Cammie tried out some nail art on me."

Mia held up her hands. Shane stepped into the office. He took her hands in his and examined them. A thrilled shudder shot through Mia's entire body, followed by a woozy sensation. "Cute," Shane said, releasing her hands.

"Thanks." Mia managed a nonchalant smile.

This is becoming a problem, she thought, melancholy. *I may have to fire him.*

CHAPTER 10

A Knights of Columbus holiday party kept Mia at Belle View until the early hours of the morning. "I hope the teens are less rowdy than the Knights crowd," she told Doorstop as she negotiated space on the bed with the sleepy cat. She passed out, only to be awakened a few hours later by Tony Bennett blasting jazzy takes on holiday favorites. Mia stumbled out of bed. She showered and changed into warm leggings, a purple fleece pullover, and purple UGGs she'd bought with one of Madison's precious discount coupons. After inhaling a yogurt and some leftover *struffoli* honey balls, she padded downstairs. She tracked the music to the basement, where she located Elisabetta and Philip counting coins and crumpled bills. "Donations?"

"*Si*." Elisabetta stacked up quarters. "I admit it's tough to compete with that Jacinta and her Tony Benne-Santa, but with all the attention on our block, we gotta have a bead on donations. I haven't checked the Levines' box in a few days because I couldn't find their keys."

"They were hidden under a pile of wrapping paper." Philip held a keychain. A silver *hamsa*, the hand-shaped amulet representing the hand of God, dangled from it.

"I was sure the Levines' box would be loaded thanks to all the looky-loos checking out the crime scene," Elisabetta said.

"Yes, I noticed you replaced the crime scene tape as an added draw," Mia said, amused.

Elisabetta tallied up figures she'd written on a piece of scrap paper she'd created from an old paper menu trumpeting pizza prices that hadn't been around since the 1970s. She frowned. "Not even twenty bucks." She narrowed her eyes. "It's those *cretini* from Forty-fifth Place. I bet they're talking people out of coming on our block."

"Not to boast," Philip said, boasting, "but we've received almost two hundred dollars in our box already. I guess the neighborhood was more ready for a modern twist on holiday decorations than *some* people thought." He directed this at Elisabetta, who shot him a dirty look.

"Nonna, you might also want to take a look at your past with the other blocks," Mia said. "I seem to remember a certain *someone* spreading a false rumor that the brownies Forty-third Place was selling as part of their fundraising efforts were laced with a diuretic."

"Some of them were made with *carruba*, carob," Elisabetta said, offering a weak defense. "It can make you go."

This engendered an eye roll from both Mia and Philip. "My advice, Nonna? Make nice with the neighbors on the other blocks: Forty-second, Forty-third, Forty-fourth. That'll counterbalance your feud with Jacinta." Mia kissed her grandmother on both cheeks, then took off to meet Cammie at Rejuve.

The Rejuve lobby managed to give off a vibe of combination doctor's office and yoga studio. White leather chairs ringed three walls. A pretty young receptionist clad in a white medical gown sat behind a white desk. The kind of tinkling music that usually accompanied a sleep app wafted in from hidden speakers. The sound served as background noise to a stone fountain burbling in the room's center. The whole place reminded Mia of movie scenes depicting the waiting room for Heaven. "Welcome to Rejuve," the receptionist said.

Her thick Queens accent broke the mood. Mia got a jolt of recognition at the sight of her perfectly made-up face, with its bow-shaped lips and powder-blue eye shadow. She knew the receptionist from somewhere but couldn't place where. "I'm Mia Carina. I scheduled appointments for myself and my friend Cammie Dianopolis. With Renata for facials and Aida for massages."

The receptionist checked a tablet. Mia noticed she was wearing a name necklace and adjusted her position so she could read it. *Zoe. Nope, doesn't ring a bell,* she thought.

"Ms. Dianopolis already checked in," Zoe said. "She's with Renata getting a four-step resurfacing and antiaging nourishing radiance facial."

Mia's eyes widened. "Huh? I thought I booked a plain old regular facial."

"She traded up. She instructed us to put the difference on a credit card belonging to a Pete Dianopolis. We called him to verify, and he said yes. It sounded like he was choking."

"I bet it did." Mia couldn't help chortling at the image of Pete hearing the cost of Cammie's latest punishment.

"Aida is finishing with a client. As soon as she's done, she'll take you for your massage. Help yourself to cucumber water and organic trail mix."

"Yum," said Mia, who was not a fan of either.

She was about to sit down when a woman wearing a blissful expression exited through the door leading to treatment rooms. Aida, dressed simply in a white T-shirt and matching drawstring pants, walked behind her. "If you're here for Aida," the woman said to Mia as she passed, "you're in for a fabulous experience."

"Can't wait." Mia rubbed a crick in her neck. She was looking forward to combining sleuthing with a much-needed massage.

"Hi, Mia." Aida gave her a warm grin. She held the door open, and Mia followed her down an incense-scented hallway. "I saw you booked appointments with me and Renata. That was nice. We appreciate it." She led Mia into a small room featuring a massage table. Bottles of oils lined a shelf. One bottle rested inside a massage oil warmer. "You can hang up your clothes here." Aida pointed to a row of hooks. "Make yourself comfortable under the sheet. I'll step outside. Ring the bell when you're ready."

Aida disappeared into the hallway, allowing Mia to strip down in privacy. She climbed onto the massage table, lay on her stomach, pulled the sheet up to cover herself, then rang the small bell placed by her side. The masseuse returned to the room. "Do you prefer music or quiet?"

"Quiet, please," Mia said. *The better to hear your answers to my questions.*

Aida removed the oil container from the oil warmer and squirted a dollop into her palm. She rubbed her hands together and began kneading Mia's neck with firm fingers. Mia relaxed into the treatment. "To be honest, I was surprised you and Renata were back at work so soon after Lorenzo's . . . passing." The position of her face inside the massage-table face hole caused her voice to sound muffled.

"That piece of dirt."

Aida dug her fingers into Mia's neck with force. "Ow."

"Sorry. When I think of that—that—turd, I get so angry." Aida accompanied the statement with a few angry punches to Mia's back. "He used Renata. Took money from her. Lied to her. Cheated on her."

She punched Mia's back with each word. Mia winced but soldiered on. "Do you have any idea who might have wanted to kill him?"

Aida responded with a harsh laugh. "Who didn't wanna kill him who knew him?" She pummeled Mia's back. "I swear, I was one step away from killing him myself."

"Oof" was the only response Mia could muster.

"I was hoping when that Donny Junior went after him, he'd do us all a favor and take him out."

"Wait, what?" Stunned at this development, Mia sat up. It couldn't be. Donny Junior wouldn't be dumb enough to do something impulsive like threaten Puglia. *Oh, wait. Of course he would.* "When did Lorenzo and Little Donny go at each other?"

Aida pushed her back down. "Day before Lorenzo died. Donny showed up at our apartment and started yelling at Lorenzo for destroying his family. He threw a few punches and Lorenzo threw a few back. Donny yelled 'You'll be sorry you ever messed with us,' or something like that. Lorenzo called him a jealous idiot.

Stupid me, I broke it up and told Donny to leave. I shoulda let him keep going."

Aida transferred her anger into her fists, pummeling Mia, who whimpered. "Did you tell the police about this?"

"Narc on a Boldano? Are you outta your mind? You ever hear of omertà?"

Mia had more than heard of the Mob code of silence—she'd grown up with it. Both her father and brother had passed on plea deals predicated on ratting out a colleague. She'd deeply resented the code as a child. Now she was glad it had kept the cops in the dark about Donny Junior's dustup with Lorenzo. It would give her a chance to find out more about the incident and hopefully clear Jamie's brother.

Mia's foray into uncovering clues to Lorenzo's killer had pushed a button for Aida, resulting in the most painful massage of Mia's life. A timer dinged a pleasant ping, indicated the experience was finally, blessedly, over. Aida cracked her knuckles. "Wow. I really got into that."

"Did you ever," Mia said, her voice weak.

"You can keep your clothes here and just put on a bathrobe, since you're getting a facial. I'll move your stuff to Renata's room."

Aida helped Mia off the table. The event planner wobbled, almost losing her balance. "Hard to come back to reality, huh?" Aida said this with a knowing grin.

"Mm-hmm."

Mia staggered back to the waiting room. Cammie was there, waiting for her turn with Aida. She had her feet propped up on a white leather-upholstered ottoman and was thumbing through a magazine. She munched on a

Florentine cookie. A plate of the lacy treats sat on a nearby end table. Her skin glowed. Mia lowered herself into the space next to Cammie with a groan. Cammie put down her magazine and eyed Mia. "What happened to you?"

"Aida. Talking about her daughter's late boyfriend is not her favorite subject. I learned something about Donny Junior I wasn't happy to hear, though. Did you get anything from Renata?"

"Yes. Anyone who can make my skin look this good cannot be a killer." She finished her cookie and took a second. "You have to try these. They'll make all your problems go away."

Mia reached for a cookie, moaning from the pain in her beaten-up muscles. She bit into it and moaned again, this time with pleasure. "These are unbelievable. I have to get the recipe."

Renata emerged from the treatment room hallway. Like her mother, she wore a white T-shirt and drawstring pants. "I've got your schedule for this afternoon," Zoe said, handing her a sheet of paper. Renata grunted a response. When Zoe turned away, the aesthetician fired a look of pure hatred at her back. Mia flashed on where she'd seen that expression on Renata's face before—during the visit to Hot Bods where she first met Lorenzo and the Espositos. And she realized why Zoe looked familiar. "That's where I know her from," she murmured.

"Huh?"

"Zoe," Mia whispered. "She was at Hot Bods. She flirted with Lorenzo."

Cammie wagged a finger at Mia. "What are you doing going to a dive like that? You will not find the next Mr. Carina at Hot Bods."

Renata plastered on a smile and waved at Mia. "Hi. You ready?"

Cammie patted her smooth, shiny cheek. "Prepare to be pampered."

Mia trod after Renata, who brought her to a different treatment room, one designed for facials. Like the massage room, it was painted a soothing sage green. Steam rose from a towel warmer. A variety of masques and cleansers sat atop a cabinet filled with folded towels and medical gowns. Renata handed a gown to Mia and stepped out of the room so she could change. She returned a minute later. Mia climbed into the facial chair. Renata reclined the chair, then sat on a mobile stool and rolled up to Mia. She flipped on a light bright enough to be used in an interrogation room. Mia blinked and squinted as Renata carefully examined her face. "You've got nice skin. It's pale for us Italians. Very. But still, it does a good job of hiding fine lines. You break out around your period?"

"Yes." Mia wasn't sure why she felt embarrassed admitting this, but she did.

"If you're not on the Pill, you might wanna get on it. Totally helps with breakouts."

"It's not like I need it for anything else," Mia couldn't help muttering.

"Sorry to hear that. Maybe you're better off."

Mia knew a good segue when she heard one. "I'm sorry about Lorenzo."

"Don't be. He ain't worth it." Renata took a warm cloth and slapped it on Mia's face.

Owww. "Really? How so?" Mia inhaled a mouthful of steam from the towel.

Renata swiped the towel over Mia's face and tossed it in a bin. She took an extraction tool and began digging into Mia's skin. "Jamie wasn't the only one he scammed. My family and me didn't have a clue he was faking the whole thing. But that wouldn't be the first time the SOB lied to me." She dug with more force. Mia whimpered. "*Zoe*," the aesthetician said through clenched teeth.

"The girl out front?" Mia assumed it was but wanted to confirm it.

"Yup," Renata said with an angry dig. Mia yelped in pain but the facialist didn't notice. "I found out she and Lorenzo had been hooking up behind my back. When he lost his place because he couldn't afford the rent, we let him move into our basement. They were doing the nasty there. Sometimes while me or my brother or mom was home. Santi saw her sneaking out one night when he was throwing out the garbage. He was really po'd because he'd hit on her and she turned him down."

These people are horrible, Mia thought. *And my pores are in pain.* She soldiered on. "I heard Donny Junior showed up at your place and laid into Lorenzo."

"Yeah. I wasn't there. My mom was. Donny Junior's cute. I thought he was hitting on me at the funeral lunch, but all he wanted to talk about was who didn't like Lorenzo and could've killed him. Jerk."

She accompanied the epithet with another angry go at Mia's face. "Ow!"

"Sorry. Deep blackhead."

Renata dropped the extraction tool into a container of disinfectant. She took the lid off a warming container and slathered an applicator with a muddy clay mask. She covered Mia's face with it using big, angry strokes. Mia swallowed a chunk of clay that flew into her mouth. It tasted foul. "I was so good to Lorenzo." Renata's voice trembled. "Cooked for him. Free facials whenever he wanted and let me tell you, he was very vain about his skin. Very vain. Ma even threw him a free massage sometime. And I put out. Like, a *lot*."

I so did not need to know that. "But you really had no idea that he was faking the whole long-lost brother thing with Jamie?"

Renata shook her head. She slapped a towel on top of the masque, this one hotter than the first. Mia, panicked she might suffocate, gasped for air beneath it. "And now he's gone," Renata said, "and I don't have a boyfriend. I'm *alone*."

She burst into tears and fled from the room. Mia yanked off the hot towel and bolted out of the facial chair. She spit out more clay that had found its way into her mouth and went to the room's sink. She washed her face, scrubbing it raw to remove clay that was stuck to her skin like glue. She shed her medical gown for her own clothes and made her way down the hall, limping from injuries sustained during Aida's anger-fueled massage. As she limped, Mia evaluated the potential clues she'd picked up from both women. Lorenzo had taken advantage of the Espositos as well as Jamie. Donny Junior had confronted him. Mia knew she'd have to deal with that reveal eventually but for the moment, chose to go in a different direction. Lorenzo cheating on Renata with Zoe added a new angle to his murder—revenge on the part of his wronged girlfriend.

She reached the reception area. A relaxed Cammie lolled in a leather chair with her eyes closed, her expression beatific. Zoe glanced up from her tablet, saw Mia, and screamed, snapping Cammie out of her reverie. She took one look at Mia and also screamed. "What?"

Zoe handed her a mirror. Mia saw her image and let out a shriek. Her face looked as if she'd been in a bar fight and her hair was matted with clay. One shoulder stood higher than the other, the result of compensating for pain inflicted by Aida. "I'm Quasimodo!" she wailed. "I can't go out in the world looking like this!"

"You have to," Zoe informed her. "Your face needs a couple of hours to settle. You can't put on cover-up or anything. You've got open wounds. They could get infected."

Cammie reluctantly left the comfy confines of her chair and came to Mia. "You need to get that mug under some cold compresses. STAT."

She took Mia's arm to lead her out of Rejuve. "That manicure," Zoe said, entranced. "It's spectack."

"Thank you."

Cammie held up her hands, flaunting her work. She'd painted a sparkly ornament on each nail, replete with glitter and rhinestones. Despite the humiliation and pain Mia was suffering, Zoe's admiration gave her an idea. "Cammie always needs people to practice manicures on," she said. Cammie sent Mia a quizzical glance and Mia shot one back, indicating she should follow her lead. One-on-one time with Lorenzo's side girlfriend might lead to clues about how the Espositos, particularly Renata, reacted to his duplicitous behavior.

"Yes," Cammie said. "Let me see your hands." Zoe held her hands out and Cammie gave them a once-over. "Nice, flat surface. And extremely healthy nail beds. I'd love to work with you. We'll make a date for you to come by Belle View."

"Here's my card." Mia pulled out a silver business

card holder, a gift from Ravello. "It's got my business number and cell."

Zoe beamed. "Awesome."

Mia and Cammie put on their coats and started for the door. "I'll explain everything outside," Mia whispered to her friend.

"Mia, wait," Zoe called. She turned back to see Zoe holding up her tablet. "You forgot to pay."

CHAPTER 11

Mia paid the exorbitant bill. She didn't want to alienate the Espositos, but given her incomplete facial, she felt no guilt in chintzing on Renata's tip. She and Cammie left Rejuve. Once outside, Cammie said to Mia, "'Splain, please."

The chilly air burned Mia's tender skin. She shivered under her coat. "Lorenzo was taking advantage of the Espositos and they were not happy about it." She detailed what she'd learned from the women. "That's why I want to get Zoe alone. Maybe Lorenzo said something to her that could point to his killer. Or maybe she has gossip about the Espositos that could incriminate one of them. Or all of them." Mia opted not to mention what she'd learned about Donny Junior getting into it with Lorenzo. Much as she hated omertà, sometimes keeping her trap shut was the sensible way to go.

Cammie mulled this over. "It's a good plan. And I wasn't lying when I said Zoe had nice nail beds. I already have a few ideas for her digits." The women walked toward the subway. "You headed to work? I'm certainly not, but I thought I'd be polite and ask."

"Not yet. I'm going home and taking a few hours to recuperate from my 'day of beauty.'"

"You're hiding out so that hottie Shane doesn't see you looking like you ran out of a burning building a little too late," Cammie teased.

"*Wrong.* You're the one who said I should apply cold compresses. This has nothing to do with Shane."

"No? Then you won't mind if I show him this."

Cammie snapped a picture of Mia with her phone. "Gimme that," Mia said, appalled. She went to grab the phone, then stopped herself. "You know what? Go ahead, show it to him. I don't care."

"Liar."

Cammie deleted the photo. Mia hid the sigh of relief she breathed.

The women went their separate ways at the corner. Cammie disappeared into a new boutique to put a few charges on Pete's credit card and Mia hailed a cab to take her home. Nonna's chubby terrier mix Hero barked at her like she was a burglar when she stepped into the vestibule. "It's me, Hero," she told the suspicious mutt. "Ignore the facial damage."

She tromped up the stairs. Once inside her apartment, she kicked off her boots, which were wet with street snow, and went to the kitchen, trailed by Doorstop. She fed him a few kitty treats, then ran a washcloth under cold water. She retreated to her bedroom, where parakeet Pizzazz tweeted a cheery hello. Mia laid down and placed the washcloth over her face. Its coolness refreshed her. She lowered it under her eyes so she could see her phone screen.

Her first order of business was checking in with Kaitlyn. She texted the teen, who reported that Dylan Schiff *like*-liked her too, confirming the news with a string of hearts and happy face emojis. *Mission accomplished,* Mia thought with a satisfied smile, *at least for now.* Next, she sent a lie to Santino Esposito that the Puglias had requested she gather Lorenzo's belongings together for them. She would rather have reached out to Aida or Renata, but given their animus toward Lorenzo, opted for Santi. He instantly responded that he'd be happy to return Lorenzo's belongings and invited Mia to retrieve them over drinks at Hot Bods. To skirt the horndog's blatant lust, she offered up the family-friendly, brightly lit Aquarius Diner as an alternate rendezvous spot. He reluctantly agreed and they settled on a time.

Her last task proved the most difficult. She tapped Donny Junior's cell number into her phone but stopped before entering the last digit. What would come from confronting him about his kerfuffle with Lorenzo? He'd either lie and deny it or worse, brag that yeah, he got in the jerk's face and he was glad he did. She could hear him proudly defending himself: "Nobody messes with my brother or anyone in the Family. Not on my watch." Not that it actually was his watch. Donny Senior managed the delicate balancing act of letting his hothead of a not-particularly bright namesake think he was in charge while surreptitiously delegating to more reliable, low-key lieutenants. Mia deleted the telephone number. She wanted to keep that troubling discovery to herself until she—hopefully—had evidence to prove it didn't lead to Puglia's death.

Mia removed the washcloth and got up from the bed. She checked her face in the mirror. The angry red had faded, except for a couple of extraction sites. She padded across the carpeted floors back to the kitchen, where she set up her laptop. Mia sent emails to Drew Puglia and Kevin Turman. Lorenzo's brother-in-law Kevin instantly let her know that he would be more than happy to schedule an appointment where they could discuss Belle View's accounting needs. However, Drew Puglia's secretary replied with a short email instructing Mia to mail the belongings to Drew's office; he would reimburse her for any costs incurred. Mia assessed this obstacle. After a few minutes, she landed on a way to circumvent it, but her plan required a favor from someone she knew she'd regret asking. She reluctantly tapped in Teri Fuoco's telephone number. "Hey, girlfriend," Teri answered.

Mia cringed. "Don't call me that."

"Why not? We're friends now."

Mia reminded herself of the reason for her call. "Yes. Yes, we are friends. And friends sometimes help each other out."

Teri chortled. "Somebody needs a favor."

She said this in a singsongy voice that grated on Mia, but she sucked it up. "Can I pretend to be you?"

"Oooh, this is good. *Ma perche?* As our people say."

"I need an in to Drew Puglia," Mia said.

"Lorenzo's brother? Interesting. Yes. I give you permission to be the fabulous *moi*."

"Thanks, I appreciate it."

"You're welcome. And now you owe me big-time."

Mia managed to get off the phone without shooting a snarky comment at Teri for the glee in her voice. She placed a call to Drew Puglia's office. When the secretary asked Mia to identify herself, she said, "I'm Teri Fuoco of the *Triborough Tribune*. We're doing an article on Long Island's top ten up-and-coming politicians and we'd love to interview Drew Puglia for the piece." She instantly received an appointment with the pol.

Mia heard her grandmother singing one of her favorite songs, "*Le Donne d'Orsogna*." She grinned as Elisabetta warbled the tune about how Orsognese women were all beautiful and knew how to dance the polka and tarantella. Mia sniffed the air, suddenly redolent with the scent of fresh-baked sweets. Unable to resist, Mia left her apartment for Elisabetta's quarters below. Her grandmother was in the process of removing a tray of pignoli nut cookies from the oven. "*Marone*," Elisabetta said with an expression of horror. "What happened to your face?"

"Believe it or not, this is way better than it was an hour ago." She snuck a cookie. "What's the baking for?"

"Gifts for friends."

Mia noted a cagey undertone to her grandmother's explanation. "As in friends you dissed and now want to suck up to?"

Elisabetta feigned shock. "Listen to you. So doubting. It's the holidays. Can't someone be a good person?"

"Of course. But I don't think that someone is you right now."

She tried to sneak another cookie but Elisabetta caught her and took it back. "*Basta*. No more cookies for you."

Mia heard a faint ringtone. "Shoot, that's my phone. It's upstairs."

She grabbed another cookie and ran back upstairs, ignoring her grandmother's scolding, and reached her phone before it went to voicemail. "Hey," she said, out of breath.

"How's your face?" Cammie asked. "Better?"

"A little."

"That'll have to do. Put on some nice clothes. Pete's on his way to pick you up. He's got some big news for the Boldanos and wants you there when he shares it."

Anxiety replaced Mia's appetite. She dropped her cookie on the kitchen table. "Any idea what's going on?"

"Nope. But whatever it is, it appears to be a major development. I gotta go. They're delivering my Peloton bike. Early Christmas present from Pete. Which he doesn't know about yet."

Mia quickly slipped into gray wool pants and a white V-neck wool sweater that she accessorized with a silver bracelet. Assuming enough time had passed to apply makeup, she covered her bruised face with base. Pete had never made such a big deal about revealing something before, which concerned her. Arresting a Boldano would certainly be a major development. Mia prayed that wasn't where this was heading.

"Mia, Pete Dianopolis is here," Elisabetta hollered from below.

"Coming," Mia hollered back.

She threw on a coat, then scurried downstairs and outside, where Pete was waiting for her in an unmarked sedan. "Let's book," the detective said. He turned on the car's siren and red flashing lights and peeled out.

Mia braced herself as Pete blew through stop signs and red lights, slowing only incrementally. "Any particular reason for the rush?" she asked, praying it wasn't for the reason she worried it might be.

"I wanna get to the Boldanos." She'd never heard Pete sound this excited. "What a twist. I can't wait to throw it into a Steve Stianopolis mystery."

"Pete, the suspense is killing me. Can't you give me a hint about what's going on?"

Mia added a whiny spin to her plea, hoping if she sounded more gossipy than investigative, he might not be able to contain his news. But Pete shook his head. "Sorry, but no dice. I haven't even told Cammie and believe me, I wanted to."

Mia gasped at this revelation. Pete withholding juicy info from the woman he would do anything to remarry? Whatever news he had was huge.

They reached the Boldano compound in record time. Pete pulled up to the gate and spoke into the driveway gate voice box. "Detective Peter Dianopolis, NYPD. The Boldanos are expecting me."

The gate slowly and silently swung open. Pete drove onto the property. He parked in front of the home's columned front entrance. He and Mia exited the car. They approached the front door, where Aurora and Donny awaited them. The foursome exchanged greetings, then the Boldanos led Pete and Mia into the living room. Donny Junior and Jamie were already there, as were their Aunt Vera and Uncle Stefano, who were on the flip side of their Bermuda cruise. "Coffee?" Aurora asked her guests.

"Or something stronger?" This came from Donny Senior, who Mia sensed could use something stronger himself. A visit from the police to the Boldanos had never been classified as a social call.

"Maybe later." Pete cast a hungry eye at an elaborate tray of desserts taking up most of the coffee table. "Same with those. But first, let's get down to business."

Donny Senior and Aurora sat down on the couch between their sons. Vera and Stefano opted for the room's love seat and Mia chose a side chair. Rather than sit, Pete paced. The room buzzed with the electricity of a downed wire. Mia noticed Aurora grip her husband's hand. "I'm not here to arrest you," Pete said.

The room's occupants blew out a collective breath of relief. "*Grazie dio*," Aurora murmured.

"Don't get too excited. I haven't ruled out any of you as suspects. Anyway, when we found Lorenzo Puglia and learned of his attempt to worm his way into your family—"

"Good description," Donny Senior said.

"Thank you. I brought your pal Mia with me tonight because she encouraged me—well, *nagged* would be a better word for it; she nagged me to look beyond the obvious, even though I've learned through my long career that the obvious is usually the answer."

"Did you find Lorenzo's killer?"

Jamie did a poor job of hiding his impatience, unnerving Mia, who was afraid Pete might be annoyed back into placing the Boldanos in first position on the list of suspects. But Pete was on a roll. "We found evidence that Puglia engaged in a physical fight before his death, so we tested DNA discovered in one of his wounds and cross-checked it with our database. Donny Senior, yours was in the system. You've been in there I don't know how long. We got samples from your sons off glasses from the funeral luncheon. There was no DNA match to Puglia with any of you, proving he was a fraud."

Donny Junior exhaled a deep breath. "Phew. I thought you were here to nail me for the fight me and that moron had."

And there goes my need to protect him, Mia thought with a mental eye roll.

"You went after the guy?" Exasperated, Donny Senior threw his hands in the air. "*Perché, idiota?!* Why would you do such a stupid thing?"

"Hey, it wasn't stupid. The SOB was making trouble for my brother." Donny Junior thrust out his chest. "Nobody messes with my brother or anyone in the Family. Not on my watch."

And there it is.

"You did that for me?" Jamie asked, touched.

"Yeah." Choked up, Donny Junior laid a hand on his brother's shoulder. "I love you, bruh. I'd kill for you." The entire room groaned, included Pete. "Not that I did," he quickly added.

"Can we focus here?" Pete said, annoyed. "Where was I? Proof . . . fraud . . . Right. So, we can prove that when it comes to calling himself a Boldano, Lorenzo Puglia was full of it. But . . ." Pete halted his pacing and paused for dramatic effect. Mia, anxious, chewed on a Rudolph-manicured fingernail. "We discovered something else that surprised us. Something we never expected. The DNA testing showed us that you"—Pete pointed at Jamie—"and you"—he pointed at Donny Senior—"share a lot of markers. Enough to tell our forensics experts that Mr. Boldano here is Jamie Boldano's biological father."

Mia thought of the old cliché, silence is deafening. For the first time in her life, she now experienced it.

Pete puffed out his chest. "I know there have been issues vis-à-vis Jamie Boldano's parentage. I'm glad I could deliver good news." He sat down in front of the dessert spread and helped himself to a custard-filled pastry.

"Good news?" Aurora said this in a guttural voice. Mia swore she felt the earth rumble. "*Good news?*" The Boldano matriarch rose from the couch. She reached down, grabbed her husband's shirt, and yanked him to his feet. "Who was she?" she screamed at the quaking man. "Who did you sleep with, you sonuva—"

Jamie and Donny Junior tried separating their parents, but Aurora wouldn't let go of her husband. She shook him like a rag doll, screaming in Italian. "*Chi era, chi? Dimmi, dimmelo!*"

"Mom, stop!" Jamie yelled at her as Donny Junior wrenched their father from her grasp.

Aurora collapsed on the couch. Mia went to the distraught woman's side. "Mrs. B, I know this is . . . huge news. But I'm sure there's a logical explanation. Right, Mr. B? *Right?*" Her tone indicated there better be.

Donny Senior wrung his hands. "I—I—I—" was all he managed to get out.

"Dad. Please. Tell us what happened."

The plea came from Jamie. Donny Junior placed a protective hand on his shoulder. Mia had never witnessed a closer moment between the brothers.

"*Mi dispiace*, son." Donny Senior held up his hands in a helpless gesture. "I don't know what's going on here myself."

Mia saw Stefano and Vera exchange a look. Vera gave her husband a slight nod. "I think I can explain what happened," Stefano said. "You know about the year the family lived in Italy, right? Around thirty years ago. There was business . . . problems . . . here in the States. Then our father, who was living in Tortonia, the little village where we have our winery, had a massive stroke. Hiding—spending time—in the old country made sense. But it was a tough time for you, Aurora. You were far from your home here. Donny Junior was a toddler."

"And there were," Vera said, "baby issues."

"I couldn't conceive," Aurora said in a dull tone.

"It was all very hard on her and Big Donny," Vera explained to the others. "They fought all the time until they decided to separate."

"For a few months," Donny Senior hastened to add. "That was it."

"During which time," Stefano said to Jamie, "your father had a brief fling with our father's nurse."

Aurora drew in a breath so deep it reminded Mia of the ocean retreating before a tsunami.

"She came to me when she realized she was with child," Vera said. "Stefano and I talked, and we saw a solution to the infertility crisis tearing apart your family. We arranged for the nurse's baby—you, dearest Jamie—to be adopted by your parents. We figured the only people who'd ever know were us and the birth mother. We never counted on DNA or that Lorenzo character. God knows how he found about it."

There was the distant sound of a car horn. Stefano jumped up. "That's our cab. Happy holidays!"

He and Vera bolted from the room. Once again, there was deafening silence. Aurora sat frozen like the statue of a Roman goddess, clutching Mia's hand so hard that Mia began losing all feeling in it. Jamie stared straight ahead, in shock. Donny Junior shook his head back and forth, muttering to himself. Donny Senior muttered prayers to *Il Dio*. Pete helped himself to a pastry.

"You see, *bella*?" Donny Senior's voice was tentative when he spoke, desperately seeking a silver lining. "I had no idea about any of this. It's all on Stefano and Vera.

They got a lot of nerve. No Christmas gifts for them, huh?"

Mia heard a rumbling come from deep within Aurora. When she spoke, the scary guttural voice was back. "*You slept with your father's nurse?*" She leaped up from the couch and hurled a china cup at her husband. He ducked and it shattered against the wall. "*Hai fatto sesso con l'infermiera di tuo padre?*" she screamed. "*Mostro! Bastardo imbroglione, ti ammazzo!*"

Aurora continued to rant and throw things at Donny Senior while her sons tried to calm her down. Pete watched with consternation while he munched on a Florentine lace cookie. "What's she saying?" he whispered to Mia.

"You don't wanna know."

"Should I do anything?" he asked as the family fracas continued.

"Yes," she said. "Leave." She got up and motioned to the detective to follow her. They dashed out of the house to Pete's car and zoomed off.

Mia and Pete were quiet on the ride back to Astoria, each using the drive to process the evening's drama. Mia thought about how Jamie's life had been completely upended in a few short weeks. First Lorenzo's deception, then learning he was adopted, to the evening's reveal that Donny Senior was actually his birth father due to a brief affair—she couldn't imagine what her friend was going through.

Pete broke the silence. "I've never been to an Italian opera. Is that what they're like, only with singing?"

Mia recalled her final sight of Aurora shaking her fists to the heavens as she declaimed her husband's treachery to the heavens. "Pretty much."

CHAPTER 12

Mia saw this latest development as an opportunity to deflect Pete's suspicions away from the Boldanos. "So, Stefano and Vera rigged the whole thing with Jamie's birth. Donny and the rest of the family had no idea what happened. And if they didn't know, they had no reason to kill Lorenzo."

"He was scamming them."

"Yeah, but Donny Senior wasn't trying to keep a secret, and Jamie or Donny Junior didn't have a reason to go ballistic on a scammer."

"Donny Junior announced to the whole room he had a dustup with said scammer."

Mia frowned at him. "You have a very skeptical nature."

"I'm a detective. That's my job."

Unable to argue Pete's point, Mia turned away. She stared out the window. The suburbs of Long Island disappeared as they transitioned onto the Grand Central Parkway. A passenger jet rumbled overhead, making a slow descent to LaGuardia. "You can drop me at Belle View."

"You got it."

Pete pulled into the parking lot that fronted the catering facility. "Thanks for bringing me with you," Mia said. "There wasn't much I could do, but at least I was there if the Boldanos needed me."

"I hope they know how lucky they are for that." Pete unlocked the car doors. "We're looking at this case from all sides, Mia. Which means I gotta keep the Family in the mix."

"I know."

"All of them, Mia. Little Donny. Big Donny. Jamie. If anyone had a motive, it's him. And after seeing Mama Boldano in action, she's going on the list too."

Mia, dispirited, got out of the car. She went to her office and only managed to get one arm out of her coat sleeve before Shane appeared in the doorway with more bad news. "We lost our animals. For both parties."

Mia gaped at him. "No."

"They got higher-paying gigs." Shane's face flushed with anger, which made him look like the brooding hero of a trashy romance novel. "You wouldn't believe how much money the churches around here are willing to spend on camels and donkeys for their living Nativity scenes. I'm never dropping bills into a collection plate again." His limpid green eyes flashed. "I've spent all morning calling around for replacements. All I came up

with were a few rabbits and chickens. We need big animals, dammit!"

Shane slammed a fist into the palm of his opposing
hand. His dedication to the job almost brought Mia to
tears. She finished taking off her coat, then sat down at
her computer. Shane peered over her shoulder. Mia could
feel his breath on her neck and fought back the chills it
sent coursing through her. She typed in a search and
scanned it, stopping at a site titled Friends Forever Animal Sanctuary. The home page featured a couple of smiling women in their forties. One hugged a goat, another
had her arm around a donkey. "Here. Call them."

"I did. They said no."

"Go in person."

"But—"

"Trust me on this."

Shane hung his head and nodded. He took a slow walk
out of the office. Mia felt terrible for putting Shane in the
position of milking his looks for the business, but if they
didn't lock down animals, both parties would be a dis-
aster. *I did what I had to do and he knows that*, she told
herself, trying to assuage her feeling of guilt. She redirec-
ted her energy to the Boldano situation, shooting Jamie a
text to see how he was faring post-blowup. Instead of
texting back, Jamie called her. "Hey. Oh man, you would
not believe what's it's like here right now."

"I bet. How are *you*?"

"Still in shock. It's going to take me a while to process
this. Right now, I'm more worried about my parents.
Mom kicked Dad out of the house. He's going to be camping out in the pool house until she cools off. Little Donny
and I are gonna stay here for a few days. I'll use the time

to research my birth mother. I'd like to meet that side of my family. Hopefully by the time I connect with them, the police will have nailed Lorenzo's killer and I'll be allowed to leave the country. If not . . ."

He didn't need to finish the sentence. Mia knew that until this happened, every single Boldano would live under a cloud of suspicion. Aside from her lifelong personal connection to the family, there was the business angle to consider. Technically, Donny Senior was the owner of Belle View and her father's boss. If he needed funds for a legal defense, or God forbid, a divorce, might financial pressures force him to put Belle View up for sale? Mia didn't think it was her place to meddle in the Boldano marriage, but she did have an idea how to garner more clues about Lorenzo's murder. "Take care of your family, Jamie. If you need me, I'm here for you."

"Thanks, Meems. I'll keep you posted. Oh, and Madison told me to tell you she can get you into Spring Fashion Week as her guest."

"James Anthony Boldano, never, *ever* let that girl go," Mia said with intensity.

She put down her cell and did a quick computer search, then picked up the business phone and tapped in a telephone number. "Sorrento Deli and Pasticceria," a male voice answered.

"Yes, hello, this is Mia Carina from Belle View Banquet Manor."

"Mia, hello. It's Pauly. Great to hear from you. What can I do you for?"

"I know this is last-minute, but I have some free time and wonder if you could put together a light tasting for me. Nothing fancy, just samplings for deli and dessert platters. We have a couple of morning and afternoon events where it might make more sense to bring in than have our own staff put them together."

"We do exactly that for several nearby catering facilities. I can have a tasting ready for you in half an hour."

"Perfect. I'll see you then."

Mia hung up and left her office for her father's. Ravello was on the phone. He held up a beefy index finger to her. "Okay, Donny. I'll give it a day, then call her."

"You heard about the Boldanos?" Mia said to her father when he got off the phone.

Ravello nodded. "I don't know what Stefano and Vera were thinking, keeping a secret like that."

"I can see it. If Donny and Aurora's marriage was teetering at the time, his fling would have pushed it over the edge. There was a good chance no one would have ever known the truth if it hadn't been for that idiot Lorenzo, may he rest in peace. Hey, would you watch things here for a couple of hours? I need to run an errand and I sent Shane off to see if he can talk his way into replacing the animals we lost for the Bianchi and Venere events."

"You mean *handsome* his way into it."

"Yes," Mia said, ashamed. "I feel bad for pimping him out, but we need those critters."

"So you admit he's a looker," her father said with a sly smile.

"Well, yeah." Mia went on the defensive. "I mean, that's a fact, not an opinion, and he's got the Italian magazine covers to prove it. Stop giving me that look. I'm leaving. And since I don't have my car here, I'm borrowing yours."

"Struck a nerve," Ravello said with a chuckle. Mia

gave an annoyed grunt, grabbed his keys, and marched out of the office.

Sorrento Deli and Pasticceria was housed in a single-story brick storefront. Neon Italian flags decorated each side of the store's sign, which featured its name, also in neon, with PASTICERRIA in smaller letters than DELI. A large glass window decorated with ads for specials fronted the street and gave a glimpse at the wide array of goods inside. The minute Mia entered, she was assailed by the warm, rich scent of Italian cheeses and meats, many of which hung from the ceiling over the deli counter, where customers were giving orders to Ralph, who was manning the counter with another employee. He acknowledged Mia with a smile as he lowered a giant provolone from its ceiling perch to slice up.

"Mia, *buon giorno*." Pauly approached her from the back of the shop. Like Ralph, he wore a white butcher's apron. She and Pauly exchanged greetings, then he said, "We have a small seating area in the back of the shop. I set up for us there. *Vieni*. Come."

Mia followed him, passing shelves of Italian boxed, canned, and bottled foodstuffs that lined the wall opposite the deli counter. The seating area doubled in width from the front of Sorrento, spilling into the shop next door. "It's spacious back here."

"Yeah. We took over the bakery next door when the owner retired. That's when we added the *pasticceria* to our name." Pauly gestured to a table where two platters sat. One featured a tantalizing collection of Italian deli antipasti and cold cuts, the other a spread of pastries and dessert.

Mia's mouth watered. "I'll start with the antipasto."

She ate while Pauly walked her through a variety of price points, including one for a six-foot hero that would be the perfect appetizer for Kaitlyn's party. Ralph joined them, adding additional input about the shop's myriad of edible options. "We put together a list of pricing packages we can offer you as a fellow catering facility." Paul gifted her with a two-sided folder that featured the Sorrento logo on the cover. He had the rough, arthritic hands that came with the hard work of hoisting heavy boxes loaded with foodstuffs.

The antipasto platter was so good Mia hoped no one at Sorrento was involved in Lorenzo's death. Still, that was the real purpose of her visit, so she reluctantly segued to the topic and the dessert platter, after showering the shop owners with compliments. "I need to say again how sorry I am about the loss of Lorenzo."

The two men exchanged a look. "Between us," Pauly said, "we're pretty sure Lorenzo stole from us. Ralph did inventory yesterday. Things didn't add up."

Mia found this on par with Lorenzo's pattern of behavior, but to be sure, asked, "What about your other delivery guy? Could it have been him?"

"Brad?" Pauly shook his head. "Timing's all wrong. Right, Ralph?"

"Nothing went missing until Puglia showed up," Ralph said in a gravelly, matter-of-fact voice. "And nothing's gone missing since he died."

Having grown up with an assortment of miscreants in and out of her life, given her father and brother's connections, the timing didn't absolve Brad in her eyes. If things went missing under his watch, here was a good chance he was either in on it or being paid to turn a blind eye.

"For the vegetarians."

Mia, embarrassed, realized her mind had drifted. She had no idea what Ralph was talking about. She did her best to cover. "Yes. The vegetarians. Have to keep them happy. We have a Kiwanis Club luncheon coming up. No vegetarians there, ha-ha. Anyway, I'd love to try you out for it. I'll have our chef call you and run the guest numbers."

Pauly, the more outgoing of the owner-partners, beamed. "*Perfetto*. We'll start small and work our way up to the big sandwich."

Mia laughed too loudly at Pauly's slight joke. "Small to big. Good stuff. By the way, is Brad here? I want to run a few thoughts by him regarding delivery."

This sounded lame even to Mia, but fortunately neither Pauly or Ralph questioned it. "He's in the back in the stockroom," Pauly said, motioning to a door behind them. The two men stood up. "Go give him a holler and tell him we're working together." He extended a hand, as did Ralph. She shook with both, then the men returned to business.

Brad wasn't in the stockroom. Mia located him in the alley behind the store having a smoke, despite the bitter cold. "You're the girl from the funeral lunch place," he said, surprised to see her.

"Yes. Belle View is going to be using Sorrento for a luncheon."

"Cool. Smoke?"

He offered Mia a cigarette. "No, thank you," she said. "I just need to confirm Belle View is on your delivery route." *I really have to do a better job of coming up with this stuff,* Mia thought.

"My delivery route is wherever Pauly and Ralph tell me to go." Brad accompanied this statement with a deep drag on his cigarette.

"With Lorenzo gone, having all the deliveries fall on you must be hard."

"Makes no diff at all. Guy was worse than useless."

"Really? How so?"

"Just was."

The terse response made Mia fear she'd come across as digging for information rather than a nosy gossip. "Ugh, people like that make me crazy," she said, hoping to redeem herself with the generic comment.

It worked. "Man, don't I know it." He dropped his cigarette to the ground and stubbed it out with the toe of his work boot. "But the good news is, with that scum gone. Renata's free and hopefully in need of some comforting, if ya know what I mean."

The lewd spin he put on this made it impossible not to. Mia felt sorry for Renata, but given the painful facial she'd endured at the aesthetician's hands, she didn't doubt Lorenzo's "almost widow" had the tools to ward off any unwanted advances.

Mia's phone pinged a text. She checked and managed not to groan out loud. Santino Esposito had messaged that he was at the Aquarius Diner with a box of Lorenzo's belongings. She'd forgotten about the meeting—or subconsciously blocked it from her mind. It was her turn to fend off unwanted advances. She left Brad lighting another cigarette and headed off to meet Renata's brother.

Diner owner Ron Karras greeted her like a rock star when she showed up, which in his eyes she was, since Mia had helped him beat a murder charge only months earlier. After cooing over a dozen photos of Ron's grand-son, who also happened to be Mia's godson—the baby's mother was one of her best friends—Ron delivered her to Santino's table, not an inch of which was visible under a collection of appetizers and main courses. Mia took the seat opposite Santino, hoping the dozen or so Greek dishes would serve as a food wall between them. "When I told the owner who I was meeting, he said anything we ordered was on the house," Santi said.

"I see you took him up on that."

Santi smirked. "Gimme to-go containers and I got food for a week here. I might even throw a few of the stuffed grape leaves Mom and Renata's way, if they ask nice."

His smug pride in taking advantage of Ron and hold-ing it over his family irked Mia. "I'm sure they'd appre-ciate more than a few grape leaves. I saw them recently and they're having a bad time right now."

"Yeah. Renata took a break from her job. Said she's too upset about Lorenzo to do good work right now."

"I bet," Mia said, her face still painful in spots from Renata's ferocious facial. "Thanks for bringing Lorenzo's stuff. I don't have time to hang around, so if you don't mind just giving it to me, that would be great."

Santino pulled a large black trash bag out from under the table and dropped it onto a chair. "Here."

Mia felt a sudden pang of sadness. "A life stuffed into a garbage bag. Is that what it all adds up to?"

"Sounds like somebody could use a little cheering up. How's about I get those to-go containers and we dump this place for the nearest bar?"

There was no ignoring the suggestive tone in Esposito's voice. "I appreciate the invitation, but I'm not looking for a relationship right now and I don't want to lead you on."

"Hey, I'm happy to be led if the final stop is you-know-what." In case Mia missed his meaning, the libidinous Esposito held the thumb and index finger of one hand together to form a circle and poked the index finger of his other hand in and out of the circle. It took Mia's last ounce of willpower not to scream, *Eww, you disgusting creep!*

"It's nothing personal." She congratulated herself on saying this without clenching her teeth.

Santino dropped his vulgar sign language. He spoke with a note of understanding. "It's that Shane guy from the place where you work, isn't it?"

Mia's eyes widened. "What? No. My husband cheated on me and then disappeared in a boating accident in Florida. I'm still recovering from the shock and loss."

"Right," Santino said, oozing skepticsm. "Word of warning: Renata's got an eye on him too. And you do not want to get in my sister's way when it comes to a hot guy."

This warning intrigued Mia. She flashed on Renata's fury at Zoe and wondered if she was equally angry at her late boyfriend. *I hope so*, she thought. *I hate it when women only blame the other woman and not the guy.*

Mia's text alert beeped with a message from her father: **Where's my car? Taking Lin to dinner.** She typed back she was on her way, and stood up. "I need to run. Thanks for bringing me Lorenzo's things. The Puglias will be grateful, I'm sure."

"If they wanna show their gratitude, that'd be fine by me."

Esposito rubbed his fingers together to indicate money. He followed this with a "make it rain" gesture. *The guy's a regular mime*, Mia thought, disgusted. She grabbed the garbage bag and made a quick departure— after a stop at the cash register to warn Ron to cut off the flow of free grub to the greedy opportunist.

Mia brought Ravello's car to him and he dropped her off at home on the way to Manhattan. "What do you think of this idea?" he asked as she started to exit the car. "A gift card for a year of dinners at our favorite restaurant?"

Still searching for the perfect Lin gift, he ran this by Mia. She shook her head. "Sounds like something you'd win at one of those school silent-auction fundraisers we sometimes book at Belle View."

Ravello gave a frustrated groan and dropped his head onto the steering wheel. "I'm hopeless. I'll never come up with a good gift for her, which means I don't deserve her, which means, we should break up. I should free Lin for a man who knows how to buy her a decent present."

"Dad, whoa, calm down. If Lin heard this, she'd break up with you for thinking she'd judge anyone by their gift-giving talent. As someone who's gotten awesome prezzies from you, I guarantee you'll eventually find something perfect for her."

"You think she'd go for a Littlest Pet Shop Treehouse?" Ravello said this with a glint of humor in his eyes.

"No, and she's not getting mine. I'm holding onto it for my own kids. Here's hoping I have them before I get so old my mind goes and I think the tree house is my actual home."

She gave her father a peck on the cheek, then dashed up the steps of her house, trading the arctic cold for the suffocating warmth of steam heat. Elisabetta was in the kitchen counting loose change with a grim expression. "There's eggplant parm on the stove."

"Oh good, I'm hungry."

Mia plated herself a serving and sat down at the sixty-year-old dinette set across from her grandmother. "That the take from the donation box?"

Elisabetta grunted in the affirmative. "Someone's stealing from it."

Mia dropped her fork. "What? No."

"*Si*. I'm sure. Nina Delfino told me she donated twenty bucks in memory of her late husband, Bernardo. There wasn't no twenty in here."

"Maybe she lied."

Elisabetta gave her head a vigorous shake *no*. "She and Bernardo hated each other. They slept in separate bedrooms for the last thirty years of their marriage after he caught her trying to smother him with a pillow. But she would never dishonor his memory by lying to me."

"Maybe your cookies weren't a hit?"

Elisabetta, offended, scowled at her granddaughter. "*Ehi, che stai dicendo?* What are you thinking, talking like that? You love my pignoli nut cookies."

"I do. I wish I had one right now."

"For your information, missy, I got two requests for the recipe. Which is going to my grave with me." Her eyes narrowed. "It's that witch, Jacinta. I know it. She's—what's it your brother says about sports? She's playing to win." Elisabetta pounded the table, startling Mia and making her jump. The last bite of her eggplant parmigiana flew off the plate onto the floor. Hero, who was napping under the table, began barking. He then noticed the errant eggplant and lapped it up. Elisabetta held up a hand and formed the sign of the evil eye. "*Maloc-*

chio! I curse you, Jacinta Benedetto! I'm gonna get back at you if it's the last thing I do on this earth."

"Nonna," Mia cautioned, "Stand down. Do *not* do something impulsive that could get you in trouble. There's too much of that going around these days. Don't accuse Jacinta of anything until you have proof she's the culprit."

Elisabetta gave a dismissive wave of the hand. "You, always with the proof." She colored the word with a derisive, mocking tone. "My proof is here." She pointed to her heart. "And there—" She pointed an accusing finger in the direction of Jacinta's house.

"Fine," Mia said, giving up. "*Basta.* Enough already. Do what you want." She put her plate in the sink, muttering, "*Testardo.*"

"I heard that and I am *not* stubborn," Nonna said in the most stubborn tone possible.

Mia left her grandmother fulminating over her competitor's assumed dirty playbook. She changed into comfy lounging-around clothes, after which she batted cat toys back and forth with Doorstop and let Pizzazz out of her cage to fly around the apartment. She gently scolded the bird for teasing the annoyed cat with a parakeet dive-bomb. Mia checked the time on the plug-in wall clock that was almost as old as Elisabetta's dinette set, in keeping with the Carina family philosophy: If it ain't broke, keep it forever. While the day felt endless, it was only seven p.m., offering no excuse not to call her mother and have the conversation she'd been putting off about the real reason for Gia's sudden visit. Much as Mia dreaded it, it was time for a mother-daughter heart-to-heart. She inhaled a deep breath, exhaled, and tapped Gia's telephone number into her cell. The call immediately went to voicemail, followed by a "mailbox full" alert.

Typical, Mia thought, aggravated. *I can't even leave her a message.* She did a search on her phone and located the telephone number for the LaGuardia Marriott. Mia clicked on it. "New York LaGuardia Airport Marriott," a chirpy voice answered.

"Yes, hi. Gia Gabinetti's room, please."

"Hold on," a desk clerk said. Mia stroked Doorstop's orange-gold fur while she waited and he purred with pleasure. The old wall clock ticked. The desk clerk came back on the line. "I'm sorry, we have no guest registered with that name."

Mia, taken aback by the clerk's response, stopped petting Doorstop. "Really? Are you sure?"

"Positive."

Mia tried to make sense of this. She had a thought. If Gia's marriage was on the rocks, maybe she registered under another name. "Can you try Gia Carina?"

"Sure." A pause. "I'm sorry, we have no guest under that name either."

"How about Gia Cornetta?" Mia asked, using her mother's maiden name.

Another pause. "No guest under that name."

Mia stared at her cell phone, dumbfounded. If her mother wasn't staying at the hotel she'd mentioned . . . where was she?

CHAPTER 13

Mia's head throbbed. She rubbed her temples as she tried to process the strange development. "Gia is my mother. She said she's staying with you. If she's not, I don't know where she is."

The desk clerk took pity on her. "Just because she's not here now doesn't mean she didn't stay here. Give me a minute." Mia's anxiety level climbed with each passing second. "Ah. Here we go. A Gia Cornetta was staying here."

"Can you tell me when she checked out?" The clerk named a date Mia recognized as the day after Lorenzo Puglia's body was discovered. "Thank you so much for looking that up. I really appreciate it."

"I'm glad I was able to help. I hope you find your mother."

"Me too." *If only to find out what in the world is going on with her.*

Mia sat back against the plastic-covered pillows of the gaudy red velvet couch she'd inherited from a neighbor who'd moved to an assisted living facility on Long Island. Where was Gia? Why was her voice mailbox full? Why had she checked out of the motel without telling Mia? And since her mother's marriage was obviously over, hence the maiden name, what happened to end it? Her mother had put up with a lot from Angelo since hooking up with him. What had he done that was egregious enough to prompt Gia to not only walk out, but cross an ocean to get away from him? The only person who might have some answers was Posi, but visiting hours at the correctional facility were over. All Mia could do was text her mother. She tapped out **WHERE R YOU???** on her cell, knowing the chances of Gia responding were slim. Angry and experated by her problematic parent, Mia tossed her phone aside and went to the kitchen, where she mitigated her emotions with a big pour of white wine.

The wine made Mia sleepy, so she went to bed earlier than usual. Unfortunately, this led to her waking up earlier than usual. Five a.m. found her staring at the ceiling, eyes wide open. Having given up trying to fall back asleep, she decided to embrace being awake. She took a quick shower and slipped into her warmest leggings and fleece pullover. After putting on a hooded navy puffer jacket, she made a quiet exit from the house to the garage, her heavy boots leaving Sasquatch-like footprints in the few inches of snow that had fallen overnight. She retrieved her bicycle and wiped off the dust that accumulated from months in storage. Mia tested the bike light and was happy to see the battery hadn't lost its charge. She wheeled the bike out of the garage, hopped on, and set off for a bracing predawn spin.

Cold air slapped Mia's face as she rode, but she found it rejuvenating. It was dark out, so the decorations in the small front yards she passed block after block were still lit up in all their glitzy glory. *Even without Jacinta, Nonna's got some serious competition for the design trophy this year*, Mia thought as she biked up and down the streets. She paused in front of Tony Benne-Santa to catch her breath. He was immobile, his dulcet tones silenced until the evening. Given how so many neighbors coveted the animatronic local hero, Mia wondered why Jacinta didn't take him in at night as a security measure. She chalked it up to hubris on Jacinta's part. Why miss a minute of holding her holiday treasure over her competitors' heads?

Mia's nose and ears began to tingle and burn, so she biked up from the bottom of her own block toward home. As she passed the Levines' house, she thought she saw a light inside. She braked and backtracked. Mia knew the Levines were still in Florida. Elisabetta hadn't mentioned they had guests staying in their home while they were out of town. She parked her bike against a light pole and snuck around the side of the house to double-check. With the thousands of lights on the block's homes, it would be easy to mistake a reflection from another light as one coming from the Levines' home. Mia stayed low below the kitchen window and glanced up. A weak light, the kind a flashlight might produce, flickered. Mia's heart pounded. She pulled out her phone to text an alert to 911. Then she saw a shadow in the kitchen window—the shadow of a woman—and Mia knew exactly who was squatting in the Levines' house. She slammed her phone into the pocket of her jacket, stomped to the front of the house, stormed up the steps, and banged on the front door. "Open up, Mom! I know you're in there."

There was no answer, so she banged again. The door slowly opened, revealing Gia. An expression of guilt and pain colored her face. "I'm sorry," she said.

Mia lit into her mother. "You are unbelievable. What kind of grifter are you, lying about why you're here? Crashing in a stranger's house? What is *wrong* with you?" Mia gasped. "The donation box. You've been stealing from them."

"Only ours. And this one. I'm gonna pay it back."

"Don't you dare call a box 'ours.' Someone who steals from her own family doesn't deserve to be part of that family." Mindful she might wake the neighbors, Mia lowered her voice and spoke through clenched teeth. "Get out of the Levines' house. *Now.* I don't care where you go, just go."

Mia stalked back to her bike. Dawn was breaking by the time she returned it to the garage. She showered and dressed. As soon as the church bells at Perpetual Anguish chimed eight a.m., she took off for Triborough Correctional Facility.

"Mom broke into the Levines' house and has been camping out there for I don't know how long," she said to Posi as soon as she sat down.

"Not broke in, really. Borrowed their keys from Nonna, made a copy, and returned the originals."

Mia gaped at her brother. "You knew. Wait—it was your idea. The whole thing. Even stealing the donation box money."

"Not stealing. Borrowing. She's gonna pay it back.

She and Angelo are having problems. But it's not my story to tell."

Mia glared at her brother, furious. "Why am I surprised? Of course this is all on you. Takes one to know one."

"What's that supposed to mean?"

"You know exactly what it means." Mia threw open her arms and circled in her seat, encompassing the entire prison visiting room.

"Oh, that we're both thieves?"

"File that under the category of *duh*."

Posi glared back at his sister. "I was trying to help a family member, something you never seem to have time to do anymore. 'Tis the season to be giving, or did you forget that, Miss Big Shot Businesswoman?"

Mia slammed a fist on the table, earning a warning harrumph from guard Henry Marcus. "Sorry, Henry. He just makes me so mad. Everything I'm doing, I'm doing for the family, Positano. But if you don't care about Belle View being a success and keeping Dad doing legal stuff instead of illegal stuff, that's your problem, not mine."

She shot an obscene Italian hand gesture at her brother and blew out of the building. By the time she reached Belle View, Mia was in a state, ready to explode with anger and disappointment in her mother and brother. She hurried to her office, closing the door behind her, not ready to see anyone until she was in control of her emotions. Her cell rang with a call from Kaitlyn. She took a deep breath. "Hi, Kaitlyn."

"I have a break between classes and had to tell you what happened with Daniella. If you have time."

"I always have time for you." Mia fought back the quaver in her voice.

"Are you okay?"

"Yeah."

"You don't sound it."

"Because *I'm not.*" Mia gave up fighting and sobbed out the story of her mother and brother's dodgy doings, finishing with an emotional, if childish, "I hate them *both.*"

"I don't blame you," Kaitlyn said. "I'd hate them too. Except at least you have a brother."

"Sometimes I wish I didn't."

"I have friends who say that about their brothers and sisters. But they don't really mean it."

"I do," Mia insisted, despite knowing Kaitlyn was right.

"Do you know what's going on with your mom?"

"No," Mia said. "I was going to ask her, but I've been busy." Kaitlyn chuckled, earning a defensive "What?" from Mia.

"Nothing. It's just I say that when my mom or dad wants me to do something I don't feel like doing. 'I'm busy, Mom.' 'I'm busy, Dad.' "

"Well, I am," Mia said, sulking.

"OMG, I say that too. And I totally sound like that. Look, I know you're mad at everyone right now. But, it's like . . . I have this pillow. It's my favorite. It has these cute little dancing bears in different colors on it and says, 'Truckin.' "

"That's from the Grateful Dead."

"Huh? What's that?"

"A band," Mia said, feeling her age. "My dad had an album by them. Don't know why. He was more into disco. Must have been a present from someone who didn't know him that well."

"Whatevs. Anyway, I love the pillow so much. Because sometimes if I'm having a bad day, I tell myself to do what the pillow says. Instead of being all negative, I should, you know, be 'Truckin'."

"The Grateful Dead version of 'power through and move on.'"

"For you, I was thinking more like you could truck on over to your mom or your brother and make up with them," Kaitlyn clarified. "But what you said is good too." A bell blasted in the background. "That's next period. I gotta get to class. I'm sorry you had a bad morning. But you're an awesome person. Love you."

"Love you too. And sweetie . . . thanks."

Kaitlyn signed off. Mia whipped a tissue out of a box on her desk and wiped away her tears. She took a compact mirror from her desk drawer and used the task of reapplying her makeup to calm herself down. *Out of the mouths of babes*, she thought as she patted concealer onto the shadows under her tired eyes. Kaitlyn had made a convoluted point. Mia couldn't imagine life without her brother. And she'd waited too long to have a candid conversation with her mother. She dropped her head in her hands, overwhelmed with regrets and fatigue.

There was a gentle knock on the door and it opened a sliver, enough to expose one of Shane's incandescent eyes. "I heard you in my office. I wasn't listening in, I swear."

"I'm sure you weren't. It was pretty hard *not* to hear me."

She waved Shane in. He closed the door behind him and leaned back against it, arms folded across his chest. "Family drama, huh?" Mia nodded, trying not to well up again. "I get it. My mom died when I was little and my dad had a lotta girlfriends. Like, a *lot*. He was a good-looking guy."

I bet, Mia thought.

"Way better-looking than me."

Mia couldn't hold back a skeptical snort she managed to disguise as a cough. "Sorry. Swallowed some of my own spit the wrong way." *No! Did I really say that? Tell me I didn't say that! I hate myself!*

"He finally remarried when I fourteen," Shane continued, "and had another kid, my sister Olivia. But I decided I didn't like my new family and became a giant pain. Skipped college, went to Rome, modeled. Did things I'm not proud of. Basically, I became an a-hole, pardon my language."

"But you're not anything like that now," Mia said. "What happened? Why did you do, like, a one-eighty?"

"My dad came to Italy, where I was busy being that a-hole—again, pardon. He said he was sorry for anything he did wrong and all he wanted in this life was a relationship with me. So, I came home. I got to know and respect Lena, my stepmom, and my little sister. And I got to spend a lot of quality time with my dad until he passed away last year."

Shane's story so moved Mia that she realized she'd held eye contact with him the entire time. "Thank you so much for sharing that with me, Shane."

"Sure. Oh, by the way, I got all the animals we need for as long as we need them from Friends Forever Animal Sanctuary. They even gave me a good price."

Mia smiled at him. "You're a miracle worker."

Shane blushed. "Just doing my job. Which I better get back to."

He left for his own office. Mia reached for her cell and texted two words to her mother: **Let's talk.**

She was in the process of debating how to convince

Elisabetta to let Gia, her mortal enemy, move into their basement, when her mother called. "*Bellissima bambina*, I love you so much," Gia said, weeping. "I left Angelo. I'm so sorry I hid the truth from you, but you're doing so well right now after all you went through with that low-rent husband of yours in Florida and I didn't want to drag you down with my problems."

"Mom, you never have to feel that way. I'm sorry I lost it this morning. I'm gonna talk Nonna into letting you stay with us."

"You don't have to. I went across the street and asked that nice couple for advice, you know, Philip and Finn. Their nanny Miranda is on vacation for the holidays and Philip wouldn't mind some help with their little ones. I'm gonna stay in Miranda's room until she returns. I kept track of the money I borrowed from the donation box and already replaced it with an advance I asked for."

"That's great, Mom," Mia said, vowing to thank Philip and Finn in a big way for their kindness and generosity.

"I know I haven't been a good mother. Or a good person. But I'm working on it. *Ti amo*."

"*Ti amo anch'io.*"

Having made amends with her mother, Mia moved on to her brother. She entered a number she had on speed dial and was immediately connected to her brother's correctional facility. A moment later she had guard Henry Marcus on the line. "Henry, if you don't mind, would you let Posi know that I'm sorry I acted out on him and everything is good with me and Mom now?"

"You got it," Henry said. Mia could hear the smile in his voice. "Makes me happy to see y'all making up like this, especially at the holidays."

The calls completed, Mia searched her phone for an image of Grateful Dead bears. She landed on a particularly cute one and was about to text it to Kaitlyn with a "thank u" and a string of hearts when the phone rang with an unusual morning call from Philip. Concerned something might be wrong with Elisabetta, Mia instantly responded. "Philip, hi. Is everything okay?"

"Nothing's happened to Elisabetta, but . . ." Mia heard panic in her neighbor's voice. "We have a problem. A big one. I need your help. Now."

CHAPTER 14

As Mia raced home, she ran through a list of crises in her head that might have prompted Philip's emergency phone call. As she zipped past Forty-fifth Place, it only took a glance out the window to land on what had sparked the crisis.

She screeched into a parking spot in front of her house. Philip waited for her at the foot of the steps. Clad in athletic wear, he jogged in place to stay warm. Mia jumped out of her car, slamming the door shut behind her. "I saw Jacinta's yard."

"Then you know what's going on," Philip said. "I was jogging down the alley when I saw her with him."

"Do you know where he is?"

"Your garage."

"Get him and bring him into the house through the back stairs to the kitchen."

Philip gave a quick nod and jogged off. Mia tromped up the steps into the house and through her grandmother's hallway into the living room. Elisabetta was parked on the couch, one of the few people left in America watching a soap opera. She let out a squawk when Mia picked up the remote and turned off the TV. "Hey! My stories."

Mia fixed her grandmother with an angry stare. "I know what you did."

Elisabetta affected confusion. "Huh? What are you talking about?"

"Don't give me that. Tony Benne-Santa."

"What about him?" Elisabetta asked, all innocence.

Philip appeared in the doorway behind Mia carrying the animatronic legend. "I saw you, Elisabetta. Sneaking Tony into your garage." Disappointment in his friend's larcenous action colored his tone.

Elisabetta wasn't ready to admit she'd been busted. She held her hands over her mouth, gave a theatric gasp, then dropped her hands. "Tony was in our garage? *Ma che successe?* How did that happen?"

"What happened," Mia said, her glance withering, "is that you stole him."

Elisabetta finally gave up her act. She crossed her arms in front of her chest like a recalcitrant child. "I didn't steal him, I rescued him from that horrible woman."

"What you call rescuing, the law calls stealing, Nonna."

"Okay, fine," Elisabetta snapped. "I 'stole' him. But only because Jacinta stole from us. *Un occhio per un occhio.*"

"An eye for an eye," Philip said. He grinned with delight. "Oooh, I translated that. I have to tell Finn. He'll be so proud."

Mia, on the verge of losing it, emitted a strangled sound. "There is no eye, Nonna, because Jacinta didn't steal from us. Gia did."

"*Mi scusi? Gia?*" Elisabetta's eyes widened, then darkened. "Gia. *Naturalemente.*"

"It's complicated," Mia said, understanding Elisabetta's reaction but beset with a need to defend her mother. She recounted her conversations with Gia and Posi. "If you check our box or the Levines, you'll see that Mom already replaced the money with the advance from Philip and Finn, who are my personal heroes. Philip, I can't thank you enough for helping out my mother."

"Don't worry about it. *Fa niente.* Ooh, listen to me. I'm practically a native."

"Now we have to figure out how to get Tony Benne-Santa back in Jacinta's yard without getting caught," Mia said. "Not the easiest thing to do midmorning in Queens, which isn't exactly in the isolated countryside. I'd be surprised if Jacinta hasn't already called the theft into the police."

"She's a night owl," Elisabetta said. "Stays up late, sleeps late. She's still in bed, I'm sure."

"Oh, oh." Philip jumped up and down, waving his hand like an elementary school student who knows they have the correct answer. "I have an idea. Our car is in the shop for a tune-up, so we have one of those boring sedan rentals. No one would be able to ID it as one of our cars. We dress in all-black with masks we have left over from the pandemic, then circle around the neighborhood to come from a different direction. I'll drive and Elisabetta and I can both be lookouts while you jump out with Tony and put him back. You get back in and we take off in the opposite direction, drive around a little bit like we live somewhere else, then I drop you off in the alley and go park in our alley."

"Wow," Mia said, impressed. She applauded. "Philip, that's brilliant. You would have made a great spy. Or criminal."

"I'll take the former." He affected a James Bond British accent. "Barnes-Webster. Philip Barnes-Webster. I like my martinis shaken, not stirred." He dropped the accent. "It works much better with single-syllable names."

The three went off to change into their disguises, reconvening ten minutes later when Philip drove into the alley. Mia brought Tony Benne-Santa to the waiting car. "I don't know how you carried this thing, Nonna," she said as she hefted him into the back seat. "He's almost your size. I think he may even have a few pounds on you."

Elisabetta climbed into the front passenger seat. "*Dove c'è un testamento, c'è un modo.*"

"Where there's a will there's a way indeed," Mia said. Philip began driving down the alley. "We're moving already? I didn't even know the car was on."

"We got a bit of extra luck because this car is a hybrid. No one will hear us coming."

Philip followed the plan he'd laid out, driving away from the neighborhood to approach Jacinta's home from another direction. As soon as they reached the place, Mia got out of the car, threw open the front yard gate, and returned Tony Benne-Santa to his center stage perch. She ran back to the car. "Go, go!"

Philip silently took off. Rather than circle again, Elisabetta suggested they make a coffee and doughnut run to justify why they were out, should they run into anyone who might ask on the return home. Having worked up an appetite with the subterfuge, Philip and Mia agreed. Doughnuts and coffee were purchased and the three headed back to Forty-sixth Place. Philip slowed down as they approached Elisabetta and Mia's home. The three stared out the window at the sight before them. Philip gulped. "Uh-oh."

Mia seconded this with an unhappy nod. "I guess Jacinta was awake after all."

Jacinta and her minions were in the Carina's front yard laying waste to it. Fake trees sprawled across the small space, denuded of their decorations. Women were pulling down whatever lights they could reach. Elisabetta threw open the car door and almost tumbled onto the sidewalk. Philip and Mia followed. "What do you think you're doing?!" Elisabetta screamed.

Jacinta held a string of lights up to the heavens and shook it. "You stole Tony! Revenge!"

"No, I didn't," was Elisabetta's lame response.

"I saw you," said a Jacinta follower. "I was doing my silver sneakers seniors walk. You got some nerve, Elisabetta Carina, stealing Tony Benne-Santa. Who does such a terrible thing?"

This elicited a chorus of sympathy for Jacinta. Mia was about to intervene when Elisabetta's "army" rounded the corner. "We heard what was going on," Phyllis said, out of breath from hurrying. "Nobody messes with our 'Betta."

Before Mia or Philip could make a move, Elisabetta and her friends descended on Jacinta's crew. The opposing sides yelled at each other in a Tower of Babel language selection—Mia even heard Arabic coming from Miriam Bashar—and began a tug-of-war with fallen light strings.

"This is like the rumble in *West Side Story* if the Jets and Sharks had been gangs of women on Medicare," Philip said of the melee as he watched with Mia.

"We have to stop this. Hey. HEY!" Mia put two fingers in her mouth and unleashed an ear-splitting whistle. The women froze, several wincing at the sound. "You all should be ashamed of yourselves, and yes, starting with my own grandmother. It's the holidays. But instead of bringing joy to world, you're bringing shame to the neighborhood with your competitiveness. Look." Mia gestured to a small group of children across the street who had stopped their snowball fight to watch the brouhaha between the warring factions. "Is this the example you want to set for these children? One of anger and destruction and revenge? Is it?"

All the women were silent. Elisabetta finally spoke up. "My beautiful and single granddaughter is right. We are behaving like animals. At the holidays! And it's all my fault." She turned to Jacinta and bowed her head. "Jacinta, there are no words to express how sorry I am for what I did. I made two terrible, terrible mistakes. Someone had been taking money from our donation boxes and I thought it was you." Women on both sides of the fight gasped. "I know now that it wasn't. But I followed that mistake with another. In a fit of anger, I took Tony. I apologize for my evil thoughts and actions with all my heart." Tears rolled down Elisabetta's cheeks. "You were right to tear down my decorations." She began to sob. "*Misericordia.* I beg for mercy. But I have not earned it. I don't deserve to help my block go for the trophy."

Jacinta gestured to her clique. They grouped around her, conferring in quiet voices. Then their leader spoke up. "Elisabetta, your beautiful but single granddaughter made points none of us can ignore. Here it is the holidays and all we *nonnas* are doing is fighting over decorations. What kind of role models are we? I accept your apology. I know I have not been the nicest when it comes to competing myself. You've been a valued member of our little community for years and deserve decorations as much as any of us. We will put back everything we tore down. And we will even make it better."

Elisabetta clutched her heart. "*Oh, Jacinta. Grazie. Mille grazie. Grazie a tutti.*"

She embraced her now-former enemy. The rivals "awwed" and applauded. "Now," Jacinta said, "let's get to work fixing what we broke."

Mia held up a hand and called to the assemblage. "Very important question before you start. It's in the high thirties out here. Who here has had a pneumonia vaccine?" All the women except for one raised their hand. "Phyllis, go home. Everyone else, you're cleared."

The women began uprighting trees and gathering lights. "That was genuinely moving," Philip said. "I'm so impressed by how Elisabetta owned what she did."

"Don't be." Mia gestured to her grandmother, who was fiddling with a strand of lights, a small smirk on her face. "That one knows how to cry on cue and her Oscar-winning performance just bested Jacinta and got Nonna a stepped-up Christmas display."

"Really." Philip, bemused, shook his head. "Well, that kind of masterminding is also pretty impressive."

* * *

Having turned down the heat between Team Elisabetta and Team Jacinta, Mia returned to Belle View, where she finally sent the Grateful Dead bears image and string of hearts to Kaitlyn, who responded with her own string of hearts. Mia leaned back in her office chair, threaded her fingers together, and placed her hands behind her head. She closed her eyes and enjoyed a well-earned feeling of satisfaction. It wasn't even noon and she'd repaired relations with her mother and brother and thwarted a senior citizen rumble. Plus, Shane had delivered on scoring animals for two important upcoming events.

"Knock, knock."

Mia opened her eyes and saw *Tri Trib* reporter Teri Fuoco standing in the doorway. Her feeling of well-being trended downward. "Are you here to see Evans?" she asked hopefully.

"Nope. It's time for us to snoop on the Puglias. Remember?"

CHAPTER 15

"What do you mean, *we*?" Mia asked, annoyed. "All I remember is I'm supposed to be you."

"You've obviously been too wrapped up in Belle View business to see the flaw in your plan." Teri came into the office. She gave Mia's chair a push and it rolled backward. Teri typed her name into the search engine of Mia's computer browser, then clicked on *Images*. The screen filled with photos of the reporter, many of which showed Teri running away from an angry recipient of her investigative skills. "All Drew Puglia or anyone in his office needs to do is look me up and you're busted."

Mia hated to admit Teri was right—but she was. "Pivoting here," she said. "You come with me and interview Drew."

Teri deposited herself in the room's spare chair and put

her feet up on Mia's desk. "That's exactly why I'm here, but feel free to make it sound like it's your idea."

Mia gritted her teeth. "While you're interviewing him, I'll bring Lorenzo's belongings to Drew's house and see what I can get out of his wife Bridget. Then I'll drive over to Kevin Turman's office to talk 'accounting.' I can pick you up when I'm done, or you can rideshare to meet me."

"Sounds good, except since I'm doing you the favor, I get to drive." Mia started to protest. "Or we can skip the whole thing."

"Fine," Mia said, fuming. "You drive."

The ride to Hempstead and environs in Teri's Smart car terrified Mia, who closed her eyes and prayed to Saint Christopher, the patron saint of travelers. Teri dropped her off in front of Drew and Bridget Puglia's home, an immaculate Tudor on a tidy suburban Long Island street. Mia had transferred Lorenzo's meager belongings from the trash bag into a box that she balanced on her hip as she rang the doorbell.

"Right on time," Bridget said with a note of approval but without a hello when she opened the door. She wore a navy power suit accented with elegant gold jewelry, and her gleaming blond hair sat wrapped in a tight bun atop her head.

"Are you on your way out?" Mia asked. Given the woman's business attire, she worried she might lose an opportunity to elicit information from Bridget.

"No."

Oh, so you're just anal, Mia thought, relieved.

"I'll take the box." Bridget reached for it.

Mia handed over the box and was about to come up with an excuse that would gain her entry to the Puglia home when Joan, Lorenzo's mother, and Bridget's mother-in-law, appeared behind her. "Mia, hello. This is so thoughtful of you. Bridget, why are you making her stand outside in the cold? Invite her in."

"Of course. Come in." Bridget said this with such a lack of enthusiasm Mia wondered if Joan was holding a gun to her back.

Joan moved out of the doorway and Mia stepped into a room featuring a meticulously curated arrangement of antique and contemporary furniture in neutral tones. The room was roped off from a neighboring den by the kind of velvet rope stanchions used at museums. Mia half-expected to see a DO NOT ENTER sign swinging from it.

"I'll fix us coffee," Bridget said.

The women walked past the living room into the kitchen, which had a forced country casual feel to it. Bridget used pods to make them each a perfectly measured cup of coffee that they took to adjoining dining room. *No pastries?* Mia thought. *What kind of Italians are they?*

"Bridget, how about putting out the biscotti you got from the neighbors?" Mia silently saluted the hint of reproach in Joan's voice. "People have been so kind about our loss."

Joan directed the latter statement to Mia, who gave a sympathetic nod and tamped down a feeling of guilt that she'd shown up empty-handed. *What kind of Italian am I?* She forced her attention back to the women. "How are you holding up?" she asked.

"Meh." Joan shrugged. "Lorenzo had his problems, but he was a good boy at heart."

Bridget, who was setting a plate of biscotti on the table, made a gurgling sound that Mia swore disguised a rebutting profanity to Joan's claim about her son.

A little girl around six dressed in a pink leotard, tutu, and ballet slippers, bounded into the room. "Nonna, I'm ready."

"*Va bene*, baby doll." Joan gave the girl an affectionate chuck under the chin. "It was nice to see you again, Mia. I need to take Lucia to dance class so Bridget can get some work done."

"I get to go to ballet." Lucia bounced up and down with excitement, then twirled until she made herself dizzy. "I couldn't but now I can because Mommy has more money."

Mia couldn't restrain from raising her eyebrows at this news. In her experience, a sudden influx of funds often came from suspicious sources.

Bridget threw a winter jacket on her daughter and hurried the little girl and her grandmother out the door. "You need to go, or you'll be late, Lulu. Bye, love you."

Mia welcomed the chance to get Bridget alone, but could sense the woman was impatient to get rid of her. She sipped her coffee and toyed with a biscotti, sending the message she wasn't going anywhere soon. "What do you do for a living?"

"I rep an online jewelry line."

"You do? I'm always looking for new things. Is what you're wearing from the line? I love it."

"Yes," Bridget said, finally warming to her. She practically sprinted across the wooden dining room floor and disappeared into another room, returning with a portable display case. She snapped the case open, revealing a line of delicate gold and silver jewelry that Mia didn't hate. "The silver is sterling, and the gold is twenty-four-karat gold-filled. This is our new line of layered necklaces. We

can personalize the middle charm with your initials."
Bridget examined her with a critical eye. "With your
combo of pale skin, dark hair, and blue eyes, I recommend a cool metal. Silver or white gold."

"I love both."

The two women chatted as Mia tried on a selection of
accessories. Sensing Bridget was as relaxed as she'd ever
be, Mia broached the subject of Lorenzo. "So, your mother-
in-law . . ." She said this in conspiratorial tone. "Between
us, she seems kinda clueless about Lorenzo."

Bridget's expression telegraphed she had strong opin-
ions on the subject. Rather than voice them, she responded
with a bland "Mm-hmm," then quickly maneuvered the
conversation to jewelry. "Oh, that's perfect on you."

She held up a mirror so Mia could admire herself in a
layered silver necklace made up of three different chains,
each sporting a heart ranging from tiny to about an inch
long. Mia caught the corner of a family photo in the mirror's reflection. She angled the mirror to get the entire
photo into frame. It was a group shot of the entire Puglia
clan. Bridget had a hand on the shoulder of a boy around
ten years old. Mia noticed Lorenzo had a hand on the
boy's other shoulder. "Lorenzo once told me you had a
son," she lied. "And they were close."

Bridget pursed her lips. "A little too close."

Leakage! Finally. "Yeah, Lorenzo's not exactly the
role model you want for a kid," Mia said, commiserating.
"Especially when your husband is a public figure."

"Exactly. Nobody else in the family understood why it
bothered me so much. Even Drew." Having found a sympathetic ear, Bridget opened up in a big way. "They were
all, 'Lorenzo is Lorenzo.' But I saw how our boy Zachary

admired him. When Zach began talking and acting like him, I had to do something. Not kill him, of course." Nervous, she tacked this on. "Just . . ."

"Pay him to stay away."

Bridget didn't respond. Sensing she regretted sharing so much and was shutting down, Mia grabbed a pair of dangling earrings from the display case. "Oh, these are gorgeous." She held them up to her ears. "What do you think?"

Bridget's face cleared. "They're you. And so versatile. You can wear them with jeans or an evening gown."

Mia, who couldn't imagine wearing the gaudiest earrings in the case anywhere, nodded enthusiastic agreement. Having milked valuable new information from Bridget, she felt obligated to make a purchase. "I'll take them. How much?"

"They're on sale. Only two hundred dollars."

Mia blanched. "Yay," she said in a weak voice.

She retrieved a credit card from her purse and handed it to Bridget, who zipped it through an apparatus attached to her cell phone. Bridget returned the card to Mia. "Let me get you a gift bag." She left the dining room. Mia texted the new development to Teri with instructions to run it by Drew and garner his reaction. She pressed *send* just as Bridget came back into the room with a small pink gauze bag. She handed it to Mia. "You can put the earrings in the bag or change into them to wear now. Most of my customers can't wait to show off their fabulous new jewelry."

"And I'm one of them," Mia said with a big, fake smile. She removed her silver studs, replacing them with the pricey new purchase.

Mia left Bridget checking her incoming online orders.

She took a rideshare to Kevin Turman's accounting office, housed in a nondescript office building on Hempstead Turnpike. All she discovered about Lorenzo's relationship with the Turmans was that Chrissy was fond of him until he took advantage of her good nature one too many times. Mia was also disappointed to learn that under no circumstances could she write off her expensive new earrings as a business expense.

Next, she paid a visit to Chrissy Turman under the guise of a condolence call. "That's so kind of you," Chrissy said, welcoming her into the family's cozy, extremely lived-in Cape Cod home. She cleared a collection of dolls and toy trucks off the living room couch and offered Mia a seat. "Can I get you a cup of coffee?"

"No, thank you," said Mia, who was still buzzed from the strong coffee Bridget Puglia had served her.

"How was your meeting with Kevin?"

Mia, focused on Lorenzo's death, blanked for a minute. "Oh. Yes. Very productive. I have a lot to discuss with my father." *If I can remember anything Kevin recommended regarding our accounting needs.* "I also wanted to let you know that I dropped off Lorenzo's belongings with your brother and his wife."

"Really?"

The hostility underlying the response caught Mia by surprise. "I didn't notice anything valuable. But there might be something in there that has sentimental value. I'm sorry. I didn't want to give it to your mother because I was afraid it would upset her. I thought I should give it to Drew, since he's the oldest sibling, and the four of you could get together to go through the box. Was that a mistake?"

"No. Not at all. Well, to be honest . . . We're not that close to Drew and Bridget. But we'll work it out."

Mia didn't need the instincts of a private eye to pick up on the fact that "not that close" was a major understatement.

Teri picked up Mia from outside the Turmans. The reporter detailed her "interview" with Drew Puglia. "Typical pol, he spoke like he was reading off a teleprompter. *Except* when I threw the 'rumor' at him that he and his wife were paying his late brother to stay away from the family. Thanks for texting me that juicy tidbit. He was seriously shocked. Like, *whaaa? That's crazy.*"

"That's gonna make for an interesting convo at the Puglias tonight. You sure he wasn't lying?"

"Positive. I knew he was telling the truth because most politicians, except for the real psychopaths, are terrible liars. There's always some tell that gives them away. Like when I asked Puglia if his political aspirations extended beyond Hempstead. He gave me some rote answer about how his only concern was serving the good people of Hempstead. His eyes looked sideways before he looked me in the eye. Like this."

Teri illustrated and the car drifted. "Keep *your* eyes on the road, please," Mia said.

"I was distracted by your earrings. They look like small chandeliers. Not that small, actually."

"I know. Maybe I can palm them off on Cammie. They have that 1980s big earring feel to them."

"Did you pick up anything else from this little expedition?"

"Only that Chrissy can't stand either her brother or his wife, or both."

"Not sure how that factors into Lorenzo getting eighty-sixed."

"I know. Although I can see how Bridget might have gotten sick of paying off the guy who was turning her son into a potential mini-thug."

Teri's cell rang with a ringtone simulating an old-fashioned news bulletin. "That's a text from work. Something coming over the wire. Can you check for me?"

"Sure." Mia picked up Teri's phone. She read the incoming alert. Her mouth dropped open. "Oh. My. *God*."

"What?"

"A deliveryman was killed when the brake on his van disengaged and it rolled down a hill, pinning him against a wall."

"So? Bad luck for him, but how is that an 'Oh. My. *God*?'"

"The deliveryman was Brad Kokolakis. From the Sorrento Deli and Pasticceria." Mia held up the phone. "He was Lorenzo Puglia's coworker."

CHAPTER 16

While Teri drove, Mia searched the internet for stories relating to Brad's demise. All reported it as a tragic, bizarre accident. Mia wasn't convinced. The deliveryman worked for Aida's boyfriend Pauly, hated Lorenzo, and coveted Renata, his late coworker's girlfriend. Mia was sure the death was suspect.

"No way is this an accident," Teri declared, seconding the opinion after Mia read her several articles. "Ooh, I just got investigative journalist goose bumps."

Mia speed-dialed Cammie. "Hi."

"Hey." Her employee's voice was groggy. "Why are you calling so early?"

"It's almost two."

"I stand by my original question."

"Can you get in touch with Zoe, the receptionist at Re-juve, and see if she can come for a practice manicure today? Like, as soon as possible? And yes, it will count as work."

"I'm on it."

Mia ended the call. "Who's Zoe and what's Rejuve?" Teri asked.

"Rejuve is the spa where Lorenzo's girlfriend and her mother work. Zoe is the receptionist who had a thing with Lorenzo."

"So she might have some pillow talk to share that would help our investigation into Brad's mysterious death."

Mia shot a look at Teri. "Our? I don't think so."

Teri responded with a cackle and knowing grin. Mia readied a retort, but two incoming texts distracted her. Cammie reported that Zoe was on her way over to Belle View. Then a photo popped up. A joyful family surrounded a lovely middle-aged woman wearing a *"Buon Compleanno"* tiara who was about to blow out candles on a birthday cake. Cypress trees enveloped the group, with rolling green hills in the distance. The woman looked vaguely familiar. A text from Jamie followed the photo: **Birth family. Found them. Mom in middle. Isabella Rispetto.** That was the reason the woman looked familiar to Mia—she and Jamie shared the same dimpled smile. Mia texted her friend back a string of hearts and thumbs-ups. She ended with an inquiry about his parents: **How r Donny Senior & Aurora doing?** She received a two-word response: **Not well.** Jamie followed this with a string of tear emojis.

Half an hour later, Teri made a right into the Belle View parking lot and idled in front of the banquet entrance. "I'm gonna drop you off and go hound Pete and Ryan to investigate this Brad dude's death as a murder.

Oh, before you go, check out what I got Evans for Christmas." She reached behind Mia and grasped a large shopping bag. She extricated a black motorcycle helmet decorated with a white lightning insignia. "It's got integrated LED lights. How cool is that? You think he'll like it?"

Mia picked up on a rare note of insecurity in the pit bull reporter's voice. "He'll love it."

"Awesome," Teri said, her cockiness quickly returning. "'Cuz I got us matching ones."

"That he won't love."

Mia exited the Smart car. Cammie had alerted her to Zoe's arrival, so before joining them, Mia detoured to the banquet kitchen. She arranged a snack plate, removed a pitcher labeled *Rum Eggnog* from the refrigerator, and carried everything to Cammie's office. She hoped the impromptu party atmosphere would loosen Zoe's lips.

The pretty young receptionist greeted Mia with an excited "Look at my nails!"

She held up her left hand. Cammie had worked fast. Zoe's thumb and index finger sported images of chubby, cheery snowmen. Mia admired them. "Cammie, you have a true talent."

"I always liked to draw," Cammie responded with a modest shrug.

"Zoe, I'm so glad you could make it," Mia said.

"A free mani? I'd never pass that up. Especially such an adorbs one."

"Did you drive here?"

"Nope. Took a cab."

Mia poured a glass of rum eggnog filled to the rim and handed it to Zoe, who took it with her free hand. Mia shed her coat and hung it on a wall hook, then dragged in a chair from the hallway to join the other women. The deluge of news about Brad's bizarre death made it an easy topic to bring up. "Did you hear about that delivery guy from Sorrento deli dying?"

Cammie and Zoe responded with somber nods. "Such a tragedy," Cammie said, with a sad shake of her head.

"It's so crazy." Zoe leaned forward and spoke in a whisper. "I knew him. Well, not *knew* him. But I met him once."

"You did?" Mia made sure her tone implied, "Tell me more."

"He showed up at work," Zoe shared, happy to oblige. "He told me he worked with Lorenzo and was a friend of Renata's, but she was *not* happy to see him. She brought him into her facial room, which is next to where we keep supplies, like office stuff. I needed a pen, so I went to get one. I wasn't spying on them or anything."

"Of course you weren't," Mia said. *Of course you were.*

She topped off Zoe's half-empty glass of eggnog. Zoe took a gulp of it. "Wow, I'm starting to feel this drink. Where was I?"

"You were not spying on Renata and Brad," Cammie prompted.

"Right. So, I heard Renata say to him, 'The only reason I made out with you was cause I was mad at Lorenzo, but it ain't gonna happen again.' Then he went, 'I'm sorry to hear that. Now I may gotta go public with your brother and that idiot Lorenzo's little secret.' I remember the whole thing because I felt bad about it." Zoe looked downcast. "Renata was mad at Lorenzo because he and me had a thing. Only a couple of times and then I stopped it. I never been that girl, you know, the one who takes another girl's guy. But Renata treats me like dirt at work. Like I'm her servant or something. I wanted to get back at her more than I wanted to hook up with Lorenzo. Her mom Aida figured out what was going on between us and told Renata, and she was *mad*. I thought she was gonna kill me. Or Lorenzo."

Maybe she did was Mia's thought as she processed this new development.

Zoe brightened. "But she and Lorenzo worked stuff out and Renata made me her usual Christmas holiday cookies, these lace cookies I love, so she forgave me."

"We had those cookies," Mia said. "Florentine lace cookies. They're incredible. You reminded me, I never hit up Renata for the recipe. Not sure now's the time, though."

The receptionist giggled. "I ate them all and got so sick after, it wasn't funny. I couldn't help it. They're *so* good. They were Lorenzo's favorite too."

She hiccupped. Cammie opened a desk drawer and took out a bottle of water. "Might be time to switch to this." She handed the bottle to Zoe.

Cammie finished Zoe's manicure without Mia exacting any new specifics from the receptionist. "The snowmen on my pinky fingers are winking." Zoe said this with a childlike glee. She held up her pinkies and wiggled them, then giggled and hiccupped again.

Cammie handed her another bottle of water. "I think you could use another one of these."

When Zoe's nails were completely dry, Mia called her a cab. "When I get to work, I'm gonna take a little nappie on one of the empty massage tables," the receptionist said as Mia helped her into the cab.

"Good idea," Mia said, feeling a bit guilty for plying the girl with the heavily rummed eggnog.

After making sure Zoe was okay and on her way, Mia rejoined Cammie. "Thanks for helping me out."

"Not a problem. I really nailed my snowman design. Hey, I made a pun. Nailed—nailed." Cammie eyed Mia with concern. "What's wrong? You look unhappy. Was my joke that bad?"

Mia poured herself a glass of eggnog. She gave it a glum gaze, then took a sip. "It's all these people cheating on their partners. Donny on Aurora, even though they were technically broken up at the time. Lorenzo and Zoe. Renata and Brad. It reminds me of what I went through when I found out Adam was cheating on me."

Cammie muttered strong invectives in Greek. "I curse that man and what he put you through."

Mia grimaced. "Ugh. I hate being seen as a victim."

"But you were."

"Was I? I'm the one who married him after what, a month of dating? Who followed him to Florida. I was never happy there and he knew it. It takes two to mess up a marriage. I need to own my part in it."

"Own it, sure," Cammie said. "And move on. You're not the first person to have a starter marriage and God knows you won't be the last. Stop dissecting it and again, move. *On*. With. *Shane*."

Mia choked on her drink. "Cammie, jeez. You're as bad as my dad. Shane is a coworker. That's it. And that's all it's gonna be."

"Aw, come on." Cammie pouted. "It would be tragic to see that hunk of man candy go to waste, but I don't want some stranger dating him."

Mia frowned at her. "As your boss, I must discourage you from such inappropriate and sexist language."

"You're right. It'd be highly inappropriate for a stranger to date him when the two of you are so obviously hot for each other."

"Argh," Mia exclaimed. "That's it. I'm downloading videos about acceptable language for the workplace and making the whole staff watch them."

"Don't. Guadalupe will snap me in half like a Piero breadstick. I'll shut up."

Cammie began gathering her things together. "Are you leaving already?" Mia asked, knowing the question was rhetorical.

"I don't want to risk saying anything else that might get me in trouble."

"A new excuse. I'm impressed."

"It's good to mix things up now and then." Cammie slipped on the wool trench coat with massive shoulder pads she'd lovingly nurtured since purchasing it in the late 1980s. "And I'm gonna stop by the precinct to see if Pete's free. I'm kind of appreciating him right now. At least he had the decency to divorce me before fooling around with other women."

Once Cammie left, Mia relocated to her own office. She decided there was no harm in asking for Renata's Florentine cookie recipe. If anything, the facialist might be flattered, which would come in handy if Mia needed to approach her again about Lorenzo's death. She spent the rest of the day planning a few surprises for her teen friend Kaitlyn's sweet sixteen, including a full-size cardboard cutout of the girl's favorite singer, Harry Styles. She decided to add a second favor on top of the midway-sized stuffed animals, something that would best anything

Kaitlyn's mean girl nemesis Daniella could offer. To get the goods delivered, she called an expert. "Madison, hi."

"Mia. I'm so glad you called. I've got news. Jamie and I are moving in together."

"You are? That's fantastic." While there was a time when the news would have lodged a dart in her heart, Mia could now say this with complete sincerity.

"I can't tell you how grateful I am to you for helping us get through all this."

"That's what friends do. Help each other. Which leads to my question." She explained the situation to Madison. "I want something that will really blow out the party. Got any ideas of the favor to end all favors?"

"Oh boy, do I. Reality makeup star Rylie Kenner is doing this whole New Year, New You line of makeup and skin care products. As a special thanks for everything you've done, I'll get samples from the new line that aren't available to the general public."

"*Yaas.*" Mia held up her hand and did a triumphant finger snap. "Daniella girl, you've been served. You are now G.P.—general public."

"I'll work on coming up with something extra for the guys at the party. Anything sports-related will do. They're way easier when it comes to favors. It's not the status battle it is with girls."

After promising to send Mia samples from Rylie Kenner's line, Madison signed off. Mia checked her email and saw one from her mother. Even with their rapprochement, it was hard to shake a case of nerves when any missive arrived from Gia. Wary, Mia opened it and was instantly flooded with relief. Gia had sent a photo of her playing with Philip and Finn's little ones. Mia responded with a downloaded image of a smiling heart.

It occurred to Mia that she had yet to thank Shane for sharing the story from his past that motivated her to reach out to Gia. She left her office for his. There was no answer to her gentle rap on the door, so she opened it and peeked in to see if he'd left for the day. He was still there, taking a little personal time. He'd changed from his work clothes into shorts and a T-shirt. He had earbuds in and his back was to Mia as he worked out with twenty-five-pound weights. His T-shirt clung to his taut biceps, which bulged with each weight lift.

Mia escaped before Shane noticed her. She grabbed the wall for support and cursed her knees, which had suddenly gone weak. *Girl up, Mia!* she scolded herself. She summoned up the strength to compose herself, then retrieved her coat from Cammie's office where she'd left it and walked briskly out of Belle View to her car. Once in the car, Mia took a few deep-breathing exercises to calm herself down. Once she was confident she was in control, Mia turned on the car engine, backed out of her parking spot, and started toward home.

She didn't notice the car that pulled out immediately after she did and began following her.

CHAPTER 17

It was past rush hour, so traffic on the Grand Central Parkway was light. There was no reason for the car behind Mia to be on her tail. "Jerk," she muttered, changing lanes. The car did likewise. Mia deeply regretted not paying the extra DMV charge to get a vanity plate that read DNT TLGT. She changed lanes again. The car changed lanes with her. Fear flooded over Mia as it dawned on her this wasn't another textbook obnoxious New York driver. She was being followed.

Her heart raced. She'd only been driving a few months. Losing a tail was beyond her skill set. She kept a steady pace as she debated her next move. As a new driver, she was generally a stickler for observing the rules of the road. But not now. She apologized to the driving gods, cut across two lanes of traffic, and exited at Ditmars Boulevard without signaling. Mia cursed when she saw the car still behind her. The sudden move hadn't shaken it off. *What do I do?* she worried as she took an aimless path up and down local streets. A plan occurred to her. She used her Civic's phone connection to place a call.

"Piero's Restaurant and Bar."

Mia took comfort from the familiar voice answering her call. "Piero, it's Mia Carina. I'm being followed." The restaurant owner let a few choice Italian profanities fly. "Are any of Donny Senior's associates there?"

"*Sì.*"

"Explain the situation. I'll give them five minutes and then pull up in front of the restaurant."

With a plan in place, Mia's fear dissipated. She meandered up and down a few blocks, straining to see who was behind the wheel of the mystery car, a generic black sedan. But she had no luck identifying the driver. After about five minutes, she saw the safe confines of Piero's ahead. Piero stood outside, feet astride, arms crossed, waiting for her. Mia zipped into the parking space he'd saved directly in front of the restaurant. The black sedan hesitated and then zoomed past her. The car parked behind Mia screeched out of its parking space in hot pursuit of the sedan.

Piero helped Mia out of the Civic and ushered her inside the restaurant. "You okay?"

Mia, shaken, made a half-and-half gesture with her hand. "*Mezza.* I'm not gonna lie. That freaked me out."

"I bet."

Piero went behind the restaurant's old wooden bar. Mia claimed a barstool. Piero poured her a shot of whiskey that she gratefully accepted and knocked back. "Thank you for saving my butt."

Piero shrugged. "*Fa niente*. It's nothing. Don't even mention it. Any idea who was tailing you?"

Mia shook her head. "I couldn't make out who was driving. But I'm sure it had to do with Lorenzo Puglia."

"That guy was NG—not good. I recommend steering clear of anyone who was in his orbit."

"Too late for that."

"You want something to eat? I find pasta very comforting in times of stress."

"I wouldn't say no to a plate of something."

She smiled at Piero, whose craggy, pockmarked face was etched with concern. He poured Mia another shot of whiskey, then limped off to the kitchen. Once a driver for Donny Senior, he'd lost a leg to cancer, so Donny set him up in the restaurant business. Being a restauranteur had proven to be Piero's true calling and his humble eatery was one of Astoria's best-kept secrets—which was exactly how Piero wanted it.

Mia surveyed the restaurant. A handful of tables were occupied by couples or small groups, as were some of the booths. All she could see of the person sitting alone in the last booth was the back of a head with short, wiry black and gray curls. Could it be?

Piero returned with a steaming dish of baked ziti. He placed it in front of Mia, along with a setup. "*Grazie*." She unrolled the silverware, whipped open the napkin, and placed it over her lap. "Is that Big Donny in the last booth?"

Piero gave a somber nod. "He's been here pretty much every night since things went down with him and Aurora. I feel bad for him. Just sits there. Hardly eats. I couldn't even tempt him with a plate of my tiramisu."

Mia sucked in a breath. "He turned down your tira-misu? That's scary." She picked up her ziti. "I'm gonna see if he'll talk to me."

She walked past the other diners to Donny Senior. His head was bent over a drink, the aforementioned tiramisu untouched and pushed aside. Mia cleared her throat. He looked up and managed a wan smile. "Mia. *Ciao.*"

"Hey, Mr. B. Interested in some company?" She sat down before he could say no. "Piero's ziti." She mo-tioned to her dish. "The best in the world. You want to split it? I'll get him to bring a plate." Donny shook his head. "You should eat something, Mr. B. You're too thin."

"Not hungry." He kept his head down and batted his drink back and forth between his hands. "I made a mess of my life."

"I know it feels like that. But I'm sure it can be fixed."

Donny gave a skeptical snort. "You say that, but I don't see how. I've been trying to make it up to Aurora. I sent her a ring with a diamond the size of a rock. Then I sent her a floral arrangement the size of a car. Your dad's girl-friend Lin does nice work, by the way. And you know what's sitting in our driveway right now? An actual car. One of those Tesslers—"

"Tesla."

"Whatever. One of those cars everyone thinks are so cool right now. I even got them to make it in her favorite color, purple. It's parked right outside the front door with a big purple bow on it. For what that ended up costing me, I could've bought her an island. Which is next on my list of things to buy her."

Mia finished a large bite of ziti, then said, "I hate to be

harsh, but this isn't something you can buy your way out of, Mr. B. To find out when your kid is in his thirties that your husband is his actual father from an affair you never knew he had? That'd be a huge shock to anyone. You need to give Mrs. B time to work through it."

Donny finally looked up. To Mia, it looked like he'd aged a decade since she'd last seen him only a few days earlier. "What if she doesn't forgive me?"

Mia helped herself to another serving of the ziti. She used the time to formulate a response. "Like I said, I truly believe you can resolve this. Give Mrs. B space right now. When you see the tiniest glimmer of an opening, tell her you're willing to share every detail of what happened in the past, if she's willing to hear it. Tell her nothing means more to you than her and the family, and you'll do anything to prove how much you love them both. Share everything that's in your heart. Everything you're feeling."

Donny shuddered. "Feelings. Sharing. Ugh." He downed his drink and signaled Piero to mix him another. His phone pinged a text. He checked it. "I sent my friend Johnny after whoever was bothering you on the road. He caught up with them. Here's a picture." He held the phone up to show Mia a photo of a terrified-looking Bridget Puglia. "Look familiar?"

"Very," Mia said. "She's the late Lorenzo's sister-in-law. Her husband Drew's a politico in Hempstead with higher aspirations. I'm guessing Drew ripped her a new one for secretly paying off Lorenzo to stay away from their family. She's the Lady to his Macbeth, so I don't know why she'd risk getting in trouble by following me."

"You never know. Could be she only wanted to scare

you. You know, payback for blabbing on her. Or there's more to the story."

"That's the direction I'm going. Although what, I don't know. Thanks for looking out for me, Mr. B. I appreciate you sending Johnny after her. And not having him do anything but take her picture."

"The new me. A good guy instead of a bad guy." He gave a heavy sigh. "Too bad it don't mean anything to the woman I love."

"It will. I know it." Mia finished the last of her ziti. She made a show of eyeing the tiramisu. "That looks *so* good. Piero makes the best tira in the world."

"You want it?" Donny pushed the plate toward her. "It's yours."

"No way I can eat this whole thing. How 'bout we split it?" Donny hesitated. Mia held up the plate. She closed her eyes and inhaled. "Mmmm . . . that sweet, creamy scent. That slight hint of espresso. It's saying to the chocolate, 'Will you marry me?' And the chocolate is saying, 'Yes, yes, a thousand times yes!'"

Donny couldn't hold back a laugh. He held up his hands in a gesture of defeat. "Fine, you win. I'll split it with you." He leaned out of the booth and called, "Hey Piero, when you bring my drink, bring another fork. Mia wore me down here."

"Will do, boss." Piero caught Mia's eye and winked at her.

Mia spent the short ride home after dinner trying to come up with motives for Bridget's pursuit of her. The behavior seemed out of character for the tightly-wound politician's wife. Mia got a renewed case of jitters reliving the frightening experience, so rather than park in her home's alley garage, she opted to park in front of the house where the glow of streetlamps was enhanced by the aggressively lit front yard holiday displays. Her phone screen alerted her to a text from Teri Fuoco: **Police looking at Brad death as possible murder v. accident.** Mia texted back a thumbs-up, to which Teri responded with emoji kissy faces. "Argh," Mia said to her phone, annoyed. "Every time I think you might be an okay person you pull something like that."

She got out of her car and saw Philip and Finn down the street heading to theirs, both perfectly decked out in suits and overcoats. She called to them and both men responded with a wave. She held up a finger, indicating they wait for her, and hurried their way. "You look nice. Holiday party?"

"Yup," Philip said. "At Finn's finance firm."

He made a snoring sound and his husband shot him a look. "Again with the snoring?"

"Better now than at the party," Philip said with an impish grin.

"I'm glad I caught you before you go to this great or boring party," Mia said. "I can't thank you enough for taking in my mom."

"Please, don't worry about it," Finn said. "It wasn't charity. She's doing us a favor. We gave Miranda a month off as a Christmas present, but to be honest, we underestimated how much help we could use. Especially now that Philip is obsessed with outdoor holiday décor."

He threw another look at his husband, who wasn't remotely fazed. Philip rubbed his hands together gleefully.

"I'm bringing new levels to the expression *on steroids*. Wait until you see what I've got planned for my pièce de résistance. Even Elisabetta will be blown away."

Mia's eyes widened. "That is a very alarming statement. Hey, do you mind if I go say hi to my mom?"

"Of course not," Finn said. "Justin and Eliza are in bed, so she's free."

"She's absolutely wonderful with kids," Philip said. "She's got a gift."

"She is? She does?" Considering how little interest Gia displayed in parenting during Mia's own childhood, she was mystified by the compliments, but assumed they were inspired by her mother's determination to become a better person. *This "new me" stuff appears to be going around*, Mia thought a touch sardonically.

The men left for their party and Mia trudged up their front steps, now devoid of Philip's man-made snow. She rang their high-tech bell, which obviously revealed who she was to Gia, because her mother threw open the front door and embraced Mia. She ushered her daughter into the house. "The babies just went down, so we'll be quiet. Come, I'll make a snack."

The women wended their way through a sea of baby and toddler paraphernalia that somehow didn't detract from the down-to-the-studs renovation that had turned the usual warren of tiny rooms in Forty-sixth Place two-family homes into one large great room with a fabulous kitchen at the far end. Mia took a seat at the counter built into the large center island. She ran a hand over the smooth granite countertop. "This is my dream home." She motioned to where sliding glass doors leading out to a new deck had replaced the back wall. "If I didn't like Philip and Finn so much, I'd be hideously jealous."

"The way you're going with Belle View, I bet you'll soon have the money to do the same with your place. At least upstairs. I think your grandmother would have a stroke if you tried removing one crocheted doily."

Mia chuckled. "So true."

"Wine or coffee?"

"Water. I already had scotch and don't wanna mix the grain and the grape."

Gia filled a crystal glass with a rich red wine for herself and filled a glass with filtered water from a dedicated faucet next to a pot-filler faucet. Mia pointed to the pot filler. "That's the one thing that might get Nonna to consider a kitchen remodel. So perfect for pasta pots."

"Tell me about it. I'm teaching Finn how to make homemade pasta. Considering how many batches we've gone through, that thing is a lifesaver." Gia handed Mia her water and took a seat next to her. "I'm glad you stopped by. I know how busy you are, but I would love to spend more time together while I'm in town."

"Do you have any idea how long that will be?"

Gia looked down at her glass. Her wavy black hair fell over her shoulders, hiding her face. "No." She took a drink of wine.

Mia put her glass on the counter. "Mom, look at me." Gia reluctantly looked up. "What happened with you and Angelo? Why did you leave him? Did he cheat on you? That's been going around."

"It wasn't that. He changed. He isn't the man I married."

"He wasn't great to begin with. The man counterfeited everything from money to passports to driver's licenses for underage drinking. And bragged about it. He was an and-it-rhymes-with-stick."

"He could be charming."

"Oh, well then, forget everything I said."

Mia, losing patience with her mother, got up to leave. Gia reached out to stop her. "Don't go. Please. I'll tell you why I left Angelo."

Mia sat back down. "Okay, shoot. And I mean that figuratively. In our family, you have to be specific."

Gia took a breath. She then shared a revelation that stunned Mia. "The scheme where Lorenzo pretended to be Donny's kid? Angelo planned it. He was behind the whole thing."

CHAPTER 18

Mia gawked at her mother, floored. She opened and closed her mouth a few times, unable to find words. She finally found her voice. "What do you mean, Angelo was behind the scam? You were in Italy? Wait—did he sneak back in the country? Did he violate his deportation? Is he here?" She jumped off her stool. "I swear, I'll kill that son—"

Gia grabbed her. "Calm down. No, he's not here. Let me explain."

"Oh, you're gonna explain. But first . . ." Mia grabbed a wineglass and filled it to the rim. "Now, start talking."

Gia pinched the bridge of her nose and screwed up her face like she had a headache. Then she launched into her shocking tale. "Things were going badly for us in Italy. I worked retail, I waitressed, I drove rideshare. Angelo did the same for a little while, then went back to counterfeiting with a couple of Italian ex-cons he hooked up with. They wound up stiffing him and there was nothing he could do about it. They weren't the kind you could demand payment from if you know what I mean."

"I do. Go on."

"Angelo decided I should play on my connection to the Boldanos, so we went to Tortonia, the little village in the Abruzzo region where they have their winery. There weren't any jobs available. But while we were looking, Angelo fell into the story of Jamie's birth."

"How?"

"There was a little old man named Alfiero who's worked at the winery tasting room for years. When we dropped Donny's name, Alfiero got all sentimental. He asked how the baby was doing. We had no idea what he was talking about, so he told us all about how a young woman who worked as a nurse for Donny Senior's father wound up pregnant and the family worked out a way for the baby to be adopted without Donny and his wife ever finding out he was the birth father."

"That I know. It was Stefano and Vera's doing. Get to the headline here. How does Lorenzo fit into this whole thing?"

"When Angelo was selling fake IDs to high school kids on the Island and here in Queens before he got pinched by the cops, Lorenzo was his connection."

Mia took this in. "Huh. I need to move up the alcohol ladder. Do the guys have any scotch? I think this story has earned me a belt and they'd totally understand."

"Hold on."

Gia went to the dining area, where a variety of liquors rested on a mid-century brass bar cart. She picked a bottle and brought it back to the kitchen. Mia read the label.

"Macallan Rare Cask. Anything with the word *rare* in it has to cost a fortune. When I die, I want to come back as a rich gay man."

"Philip and Finn have the life," Gia said as she poured Mia a finger of the smooth brown liquid into an old-fashioned glass. "But they're so lovely and generous I can only be happy for them."

Mia took the tumbler from Gia and sipped the scotch. "Oh yeah. This will definitely make the nightmare you're sharing go down easier. Continue, please. Why did the brain trust of Angelo and Lorenzo think that Lorenzo pretending to be the long-lost brother of the secretly adopted son of a Mafia don was a good idea?"

"Both of them assumed that by now everyone knew Jamie was adopted. When you think about it, that's not so unusual these days. It's more unusual to hide it."

"True," Mia admitted. "That wasn't the best choice on Donny and Aurora's part."

"Angelo figured that the Boldanos would be excited to meet Jamie's birth brother and welcome him into the family with open arms. Angelo would claim credit for the reunion and all he'd ask for in return would be some kind of position at the winery or in any other venture Donny has going in Italy. I tried to talk him out of the whole thing, but he wouldn't listen. So I decided to fly over and talk some sense into Lorenzo. But Angelo warned him off and made sure we never connected."

"Why didn't you just tell Donny what was going on? You would've saved everyone a lot of problems."

"I was afraid of what might happen to Angelo if I told Donny. Instead, Lorenzo is dead. I'm so stupid."

Anguished, Gia placed a hand over her eyes in an attempt to stave off tears. Mia rose from her counter seat and went to the glass-fronted, handcrafted cabinet that held glasses. She retrieved an old-fashioned glass and poured her mother a splash of scotch. "It's there if you need it. I think we've got bigger concerns than never mix, never worry right now."

"I'm okay. You can have it."

"Don't have to ask me twice." Mia took the glass for herself. "Does Angelo know about Lorenzo?"

Gia dropped her hand and nodded. "I let him know as soon as it happened. Then, when I tried to call him again, his phone was disconnected. That set off an alarm for me, so I went to our bank account. It's empty. There was a big cash advance on our credit card and then he canceled it. Which is why I had to move out of the hotel. And borrow from the donation boxes." She began to cry. "I'm a horrible person."

"You're not, Mom. I'm not gonna lie—you made a lot of bad choices in your life. I'm still angry about some of them. But you're changing and becoming a better person, and I respect that." She glanced around the room. "I don't see tissues. I'll get you one from the bathroom."

"They don't use them. Bad for the environment. They use hankies."

Gia pulled open a drawer and took out a white cotton square. She wiped her eyes and blew her nose, then pocketed the handkerchief. "Wow," Mia said. "I haven't seen one of those since Nonno passed. I thought they were kind of gross then and I think they're gross now. I'll remember to bring my own tissues when I visit here. Back to Angelo. Where is he now?"

"I don't know."

Mia's stomach knotted. "Oh no. Are you positive he hasn't snuck back into the country?"

"Yes. Security is way too tight at the US airports. I'm guessing he's somewhere in Eastern Europe."

"Wherever he is, given everything that's happened, there is the chance Donny will have his people track him down."

"I doubt it. He used to brag about being connected to Russian and Armenian Families. Even Donny won't wanna poke those bears."

Mia finished her whiskey. She followed it with the drink she'd poured for her mother. She needed liquid courage for the question she was about to ask. "Mom, I know you were desperate to stop Angelo and Lorenzo's stupid plan. I'm sorry, but I have to ask . . . did you kill Lorenzo?"

She stilled herself for an outraged response from her mother. Instead, she received a quiet, "No. I didn't." The simplicity of the response made Mia believe her. "I wish I could say that's a crazy idea; how can you even think that of your mother? But I can't. I'm going to the police tomorrow and telling them exactly what I told you. It'll probably make me a suspect in their eyes too, but I'll have to take that chance."

"Yeah, you can't hide this anymore. And Donny needs to know. But let me handle that."

"That would be wonderful," Gia said, relieved. "The thought of telling him all this was scarier to me than talking to the police."

"I get it." For the first time, Mia saw the frail, insecure woman who lurked under Gia's beauty. She was overcome with a feeling she hadn't felt for her mother since childhood—unconditional love. She went to Gia and wrapped her arms around her. "Don't worry, we're gonna get through this. Between the cops, the Family, and me, we'll make sure the right person and not the wrong person gets nailed for Lorenzo—and Brad's—death."

Before Mia departed, there was a glimmer of good news. Gia showed her security footage from Philip and Finn's top-of-the-line nanny cam that verified she was reading to Justin and Eliza at the time of Brad's death, providing her with at least one alibi. Mia returned home and before falling into bed, she texted Ravello that they needed to pay a visit to Posi in the morning for a family confab. He responded in the affirmative. But in the morning, she woke up to an unexpected guest. She'd readied herself for work and was shopping for a fancy new cat tree—"If I can't remodel my place, I can remodel yours," she told Doorstop—when Elisabetta yelled up to her, "Mia, *vieni qui!* We have a visitor."

Mia came downstairs to find Aurora Boldano in Elisabetta's kitchen, a cup of cappuccino and an untouched plate of biscotti in front of her. The sight of Donny's elegant wife in her grandmother's homey but faded throwback kitchen, was disquieting. Mia bent down and kissed the Boldano matriarch on both cheeks. "Aurora, *buon giorno*. A visit from you is such a nice way to start the day."

"That's kind of you," Aurora said, "especially when you know I'm here for a reason."

Way to cut through it, Mia thought. Mia could see that the stress of recent events had gotten to the usual immaculately put-together woman. Her hair, the color of black coffee streaked with white cream and always contained in a neat chignon at the nape of her neck, was pulled back in a careless ponytail. She seemed to have thrown on her outfit of burgundy houndstooth wool pants and off-white pullover sweater and exuded a strained weariness.

Mia poured herself a cup of coffee and helped herself to a biscotti, then took a seat across from Aurora. Elisabetta flanked the woman on the other side. "I'm assuming Mr. B talked to you."

Aurora nodded. "He came to me gift-free, begging forgiveness. He said he was inspired by a conversation with you." She picked up a vanilla biscotti and stirred her coffee with it, then placed it on the cup saucer, uneaten. "I'm torn. I still feel betrayed . . ."

"Mr. B's . . . indiscretion . . . happened a long time ago," Mia pointed out.

"That makes it worse. I know we were separated at the time, but the fact Donny's been hiding it from me for over thirty years makes it feel like he's been keeping a guilty secret. If he'd come clean back then, we could've worked through it."

"Do you think he's stepped out on you other times?" Elisabetta asked.

Aurora made a *who knows?* gesture. "He swears he hasn't, but . . ."

"Do you truly, honestly want my opinion, Mrs. B?" Mia asked.

"Yes," Aurora responded with certainty.

"Okay then. I was married to a serial cheater. I think if Mr. B has fooled around with other women, you'd know. You'd make excuses, try to justify red flags, and make them go away. But if someone took a lie detector to you, when you said, 'He's not cheating on me,' it would go *ding-ding-ding* or honk or beep or make whatever sound lie detectors make when it picks up that someone's lying. From what I've seen—and granted, I'm an outside observer to your marriage—except for the jail stints brought on by illegal activity, Mr. B's been pretty much a model husband and father. Only you know the truth of that, of course. But I do know this: If you let the issue of how Jamie came into this world be what breaks up you and Mr. B, Jamie will feel responsible for that the rest of his life. So that's something to think about."

Elisabetta freshened Aurora's coffee. "*Grazie*." Aurora examined the back of Elisabetta's track suit, where a Christmas tree laden with sequined and beaded ornaments glittered. "That's some jacket."

"It lights up. *Guarda*." Elisabetta pushed a tiny button inside her bright green velour jacket and tiny colored lights on the tree came to life in all their kitschy glory.

"Donny loves his tracksuits," Aurora said. "This might make a fun early present."

The hint of a rapprochement between Aurora and Donny made Mia happy. Elisabetta turned off the lights on her tracksuit. "I don't wanna burn out the battery." She returned to her chair. "Aurora, my friend. At thirty-two, I was a widow with a ten-year-old son. I spent a lot more time alone than I did with my late husband. Was it a perfect marriage? Of course not. We argued. We drove each other *pazzo*. I know there were times when we wanted to wring each other's necks and wondered if marriage was worth the trouble."

"Nonna," Mia said, "I'm jumping in here to say that if you want me to get married again sometime, this is a terrible pep talk."

Elisabetta put a finger to her lips. "*Silenzio.* I'm not done." She locked eyes with Aurora. "From my husband's death to this day, I've battled with God, trying to show him love while being angry he took my Antonio away from me so early. You and Donny love each other. Work out your problems and move on."

Aurora stood up. "*Grazie mille.* I'm grateful to both of you for giving me much to think about."

She removed her coat from the back of her chair and slipped it on. Elisabetta handed her one of the old, worn ricotta containers she used for storage. "Homemade biscotti for you and Donny."

"Elisabetta, you don't have to—"

"Don't waste your time arguing, Mrs. B," Mia advised. "No one leaves a Carina house empty-handed. It's a badge of dishonor."

Shortly after Aurora left, Mia headed to the Triborough Correctional Facility to meet up with her brother and father. Ravello had beaten her there and was cooing over photos of guard Henry Marcus's baby grandson while Posi looked on. "Look at those teeny, tiny teeth." Ravello cast an affectionate glance at his offspring. "I remember when you guys were this little. So cute."

"Someday the good Lord will bless you with grandchildren too, Mr. C.," Henry said, putting away his phone.

"Only He knows when," Ravello replied with a heavy sigh.

Mia and Posi exchanged an eye roll. "Hard to knock someone up when you're in the joint, Pops," Posi said.

"'Knocked up,' *marone*," Ravello said, aghast. He glared at his son. "I don't wanna hear talk like that from you, Positano."

Mia clapped her hands. "I need to get to work, so

focus, people." She and her father sat down opposite Posi. "Mom dropped a giant bomb on me last night. The con game with Lorenzo posing as Jamie's brother? Angelo was behind it."

Posi and Ravello reacted with shock and anger, along with a stream of Italian invectives and accompanying hand gestures that drew a dismayed response from Henry. "Whoo-wee, my ears are burning, and I don't even know what you're saying."

"Now that you've got that out of your system," Mia said to her father and brother, "let's focus on the problem here. Mom was desperate to stop Angelo and Lorenzo. Lorenzo winds up dead. It would not be illogical for Pete and Ryan to consider Mom a prime suspect in the creep's murder."

"It would not," Ravello acknowledged. Posi agreed with a sober nod.

"We know Mom didn't do it—"

"We assume," Ravello said.

"Dad!" Mia said, appalled.

"I'm only trying to think like the police and operate on facts, not feelings."

"Fine. *Assume*." Mia laid a heavy dose of sarcasm on the word. "Let's brainstorm about who else might have booted Lorenzo from the planet. We can break down the suspects we know about into three groups: the Espositos, the Puglias, and the Sorrento Deli peeps."

Posi threaded his fingers together and leaned his chin on them. "Motive for group one."

"The Espositos? Renata was ticked off at Lorenzo for cheating on her, which could have also triggered Mama Bear Aida, who wasn't too happy with the guy herself. I'm not sure they were angry enough to kill, though. I'm also not sure how Santino fits into the picture. I definitely pick up on him being an operator."

"Where does he work?" Ravello asked.

"Don't know."

"I'll make myself useful by finding out."

"Thanks, Dad. On to group number two. When it comes to the Puglias, Lorenzo was obviously the family black sheep, beloved by his mother and not at all by anyone else in the family. He wore out his welcome with the sister who was fond of him, but hard to see her or her husband annoyed enough to kill him. The older brother and his piece-of-work wife—now that's another story."

She detailed how Bridget had followed her the night before. "You should have led with that," her father said.

The dark tone in her father's voice made Mia nervous. "Relax, Dad. Donny's got people on it." She quickly moved on to the Sorrento staff. "I'm convinced that Lorenzo had a side scam going with the van, one that might implicate the Espositos. We mined some intel from the receptionist at Rejuve spa, where Aida and Renata work." Mia recounted what Zoe had shared with her and Cammie. "Brad, the late delivery partner of Lorenzo's, was trying to blackmail his way into Renata's panties. He was threatening to go public with her brother and Lorenzo's 'little secret.' The Sorrento owners, Pauly and Ralph, think Lorenzo stole from them. Hmm." Mia pondered this. "Maybe Brad's death had nothing to do with the long-lost-brother scam. What if Pauly or Ralph confronted him about the stealing and ended up killing him? It could have been an accident, but Brad saw it, and they had to get rid of him too."

"Sounds extreme for a couple of salami cutters," Posi said, skeptical.

"Or not. When I saw Mom talking it up with Ralph at the funeral luncheon, I thought she was trolling for a new mate. But given the circumstances—that Lorenzo, Angelo's patsy, worked for Ralph—maybe the conversation had something to do with the Boldano plot. I'll check with Mom when I get the chance and ask Teri Fuoco to make herself useful and dig into Ralph and Pauly's pasts."

"And when I get to Belle View," Ravello said, "I'll check in with Donny and see if he's uncovered why that Puglia woman was chasing you. Speaking of work, Posi wants to talk to you about something. I'll leave you two alone."

Ravello said his goodbyes. Once he was gone, Mia faced her brother. "What's up?"

Posi flushed and stammered for a minute, a rare expression of insecurity from Mia's preternaturally cocky sib. "I'm worried about my future at Belle View once I get out of here," he finally confessed.

"What?" Mia was taken aback by Posi's vulnerability. "Why?"

"Now that Shane's working there, you got your handsome guy."

"Posi, that's nuts. Of course, you'll work at Belle View when you get out of here. You're family."

"I don't want to be a pity hire," Posi said with a pout.

Mia angled her head and gave him a look. "Okay, tell me where there's a law that there can only be one handsome guy per banquet hall. With two, we'll be booked forever. Plus, Shane hates being handsome. You own it. You love it. You *live* for it."

"I do," Posi said, cheering up. "It's my thing. My brand if you will."

"Trust me, with you *and* Shane on deck, we will own catering facilities in Queens. *Own* them."

"*Yaaass.*" Posi, his confidence restored, fist-pumped the air.

"I gotta get to work. At your future place of business."

"Awww . . ."

Posi teared up. For a moment, he forgot where he was and reached out to hug his sister. Henry held up a warning hand and stepped toward him. "Sorry, but no contact."

Posi dropped his arms, abashed. "Right. My bad. Curse my emotional nature. What's on deck at Belle View, sis?"

"We've got a first birthday this afternoon with a Nativity theme. Don't ask." Mia got up. She blew her brother a kiss. "Love you, P."

Posi blew a kiss back. "Love you too."

Henry alerted another guard that it was time to walk Posi back to his cell. Mia waved goodbye to her brother. When she was sure he was out of earshot, she turned to Henry. "Was that the craziest conversation you ever heard?"

"In this place?" Henry said. "Not even close."

Mia's phone pinged a text. She read it and burst out laughing. "I have to show you this. It's from my coworker, Shane. He texted me, 'The animals are here. Camel poops are ginormous.' And sent this picture."

She held her phone up to Henry so he could see the photo. He squinted, and then his eyes widened. "Now that," he said, "is *crazy.*"

CHAPTER 19

On her way back to work, Mia stilled her nerves and called her mother to hear what happened when she confessed to the police that her husband was behind the whole plot to ingratiate Lorenzo into the Boldano family. She was relieved Gia answered the call. At least she hadn't been charged with Lorenzo's death—yet. "Pete immediately sent out his partner to interview the hotel employees," Gia said. "I'm sure he was hoping to find evidence that would put this whole case to bed. But one of the desk clerks remembers me coming in the night before and not leaving my room until it was time to meet you, at which point Lorenzo was already dead. They're checking security cameras for backup, but I think I'm gonna be okay."

"I'm glad, Mom. I have enough trouble fitting in visits to one jailed family member. I don't know how I'd squeeze in two."

Gia laughed. "I'm flattered you'd even consider visiting me. That's progress, *bella mia*."

"It is," Mia said, swallowing her emotions.

By the time she returned to Belle View, volunteers from the Friends Forever Animal Sanctuary had set up a comfortable home for their four-legged charges. A large section of the parking lot was covered with a carpet of hay and lined with hay bales. The temperature hovered around the high forties, and Mia thanked the universe for a break in the cold weather. Carpenters were putting the finishing touches on a wooden lean-to that would serve as the Nativity scene's stable. A wooden crib sat on the sidelines, ready to complete the mise-en-scène.

Mia approached Shane, who had shed the sport coat he usually wore at work to lend a hand with the lean-to. "Shane, this is amazing. I'm actually getting excited about the Bianchi party."

Shane used his shirtsleeve to wipe sweat from his brow. "Yeah, it's coming together." He and Mia watched the sanctuary volunteers lead a donkey, a sheep, and a fat pygmy goat from the transport truck to their temporary home. "The camel is coming separately."

"If I ever write an autobiography, that will be the title. *The Camel is Coming Separately: My Life as an Event Planner*."

Shane chuckled. "I think the title of mine should be, *If I Had a Dime for Every Time Someone Accused Me of Watering Down the Liquor, I Wouldn't Have to Do This Job*. But it's long."

"A little."

"I do love my job," Shane added, suddenly nervous. "The title's a joke."

"I know. No worries." Mia instinctively patted his arm to reassure him, then pulled her hand away. Flustered, she blathered a string of meaningless words. "Okay, well then, there you go." She regained a modicum of self-control. "I'll let you handle things out here. I'm going to check in with Guadalupe and Evans."

Mia turned to go. She noticed the sanctuary volunteers, attractive young women in their early twenties, admiring Shane and exchanging giggling whispers with each other. She scolded herself for a sudden sense of possessiveness and exited for her office.

As she walked, Mia put in a call to Teri Fuoco. "Hey, it's my new BFF," Teri said.

Mia gritted her teeth. "Stop that or I'll hang up."

"You would if you could, but you can't. You need me again. Am I right?"

"Yes," Mia was forced to admit. "Could you take a deep dive into the backgrounds of Pauly D'Annunzio and Ralph Mastacciolo? They're the only suspects with connections to both dead guys and we know the least about them."

"You used *we*! I love it."

Mia cursed herself. "I'm gonna send you a list of everyone I can think of whose names come up in conjunction with the murders and fake brother racket over the last couple of weeks. Run them through whatever you run stuff through and maybe some links will come up we—I—never knew about."

Mia typed up the list of names for Teri. As an afterthought, she added one last name. It was a reach, but why not explore every name that had popped up in the last few weeks for a possible connection? Mia emailed the list to the reporter and went to meet with head chef Guadalupe. In the banquet facility's large kitchen, the air was redolent with the scent of the Middle Eastern theme the Bianchis had chosen for their buffet cuisine, in keeping with the original Nativity location of Bethlehem. Even the cake Evans created was on topic: a chocolate manger holding a swaddled baby doll.

"You guys got it on lock here," Mia said, admiring her staff's work. She helped herself to one of Guadalupe's homemade stuffed grape leaves. Cammie had beat her there. She held up a grape leaf. "I'm on my third. They're *nóstimo.*"

Guadalupe glared at her. "I'm glad you think they're delicious. You get to explain to the guests how much they would've liked them if you hadn't eaten them all."

"Sorry," Cammie said, sheepish, adding in a low voice to Mia, "She speaks Greek?"

"Who knew?" Mia replied with a shrug.

Cammie wandered the kitchen looking for additional snacks to sneak behind Guadalupe's back while Mia and the chef went over the party details. "The waitstaff's already in costume," Guadalupe said.

"Another questionable choice on the part of the Bianchis, but the customer is always right. Do they look like shepherds?"

"When they spit out their gum and take out their ear pods, they kinda do."

Their meeting was interrupted by a scream from Cammie. "Help! A fingernail fell into the soup!"

"That's not soup, it's cake batter for the sweet sixteen

party tonight," Evans said. He began a fierce search in the bowl. "I don't have time to remake it."

Cammie wrung her hands together. "I'm sorry. I broke a nail and had to replace it with a fake one. I wasn't happy about it, believe me."

"Whoever finds it in their piece of cake will be less happy," Evans said, peering into the bowl and stirring some more.

Mia noticed a glint from something on the floor. She bent down and picked up a thumbnail painted with a glittery snowflake. "This yours?"

She handed the nail to Cammie, who stuck it back on her thumb. "Bless you. False alarm, people, false alarm."

Guadalupe held a spatula over her head. "That's it. Everyone outta our kitchen. *Now.*"

She chased the women out. Cammie went to her office to secure the errant thumbnail while Mia stopped by Ravello's office. "I talked to Donny," her father said, "and got an update on the Bridget Puglia situation. It appears some of the funding for her Get Lorenzo Out of Our Lives campaign came from her husband Drew's actual campaign funds, which is a big, illegal no-no."

"Huh. I guess when her husband laid into her after finding out about the secret payments, she must've put it together with the questions I asked during my visit, figured out I was onto her, and tried to intimidate me into keeping my mouth shut with that car chase."

"I disagree. I don't think her goal was intimidation. You'd already blabbed, so I think it was forcing you into an accident. Hopefully fatal. I have an appointment with Pete Dianopolis to fill him in on all this."

"I think Bridget just moved to the top of the suspect leaderboard."

"Probably. Oh, and there's good news on the Boldano personal front. Aurora took Donny back. He's eternally grateful to you and said he's sending over a present."

"He doesn't have to do that. I'm only glad they're moving through things." Mia checked the time on the gold filigree watch her father had given her as a high school graduation present. "The Bianchis will be here any minute. I better hup to."

Ravello gazed at his daughter with affection. "Look at you. All businesslike and everything. I'm so proud." He came to Mia and gave her a bear hug.

"Here's hoping you still feel that way after we get through today," Mia said. But she hugged her father back, hiding the happy tears his compliment engendered.

The Bianchi birthday party proved a smashing success. Mia's skepticism about the event's theme dissipated when she heard the inspiration behind it from Bruno and Angela Bianchi, baby Bruno's parents, a couple in their early forties. "This day means so much to us," Angela said, adjusting the headdress she wore as part of her Mary costume. "We've been trying to have a baby for ten years."

"We lost track of how many times she miscarried," Bruno, who was dressed as Joseph, said. He nodded to the baby in his arms, who'd fallen asleep with a non–Nativity-themed binky in his mouth. "He's our miracle baby."

"Like the one born on Christmas Day two thousand years ago."

Angela kissed her son's forehead and gently stroked his fine baby hair. Mia was surprised to find herself moved to the point of choking up. She swallowed and said, "We're so thrilled the party is everything you dreamed of. The photographer's ready for you now. You'll be able to relive today through pictures for the rest of your lives."

Angela's lower lip quivered. "You're gonna make me cry and smear my mascara. I know I shouldn't be wearing it because Mary didn't, but I have thin eyelashes."

"I'm sure if Mary could wear mascara, she would have, sweetheart," Bruno said to his wife.

While the family posed for pictures in the Nativity scene under the heat lamps Belle View provided for their comfort, as well as the animals, Mia replayed the Bianchis' story. It brought to mind the Boldanos' anguished quest for a second child. Birth was certainly the theme of the season. Even Lorenzo Puglia could be cast as prodigal son Cain.

She heard a loud guffaw. It came from Shane. The camel had finally shown up and he was feeding it hay, under the supervision of the camel's handler. The camel made grunting noises and his huge mouth moved back and forth as he chewed. "I love this guy," Shane said with the endearing delight of a child.

Mia watched Shane, amused. Her mind drifted. *I wonder what our kids would look like?* Horrified, she gasped out loud. *Stop it right there, missy!* she berated herself. *Don't you dare go there.* The photo session over, the sanctuary volunteers wrangled the animals, who were all relatively chill. Only the pygmy goat, whose name was Greta, seemed restless and out of sorts.

Someone tapped Mia on the shoulder. It was Evans. "You got a delivery. They couldn't find you, so they tracked me down in the kitchen."

"Oh. Thanks. Do you mind bringing it to my office?"

"Won't fit."

Evans said this with a wide grin, stoking Mia's curiosity. He gestured for her to follow him, which she did. They rounded the corner of the lot to the front of Belle View. Parking in front of the facility was a purple Tesla, topped with a bright purple bow. Mia stared at it. "*Whaaaa . . .*"

Evans handed her an envelope and key fob. "Someone's having a very merry Christmas."

He strolled away. Mia ripped open the envelope and took out the card inside. A florid "B" decorated the front. Mia knew the Boldanos' personal stationery when she saw it. She read the card:

> *Dearest Mia,*
>
> *There are no words for my family to express our gratitude for how much you helped our family through this difficult time. The path ahead of us might not be easy, but there might not even be a path if it wasn't for you.*
>
> *Please accept this small token of appreciation from all of us.*
>
> *Donny Sr., Aurora, Donny Jr., and Jamie*
>
> *P.S. Aurora says good luck figuring out how to drive this thing. If you can't, we'll buy you a Cadillac.*

"Hey. Whoa . . ."

Shane approached from around the corner. He stopped and took in the sight of the purple car. "A thank you from the Boldanos," Mia said.

"That's our Mobbed-up tribe," Shane said, his expression wry. "When it comes to gifts, no gift is too large. Or in this case, too purple."

"I need to move it so the valet can bring people's cars to the front door, but . . . I'm scared." She examined the fob, perplexed. "I don't even know how to use this. My car is from 2014. It's old school. It came with a key."

Shane's face lit up. "I'll move it for you."

Mia was taken aback but entertained by the enthusiasm the usually reserved man displayed. She tossed him the fob. "Go for it."

"Awesome." Shane practically skipped to the car. He crossed his arms in front of him à la Aladdin, bobbed his head, and pressed the fob. "Open sesame." The car door opened. He hopped inside. A minute later, the car slid away in silence.

Shane drove to the far end of the parking lot, passing Ravello, who was returning from his meeting with Pete. While the temperature was still high for December, it was cool enough to make a coatless Mia shiver. She stepped inside to the foyer, where she waited for her father. He tromped in shortly after. "Everything's melting out there. But they say we could be looking at snow. Right on time for Christmas Eve."

"I appreciate the weather report, but what's the deal with Pete? Any developments?"

"A huge one." Ravello removed his leather gloves. "Pete's issuing an arrest warrant for Bridget Puglia."

"For chasing me?"

"Attempted vehicle assault. But that's just a stall."

Mia had an idea where her father was heading, but asked, "What's he stalling for?"

"For enough time to gather the evidence he needs to charge Bridget Puglia with the murder of her brother-in-law, Lorenzo."

CHAPTER 20

"Wow," was Mia's instant reaction. "I'm not surprised and yet I am." Mia contemplated the news.

"Why? You said yourself she'd moved into the top suspect slot."

"I know. It's just . . . if Bridget did kill Lorenzo, you'd think a clue or two would have popped up by now. Ever since she felt threatened with exposure, she hasn't exactly been subtle."

Ravello started toward his office with Mia alongside of him. "The police may have clues we don't know about, and are waiting to make an airtight case," he said.

"That's true," Mia acknowledged. She felt an unexpected sense of guilt. "The Puglias must hate me. Which is selfishly off-topic, but I opened the lid to a big box of nightmares for them."

"I wouldn't worry about it," her father said.

Mia wasn't convinced. "Drew's a politician. This will kill his career."

"Or make it, with the right spin."

Mia gawked at her father. "Dad, that's so cynical."

"You call it cynical," Ravello said. "I call it realistic."

"I guess. By the way, I've been meaning to ask—did you ever find out where Santino Esposito works?"

"Yes, sorry, I forgot to tell you. Box Club. The big-box store. He's on the loading dock at the one in Elmhurst. Not sure how that plays into things."

"Or if it does at all. I was just curious."

"Future son-in-law?" Ravello teased.

Mia scrunched up her face in an expression of disgust. "Ugh, never. Don't even joke about that. Ugh."

"You said that twice," Ravello said, giving his daughter an affectionate chuck under the cheek. She waved him off.

Once the Bianchi party wound down, Mia took a break to check her email and see if news about Bridget Puglia had made it to the internet. A link sent by a euphoric Teri proved Ravello right about Drew Puglia working his wife's arrest to his advantage. Under the subject line **SCORE!** Teri shared that thanks to her interview with Drew—which was thanks to Mia—the Hempstead councilman had come to her with his woeful tale of how his wife was driven to the brink of madness by her evil brother-in-law, who threatened to corrupt those most dear to her heart, the Puglias' beloved children. **Story picked up by Reuters, Associated Press, AND many more!!** the reporter bragged. Mia sent back a simple message: **Now *you* owe *me*.** Teri shot back, **Wrong. We're even. Until YOU need ME again. Which you will.**

Mia made a face at the computer, then pushed back from her desk until her chair met with the office's back wall. She mulled over Bridget's arrest. The woman certainly had motive for getting rid of Lorenzo. *So why does it feel wrong?* Mia wondered. She'd once told Pete Dianopolis that she understood the criminal mind because she grew up with it. Mia learned to trust her instincts at an early age and right now they were telling her something was off. But what? She closed her eyes and concentrated. "Brad," she blurted, and opened her eyes. So far, she could connect the late deliveryman to the Espositos and Sorrento staff, but there was zero evidence of any link to the Puglias. Try as she might, Mia couldn't shake the feeling that the murders were related.

Cammie opened Mia's door and stuck her head into the office. "The DJ's here, along with all the party equipment."

Break over, Mia rose from her desk. "Round up the troops. We've got the world's best sweet sixteen to throw."

While the DJ set up, Mia, Cammie, and Shane supervised the arrangement of various entertainment stations in the Marina Ballroom. There was the requisite selfie station and paraphernalia, but Mia had complemented the return-to-childhood theme with a candy bar, a craft area where guests could decorate frames with macaroni noodles, and a half-dozen video consoles featuring favorite games from the teens' adolescence. Eight p.m. finally arrived. Mia wrung her hands. Her heart pounded. "I wasn't this nervous at my own sweet sixteen," Mia said to Cammie.

"Less at stake. What's that old saying? The life you

ruin may be your own. Here, if this party's a dud, you're ruining someone else's life."

Mia gave her coworker the side-eye. "I cannot tell you how much I did not need to hear that."

A few teenagers wandered in. All managed to shed their coats without letting go of their cell phones. Most of the boys wore their version of dress-up: jeans and a button-down shirt their mothers most likely forced them into. The girls, however, didn't stint on the sequins and sparkle. All were clad in shiny micro–minidresses. The ballroom slowly filled with a sea of disaffected youth. At 8:30, the DJ stopped playing an excellent mix of tunes that had yet to lure a single partygoer to the dance floor. "Ladies and gentlemen," he announced into a microphone, "please welcome your hostess and the guest of honor, Miss Kaitlyn Venere."

He played a flourish as Kaitlyn's parents led her into the ballroom. The teen looked stunning in a red-velvet minidress and matching satin-and-beaded high heels. She waved to a couple of friends and Mia could see her hand was shaking. A decent number of her guests looked up from their phones, which she classified as a win. Kaitlyn's parents each kissed her on the cheek, then hurried away. "Kaity doesn't want us here," her mother explained to Mia as she headed for the exit with her husband. "Thank God."

The DJ put on a Drake song that did nothing to inspire energy in the room. "Tell the waitstaff to start passing hors d'oeuvres," she instructed Cammie. "Go heavy on the mini-pizzas and pizza rolls. And anything else on the menu with the word *pizza* in it." Cammie scurried off to the kitchen. Mia strode over to the DJ and motioned for him to turn off the music. She grabbed the microphone. "Hi all, welcome to Kaitlyn's awesome party," she announced, instantly regretting the forced "awesome." "Food is on the way and we have a ton for you to do tonight. But here's the big news. Remember how much you loved petting zoos when you were little? Well, tonight you get to relive how much fun they are because outside in the parking lot are the cutest animals ever, just waiting for you to show them some love." The announcement earned zero response from the crowd. "Whoo-hoo!" Mia added, desperate.

"We're wearing dresses," called out a model-thin girl clad in a tiny pink dress and six-inch platform heels. She delivered the statement with a toss of heavily highlighted long hair.

Based on Kaitlyn's description, Mia knew she was Daniella, the resident mean girl, and instantly hated her. Unfortunately, Daniella put a light on a giant flaw in the evening's plans. The guests—at least the girls—would be loath to risk ruining their best dresses to pet a donkey. Mia castigated herself for missing such a crucial concern. "If you don't want to pet them, you can at least look at them," she offered, cringing at how lame this sounded even to her. She handed the mic back to the DJ, who gave her a look of pity.

For the next hour, Mia did her best to breathe life into the party but to no avail. "Teenagers are horrible people," she muttered to Cammie after hearing a teen call for a rideshare to pick up her and three friends.

"They're not. They're just . . . teenagers."

Mia saw Kaitlyn sitting at a table for ten with one friend, the lovely British Juliet, who Mia was sure would grow up to be a sociologist famous for writing a treatise on the dystopian youth of America. "You were right," Mia said to Cammie, almost in tears. "I'm ruining Kaitlyn's life."

"There, there." Cammie gave her a sympathetic pat on the shoulder. "Not to add to your troubles, but I'm clocking out in ten."

Shane, who'd been tasked with monitoring the animals, suddenly ran into the room. Mia had never seen him so disheveled. He was devoid of his sport coat, his shirt hung out of his pants, which were stained with large wet spots. "We have a situation," he said, gasping for breath.

"No," Mia whimpered. "No situations."

"We can't get out of this one. The goat is about to give birth."

"*What?*" Mia's screech caught the attention of nearby teens. She lowered her voice and hissed, "What do you mean, the goat is giving birth?"

"A baby goat is about to come out of a mommy goat."

"I know what giving birth means!"

"I was being caustic!"

"Simmer down, you two," Cammie cautioned. But it was too late. The room buzzed with the news. A few teens faked a casual saunter to the door and then raced outside. Others followed until the room emptied. Mia and Shane ran ahead of the kids. Mia reached the volunteers handling the birth first. "Why on earth did you bring a pregnant goat today?" she asked the women, exasperated.

"Shane thought it was cute and I didn't want to disappoint him," the younger of the two responded.

The goat bleated loudly. "It's coming." The other volunteer placed a towel under the animal. "Helen, look alive."

The crowd fell silent, watching the scene with bated breath. There were a few more bleats and a tiny body slid out of the goat. The teens murmured in awe. There was a flurry of cell phone photography from the kids who weren't already filming the birth as the volunteers dried off the tiny kid. "She's cleaning her baby," Kaitlyn said as the mother licked her newborn.

"I can't believe we got to see this," Juliet marveled in her irresistible accent. "It's the cutest thing ever."

Whether she meant it or was being kind, the effect of her statement was instantaneous. There was a chorus of agreement from the teens. The posturing disappeared. They chattered happily with each other and posed for selfies with the other animals. Mia had a brainstorm. She texted the story to Teri, who instantly wrote and posted it. Within half an hour, news crews showed up to interview Kaitlyn and the other teens about the archetypal holiday feel-good story of witnessing an actual birth at a living Nativity scene. The rest of the teens hovered around the birthday girl, the only snark coming from displaced queen bee Daniella, who was ignored by the others. Being sidelined, she was the only one who noticed a limo pull up next to the site. The limo driver got out and opened the passenger door. He helped a slim twenty-something dressed in a sexy Santa suit out of the limo, then grabbed a sack from inside. Daniella let out a scream, startling the other. "Shush," Juliet admonished her, motioning to the kid, who gave tiny bleats as she tried to find his footing. "The baby."

"Sorry, but it's—it's—"

Unable to point words, Daniella pointed. Juliet gasped, and then shrieked, "Rylie Kenner! *Ahhhhhhh!*"

Rylie struck a practiced pose as the rest of the girls squealed and jumped up and down. "Where's the birthday girl?"

Kaitlyn, who appeared close to passing out, held up a weak hand. Rylie sashayed over to her, the driver following with the sack. "Happy sweet sixteen, Kait. My friend Madison thought it would be more fun if I delivered your favors in person. Selfie with the product." Rylie extricated a hefty gift bag from the sack and handed it to an awestruck Kaitlyn. The celebrity threw an arm around the teen, held up her camera, and snapped a ton of photos. Then she spoke to the crowd. "Who wants samples from my New Year, New You line?"

There was a chorus of "Me, me!" and a crowd that included a couple of the teen boys surrounded the reality star and makeup maven.

"This is the best party *ever*."

The compliment came from Daniella. *Mission accomplished*, Mia thought, satisfied.

The party ended after two a.m. Teens who'd been trying to escape hours early had to be gently booted from Belle View. Kaitlyn's parents were in shock at the sight of their deliriously happy daughter and rewarded the staff with hefty tips. Kaitlyn showered Mia with *I love you*s and made Mia swear to stay in touch, which the event planner was planning to do anyway. The animal sanctuary volunteers left with all their charges except for the new mother and kid. LouAnn, the woman who ran the sanctuary, had arrived shortly after the birth, and told Mia she'd prefer to let them rest overnight before moving them home. "Absolutely," Mia said. "I'll spend the night here too. Just in case anything comes up."

"I'll stay with you," Ravello said.

Mia could see that her father, who usually kept farmer's hours, was exhausted. "You don't have to do that."

"I don't want you manning this place alone."

Shane jumped in. "Sir, I'll stay."

Before her father could rebut, Mia said, "That's a perfect solution. Night, Dad." She kissed him on both cheeks and steered him toward the door.

Once Ravello left, Mia and Shane made sure LouAnn, the mother goat, and her kid were comfortable. "Do you need another heat lamp?" Mia asked. "And are you sure you don't want more pillows?"

LouAnn, a leathery middle-aged woman who gave the impression of placing creature comforts far below critter comforts on her list of life's concerns, gave Mia a thumbs-up. "We're good to go."

Shane and Mia policed the premises, then set up camp, she in the upstairs bridal lounge, he in the hallway outside because he didn't feel it was appropriate to sleep in the same room as Mia, much to her disappointment. Despite the late hour, Mia wasn't ready to crash. "I'm still wired from everything that went down tonight. I could use a nightcap."

"I'm really glad you said that. I feel the same way."

The two retreated to the kitchen. Mia poured them each a glass of wine. Shane held his glass up to her in a toast. "To the lady who pulled that party out of a hat. Magic, for sure."

Mia, being facetious, bowed. "Thank you, thank you. The credit really goes to Greta the goat. But at the end of the day, the teens got what teens want most: attention. And Rylie Kenner products."

Shane tapped his perfectly smooth cheek. "I could do with a little exfoliating."

"That's all gone, but I have a few Mets T-shirts left over. A couple of the boys were Yankees fans. In *Queens*. Go figure." Mia's phone pinged. "It's Kaitlyn. She's still up and so are her friends. They're all texting and social media-ing like crazy. No one can stop talking about the baby goats. The hashtag *#Kaitlynsbabygoat* is trending. Awww . . ." Emotional, Mia wiped her eyes with the back of her hand.

"Here." Shane handed her a napkin. "I'm glad the kids—the human ones, not the baby goat—got some family-friendly pictures for a change. Too many of them learn the hard way that what goes on the internet stays there forever." The dark tone in Shane's voice told Mia he had a personal connection to this issue.

"You up for leftover cake?" she asked, aiming to change the subject. "We've got hunks of it from both parties."

"You will never find me saying no to any leftover. Especially of the cake persuasion."

Mia removed two containers from one of the facility's industrial refrigerators. She cut slices and placed them on paper plates featuring a photo of Kaitlyn under the words, *Kaitlyn's Super Sweet Sixteen!* She handed a plate and fork to Shane.

"Thanks." After taking a bite, he pinched together his index finger and thumb and blew a chef's kiss. "Outstanding. If anyone ever tries to steal Evans from us, we take them out."

"Amen to that."

"Not literally, of course."

"I know. But it never hurts to confirm."

Shane dug into his slice of cake. "Speaking of taking people out, anything going on with the Puglia murder investigation?"

"Nice segue. The police like Bridget Puglia for it. Oooh, listen to me, I sound so *Law and Order*. Anyway, she's the woman who tried to run me down. Lorenzo's sister-in-law. The thing is, I can see why she'd want to get rid of him, but why take out Brad Kokolakis? I have to believe the deaths are connected. My dad trained me to second-guess all coincidences."

"Mine did too."

Mia responded to this with a nod of camaraderie. It was the first time they'd ever touched on their similarly sketchy backgrounds.

"Family is everything for us Italians," Shane continued. "Yeah, we have giant fights and can hold a grudge for generations. But at the end of the day, we'll fight for each other. Even to the death."

"So true." Something in Shane's comment niggled at Mia, but she couldn't put a finger on exactly what.

His cell phone alerted him to a text. Shane put down his fork and checked. "Wow. FedEx is working way overtime. They just dropped off a package at my apartment. I made sure to get alerts. We had a problem with porch pirates, although not so much recently."

A jumble of ideas coalesced in Mia's brain. "When did they stop?"

Shane wrinkled his brow. "I dunno. Maybe about two weeks ago?"

"Do you by any chance remember the last day something was stolen?"

"No, but I know how to check. I had to write the company and ask for a credit. Let me search my *sent* file." Shane typed on his phone, called up his *sent* history, and scrolled down. "Here." He showed the email to Mia and a puzzle piece clicked into place.

The last theft occurred the day before Lorenzo Puglia was murdered.

CHAPTER 21

"You think Lorenzo and Brad were porch pirates?" Shane said when Mia ran her theory by him.

"Lorenzo, yes. I think that was his side gig—stealing packages, tossing them in his delivery van, and selling the stuff worth selling. Whether or not Brad was in on the actual stealing, I don't know, but you can bet he knew about it. I'm guessing that's one reason he couldn't stand him. Either he didn't like what Lorenzo was up to or he wasn't getting a cut of it—or a big enough cut. I'm positive that's the 'little secret' he tried to hold over Renata's head. Hmm . . . I wonder if Santino was in on it. He works on the Box Club loading dock in Elmhurst. Loading . . ." She moved her hands back and forth. "Stuff going in, stuff going out. In Lorenzo's van, maybe?"

Shane shook his head. "I doubt it. Those big-box stores have security up the wazoo. I know because a couple of my dad's goons tried to pull off a heist at a Box Club near us in Florida and it did not go well. They're still locked away." He followed this with a yawn.

"It's almost four a.m.," Mia said. "Sorry I dragged you into playing detective with me. Let's call it a night."

"Okay, but to be honest, it was kinda fun playing detective. In my house, it was always the other way around. We did everything we could to avoid them."

"Yup." Mia nodded at another example of something they shared in common. "Same here."

They retired for what was left of the night, but Mia barely slept. Murder theories whirling around in her head, coupled with the male Sleeping Beauty outside her door, kept her awake. She finally dozed off for a few hours. She woke up under a fog of fatigue that a shower cleared. Not for the first time, Mia changed into unclaimed clothing left behind by drunk bridesmaids. The makeup she used for touch-ups between events was downstairs in her office, so she made use of face powder and blush Belle View kept on hand for guests. When she stepped into the hallway, she almost tripped over Shane, who was still asleep on the sofa pillows he'd arranged for himself. *Please let him be snoring*, Mia thought. She paused to listen and heard nothing but quiet, rhythmic breathing. *He's even a perfect sleeper*, she thought, a little annoyed.

She walked down downstairs and left the building to check on Belle View's guests, animal and human. Greta's baby was curled up next to her mom while Helen prepared the trailer for their departure. "Morning," Maggie said.

"Morning." LouAnn, obviously a morning person, sounded upbeat and energetic.

"Do Greta or her baby need anything?"

"Nope. They're doing fine, thanks."

"How about you? I was going to make breakfast in our kitchen. Can I fix you something?"

"I'm good. I always carry energy bars with me." She patted the breast pocket of her flannel shirt. "Just had one for breakfast. The other one's for emergencies."

"Okay. Well, if you change your mind or need help loading the trailer, let me know."

"Will do. And thanks a bunch for letting us camp out here last night." She eyed the kid, who was taking small steps on still-unsteady legs. "We need a name for the little one. Since she was born here, I'll let you do the honors."

Mia thought for a moment, and then said, "How about Kaitlyn? After last night's birthday girl?"

"Kaitlyn it is. Happy holidays."

"Same to you."

Before LouAnn took off with Greta and Kaitlyn, Mia forwarded her the Venere's contact information so the animal wrangler could alert the teen to the naming honor. When she returned to the kitchen, she discovered Shane scrambling eggs. The scent in the air told her he'd already put up a pot of coffee. "That's my happy smell," she said. Shane raised an eyebrow and she cringed. "Yikes, that did not come out right at all."

Shane grinned. "No worries. I'll take it as a compliment. The coffee should be ready."

Mia poured them each a cup of coffee. She watched Shane add a dash of grated Parmesan to the eggs. "Don't tell me you're an amazing cook too."

"What do you mean *too*?" Shane asked, puzzled.

Mia reproached herself for the slip. "Well, you know, like, how you're also so good at your job," she fumphered, trying to cover.

"Oh. Thanks. That's nice to hear. I appreciate it. But you're soon gonna see that I'm way better at my job than at the stove." Shane shook the pan, then divvied up the eggs between two plates, adding a hunk of Italian bread to each plate. He and Mia sat on barstools they pulled up to the island and began to eat. "Are you gonna do anything about what we talked about last night? The idea that Lorenzo might have been a porch pirate?"

Mia swallowed her mouthful of eggs, then bit off a large bite of bread. She hadn't realized how hungry she was. "I'm gonna text it to Pete Dianopolis. He's all about Bridget Puglia being the one who offed Lorenzo, but this angle connects both murder victims in a way besides them being fellow deliverymen. As far as I know, my embedded spy Cammie hasn't wheedled a link between Bridget and Brad out of Pete."

"Hah. I see what you did there. Em*bedded*. Because they go to bed together."

"Pete wishes. I don't think she's let him back in the boudoir yet. And you're giving me more credit than I deserve. That play on words was a total accident." Mia stopped eating for a minute. Nerves made her heart pound. But she took the plunge. "If you're free tonight," she said in the most casual voice she could muster, which she deemed a failure when her voice cracked, "they're judging the holiday displays in my neighborhood. People put out treats and drinks. It's like a block after–block party."

"Wish I could, but I have plans. Looking forward to tomorrow night, though."

"Right," Mia said, deflated. "The work event." To celebrate the holidays, she and Ravello were throwing a Christmas Eve Festival of the Seven Fishes party. They celebrated the Italian tradition every year, but this would be their first as Belle View's proprietors.

"I should get going, unless you need me to do anything else today."

"No. You're officially on your paid holiday break."

"Cool."

Shane went to put his plate in the sink. Mia stopped him. "You cooked, I clean. That's how we Carinas roll."

Shane held up his hands and made a show of stepping away from the sink. "Yes, boss. See you tomorrow."

As Mia washed and dried the dishes, she tried not to imagine what Shane's plans were. He'd used the B-word: boss. This was the second time he'd turned down an invitation from her. He was setting a clear boundary and she was being inappropriate. *Shame on me*, Mia thought, her face flushed with embarrassment. People may have met mates at work in the good old days, but times had changed. Like it or not, Mia needed to suck it up and download a dating app, much as she despised them. She'd put it on top of her resolutions for the New Year.

It occurred to Mia that given the drama in the Boldano household, the family might not make it to the Christmas Eve soiree. She texted Aurora, who immediately responded she and the others wouldn't miss it. The matriarch attached a photo of her entire brood in front of their Christmas tree, and a single word: *Grazie*.

Next up was a text to Pete Dianopolis espousing her theory that Lorenzo worked a sideline as a porch pirate, for which she received an eye roll. This didn't discourage her. She'd learned that while the detective balked at giving her ideas credence, he eventually, if reluctantly, gave them legitimate consideration.

Almost done with cleanup, Mia reached the last item, the cast-iron skillet where Shane had cooked the eggs. She noticed a forkful of eggs left in the pan and speared it. As she enjoyed the final bite she couldn't help thinking that on top of everything else, Shane was indeed an *amazing* cook.

Once she got home, a sleep-deprived Mia treated herself to a nap. Doorstop joined her and they fell asleep to Pizzazz's version of a parakeet lullaby. When she woke up a few hours later, it was already dark. She showered and slipped into Elisabetta's yearly gift of a tacky Christmas sweater, made more amusing by the fact that Elisabetta had no idea the younger generation wore sweaters like it with tongues firmly in cheek. Mia did a double take when she cut off the price tag on the current model, which was designed to look like the top half of an elf costume—an unfortunate choice, given where the late Lorenzo had been found. Mia held the tag up to Doorstop, who was stretched out on the floor, lazily batting a cat toy back and forth between his paws. "You wouldn't believe what Nonna shelled out for this thing. I'm in the wrong business."

She was about to go downstairs and rendezvous with her grandmother when Teri called. "I've got news," she said, excitement in her voice. "You know that last name on the list you gave me? I found an extremely interesting link to someone else on the list."

"Really?" Mia was equally excited. "Who?"

Teri told her. Mia's jaw dropped. "Wow. I did not see that coming."

"Neither did I," Teri said with a squeal. "There has to be something there. Which is repetitive, but you know what I mean."

"Yes and yes."

"I'm gonna play around with all this. I'll let you know if I come up with anything else."

"Awesome. And since this is your find, you should be the one sharing it with Pete."

"Roger that."

Mia evaluated the link. "Here's something else to run by Pete. But I want credit for it."

She shared her theory with Teri. "Makes sense to me. I'll tell him and say that if it's right, all kudos go to you. Hey, long as I have you on the phone, how should I dress for tomorrow night? Evans is bringing me as his date."

Mia had never heard Teri sound so girly. She found it disturbing. "Instead of your day khakis and polo shirt, wear your evening khakis and polo shirt."

"Shut up. I'll pick up an outfit at the new shop on Ditmars."

Mia pulled on a pair of warm black sheepskin boots and removed her black down bomber jacket from its hook in the entry hall. Thrilled by the unexpected link Teri had uncovered, Mia practically skipped downstairs to the vestibule, where an impatient Elisabetta scolded her for the delay. "What took you so long? I don't wanna miss when the judges show up."

"Sorry. Teri Fuoco uncovered a new development in the Puglia murder case."

Elisabetta threw her hands up in the air and expressed

her irritation in a string of Italian, ending with, "You wanna be a detective, go to detective school. Right now, I got a contest to win."

The women bundled up and stepped outside. The cold night air nipped at Mia's nose. She went directly to a table set out in the middle of the street, which had been closed to traffic, and helped herself to a cup of cider being kept warm in a Crock-Pot. "You want a shot in it?" octogenarian neighbor Estevan Maranulli asked in a low voice.

"Always," Mia said. The old man held her glass under the table and added a shot of bourbon. He passed it to Mia like they were doing a drug deal.

A convivial crowd filled the block with festive chatter. As was tradition, the DiMicas, who lived next door to Mia and Elisabetta, had used around a mile of extension cords to connect their circa-1970s speakers to their equally ancient stereo system and were blasting Christmas carols out their living room window. Elisabetta received many compliments on the velour hoodie embellished with three sequined wise men that she wore over several layers of sweaters. She'd perfumed herself with frankincense to really sell the image and thrust her wrists in people's faces, insisting they sniff them.

"Everyone, the judges are coming," someone cried out.

The crowd hushed. Elisabetta waved to the DiMicas and made a slashing motion to her neck indicating they should turn off the music, which they did. A group of carolers dressed in Victorian garb rounded the corner warbling about wassail. They were followed by the judges—a local newscaster, a representative from the Queens Chamber of Commerce, and the celebrity judge, a Botoxed blonde from the cable TV show, *Crazy, Out-There Christmas*, which trolled the country for the most extreme holiday home displays. She wore a full-length fur coat and a giant button that read THIS IS FAKE. Mia assumed it was to ward off animal rights activists. She also assumed the activists were smart enough to figure out the only thing fake about the coat was the giant button.

Elisabetta clutched her granddaughter's hand. "They're starting with our house and the DiMica's because we're on the corner." She squeezed her eyes shut. "I can't look. *Guarda per me.*"

"Sure." Mia observed the judges. They smiled and pointed, then made notes on pads. "Looking good, Nonna. I see happy faces."

Elisabetta, relieved, clutched her heart. "*Grazie Dio.*"

The judges moved on, taking notes, and conferring among themselves in front of each display. Neighbors from nearby blocks joined the starstruck crowd tailing the judges and soon the street was packed with people. Mia and Elisabetta stopped outside the two-family home where Evans rented the top floor from Andrea Skarpello. He'd set up a table that was now covered with empty platters. "Nothing left, huh?" Mia, disappointed, surveyed the table.

Evans bent down and disappeared behind the table. When he stood up, he held two Florentine cookies. He handed one to Mia and one to Elisabetta. "Private stash. These were the first to go. Great recipe."

"I'll tell Renata."

Fortified by the cookies, Mia and Elisabetta kept going. When they reached Philip and Finn's house, Mia saw her mother and waved. Gia waved back, then pointed to Elisabetta and made a question mark in the air.

"Nonna, I'm inviting Mom to join us. She's doing her best to be a better person. I'm asking you to declare a truce tonight. *Per me.* Please?"

Elisabetta hesitated and then responded with a slight nod. Mia gestured for Gia to join them. She weaved her way through a group of revelers. When she got to her daughter's side, she kissed Mia on both cheeks. "*Ciao, bella.*" She turned to Elisabetta. "*Buona sera, Elisabetta.*"

Elisabetta grunted. Then, to Mia's surprise and gratitude, she offered a cheek to her former daughter-in-law. Gia bent down and planted a kiss on each of the tiny woman's cheeks, then exchanged a smile of acknowledgment with Mia.

"I heard your boss Philip has a surprise for us," Elisabetta said.

"Yes. When he announces it, look up at the roof."

Philip appeared on the landing of his home steps, Finn at his side. Philip held a bullhorn. "Ladies and gentlemen," he called out through the bullhorn as if he was a circus ringmaster, "prepare to be amazed."

"It's like living with P.T. Barnum," his husband said, earning a guffaw from the onlookers.

Philip held up a giant switch that looked like a movie prop. "Count down with me. Five, four . . ."

"Three, two, one!" the crowd chanted.

He flipped the switch. On the roof of the house, a giant neon sculpture spelling *Buon Natale* buzzed to bright white life, earning screams and cheers. "He imported it from Italy," Gia shared.

"*Marrone,*" Elisabetta said, awed. "*Che bella.*"

"There's more."

A laser show shot into the sky like fireworks while

Mannheim Steamroller's "Carol of the Bells" played in rhythm with the light show. "It's a miracle!" Elisabetta screamed to be heard over the ecstatic crowd. "We're gonna win the contest tonight." She cupped her hands around her mouth and yelled to Philip, "*Brava, mio amico, brava!*"

Philip accepted the crowd's accolades with the grace of a British royal, even utilizing their screwing-in-a-light-bulb formal wave. Then suddenly the street plunged into darkness. The music stopped. The crowd quieted, confused muttering replacing cheers. "Um, everyone?" Mia couldn't see Philip, but she heard his voice coming through the bullhorn. He sounded sheepish. "It appears something has caused a blackout on the block."

"Give me that thing." Finn took the bullhorn from Philip. "That something would be us. And I've already called ConEd. They're on their way. In the meantime, enjoy a lovely view of the stars, which you so rarely get in the city." The lights of the display in the Levines' yard across the way suddenly came on. "Or that."

"Eh, look at that," Elisabetta said. "The Levines' generator went on."

"A generator is a good idea," Gia said. "We should get you one, Mia." She turned to where her daughter had been standing. "Mia?"

Mia was gone.

CHAPTER 22

When the blackout hit, Mia felt a prick in her side. "Ow." Assuming she'd bumped into a plastic utensil held by a partygoer exiting the area, she tried moving away. Someone grabbed her arm and hissed in her ear, "Don't talk or turn around. I've got a knife."

Someone grabbed her other arm. "So do I."

Mia was hustled away among the throngs of people feeling their way in the darkness. She was at the far end of the block when the Levines' lights came on, illuminating her captors: Renata and Santino Esposito. "Get in the truck," Santino ordered, using his knife to point to a pickup truck with a club cab. Renata used her knife to herd Mia into the back seat. Santino jumped into the driver's seat. "Let's get out of here fast," Renata said to her brother.

"You got it."

Santino started the engine, backed up, and attempted to pull out of the parking spot. Given how hard it was to find street parking in the neighborhood, drivers squeezed themselves into whatever space they could find, making extricating themselves a time-consuming feat. Santi yelled a stream of curses as he drove forward and back, easing himself out of the spot.

"*What part of fast don't you understand!*" his sister screamed at him.

"*You try driving this mother!*" he screamed back.

While they argued, Mia snuck her free hand onto the handle of the door she was seated next to. She was about to yank it open when Renata saw what she was doing, reached over her, and slapped down the lock. "Fuhgedda-boudit," she said, glaring at Mia.

Santino finally pulled out of the parking spot. "Yes," he said, triumphant.

He drove slowly down the street at first, so as not to attract attention. After a few blocks, he picked up speed, barreling toward the water. Renata kept the knife poking into Mia's side. Mia shook with anger and fear. "Why are you doing this?"

"You know," Renata said.

"Know what? I don't know anything." This was half true. Mia had put together a few ideas but had yet to spell out the specific link to the Espositos.

"Liar. Zoe told me you wanted the recipe for my Florentines. That could only mean one thing."

"*That I really liked the cookies!*" At her wit's end, Mia yelled this. Then it dawned on her. "Lorenzo had cyanide in his system. The cookies. They were poisoned."

Renata, who was proving to be a crier, burst into tears. "I made them for stupid Zoe, just to make her sick a little for hooking up with my boyfriend, but Lorenzo had to go sneak the ones I hadn't given her yet. I killed the man I loved!"

"No, you didn't."

Renata stopped crying. "Huh?"

"That's not what killed Lorenzo."

"Then what did?!" This came from Santino.

"I can't say," Mia demurred. "It's police business. But it wasn't the cookies. They made him sick. But they didn't kill him."

Renata put the hand not holding the knife on her heart. "Oh my God, I'm so relieved."

"Glad to hear it," Mia said. "Now you can let me go."

Mia reached for the door lock and felt a stabbing pain in her side. "*Ow.*"

"Sorry, we can't let you go," Renata said.

Santino weighed in. "You sure? She's so pretty."

"You wanna save her cuz she's pretty?" Renata, enraged, screamed this at her brother. "*You sexist idiot, we'll get arrested for kidnapping!*"

Mia jumped in. "I won't bring charges. Promise."

"There's also the cookies. You know what I did to them. It could be called attempted murder. Keep driving, Santi."

"'Kay."

"Drive to the industrial waste site between the East River and Rikers Island," Renata instructed. "We can jump out of the truck and push it into the water with her in it."

Santino took a corner so fast the pickup truck almost

toppled on its side. "*Are you outta your mind*?" he screamed at his sister. "This truck ain't even a year old. If we wanted to ditch a car, we should have taken your beater."

"No flipping way! I love Sheila. I've had her since high school."

"Exactly! She's old, and stinks like cigarettes and sex."

"Ugh, gross! Take that back!"

"No, you!"

"Wow," Mia said. "You two really didn't think this through."

While the siblings continued to argue, Mia heard sirens. The sound grew louder. She again made a play for the door lock, but Renata and Santino also heard the sirens over their yelling and knuckled down on their mission. Mia winced as Renata took another poke at her with the knife. "Drive fast, Santi!"

"I am!"

He careened around a corner. An oil tanker lumbered across the street in front of them. All three pickup truck inhabitants screamed. Santino hit the brakes and swerved. He lost control of the pickup and smashed into the wall of a warehouse, tossing Mia and Renata around the club cab back seat. Santino slumped over the steering wheel. His sister, dazed from her head colliding with the roof, groaned. A phalanx of patrol cars screeched to the scene. Mia finally managed to unlock the car door and stumbled out of the pickup as police officers, including detectives Pete and Ryan, swarmed it. She heard someone call her name. Gia shoved through the officers and ran to her. She threw her arms around her daughter. "Thank God you're all right."

Mia buried her head in Gia's shoulder. "I'm not gonna

lie. That was terrifying. How did you know where to find me?"

"When your grandmother and I realized you were missing, we called Jamie and Ravello. Your dad was in Manhattan and is on his way here. Jamie told us about the friend app you both have. He's at the Boldanos, but he's been tracking you and working with the police."

"Modern technology saves the day. Maybe a dating app will actually find me a boyfriend."

"Huh?" Gia said, confused.

Mia waved off the comment. "Nothing. Just making a joke to keep from busting out in tears."

A motorcycle suddenly zoomed up to the action and came to a stop. Teri disembarked, followed by Evans. "What a story. You are the gift that keeps on giving, my friend." She ran off to take pictures with her cell phone and badger police officers for interviews.

"You okay?" Evans asked.

"I'll live, thanks." Mia watched the police extricate Santino, conscious but dazed, from the vehicle. Renata emerged a minute later, holding up her hands. "I need to tell the cops she held a knife to me, so they know to look for it."

"She was gonna knife you?" Gia broke away from Mia. She ran to Renata screaming a stream of Italian curses and tackled her. "You could've killed my baby girl," she roared, pummeling the facialist. Two officers managed to yank her off. *Shane's right*, Mia thought, watching with affection as the officers calmed her mother down. *We Italians will fight to the death for each other. Except for a rotten-egg lost cause like Lorenzo Puglia.*

Officers led a handcuffed Santino to the patrol car next to Mia. "I didn't kill Lorenzo, I swear."

"We'll talk about that," Pete said. He directed the prisoner into the car. "Among other things, like charges of kidnapping and attempted murder. And full-on murder."

"I told you—"

"I know, I know. You didn't kill Lorenzo. But guess what? Thanks to an informed citizen"—Pete mimed tipping a hat to Mia—"we looked a lot closer at the 'accidental' death of your coworker Brad Kokolakis. We got security footage from the house next to where he was making his last delivery and got the evidence to show his death was no accident. We'll fill you in on the rest at the station."

The patrol cars carrying Santino and Renata drove off. Others remained behind to work the crime scene. Ryan Hinkle approached Mia. "If you're up to it, I need to get a statement from you."

"Sure." For the first time since the melee began, Mia realized where she was. The pickup had plowed into the side of Hot Bods, where she'd first met Lorenzo Puglia and the Esposito family. She leaned back to take in the Hot Bods neon sign, affably blazing in the night sky. A clutch of people, girls shivering in skimpy date clothes, had gathered to observe the police action. "How about we go in there? I could use a drink."

CHAPTER 23

An hour later, Mia plus family and friends, landed in Elisabetta's living room. The electricity to Forty-sixth Place had been restored. Only Philip and Finn's home was still dark. Elisabetta served everyone espresso laced with Amaretto. Evans set out more of his "private stash" cookie supply on the coffee table. Much as she loved them, Mia avoided the lace cookies. "I think it's gonna be a while before I can look at a Florentine and not think of Renata," she said, opting for a honey phyllo cookie instead.

"*Anch'io*," Ravello agreed, cracking his knuckles, and then making two fists. He'd arrived from Lin's at the tail end of Mia's statement to Ryan. She considered it lucky for the Esposito offspring that they were hauled off before he showed up. She didn't want to think about what her father might have done if he'd gotten his hands on them.

The doorbell rang. "I'll get it," Gia said.

She disappeared and reappeared a minute later with Cammie. "It's starting to snow out there. Looks like we're gonna have a white Christmas." She pulled off her pom-pommed knit pink hat and shook out her frosted hair.

Mia held up a demitasse cup. "Spiked espresso?"

"You betcha." Cammie accepted the cup and pulled one of the vinyl-covered chairs Mia brought in from the kitchen closer to the coffee table. She took a lace cookie. "I called Shane to tell him what happened and see if he could come over but couldn't reach him."

"Thanks, that was sweet, but there's no reason for him to be here," Mia said, wishing there was.

Cammie settled into her chair. "Anyhoo, Pete dropped me off and I come with updates. Santino Esposito called for a lawyer the minute he heard the security footage the police uncovered showed him sneaking up to the side of Brad Kokolakis's van, climbing inside, and jumping out while the van heads toward the Brad guy."

"He released the emergency brake on a hill."

"They don't have the actual act on film, but that's the assumption."

"*Ma perche?*" Elisabetta wondered. "What did this Brad ever do to the other one?"

"That's where his ever-lovin' sister comes into it. She's thinking if she sings, she'll be able to cut a deal. Apparently Brad got tired of being complicit—because he never ratted on Lorenzo or Santino, who came up with the whole porch pirate scheme—without getting anything out of it. And what he wanted was a) a cut of the proceeds, and b) mattress time with the fair Renata, who was N.I.—not interested. And here's something new."

Reveling in being the bearer of an unexpected update, Cammie sipped her espresso. She crossed one leg over the other and swung her foot back and forth until Mia burst out, "Tell us already."

Cammie favored Mia with an impish grin. "So impatient. Fine. It appears the person who nixed Brad getting hush money was—"

Mia raised her hand like an excited elementary school student and called out, "Oooh, ooh, I know! Aida Esposito."

"You're ruining my story," Cammie scolded.

"Sorry," Mia said, abashed. "Am I right?"

"Yes. Mama Esposito quite enjoyed the perks from her li'l baby porch pirate and had zero interest in sharing the proceeds. She was arrested at LaGuardia trying to hop a plane to Mexico."

"She'd be on the next plane back," Ravello said. "We have an extradition agreement with them."

Mia frowned at her father. "I so don't want to know why you know that."

"There was a time when information like that might have been necessary" was all Ravello would say.

The doorbell rang again. "Maybe we should just leave the door unlocked," Mia said.

"It already is." Teri's voice came from the hallway. "I let myself in."

She marched into the room humming the theme from *Rocky*, following it with the prizefighter's victory dance. "You're looking at the reporter who broke the biggest story in the city tonight." She extended a hand and bowed to Mia. "With a wee bit o' help from my friend here."

"I hate when you call me that," Mia said.

"Which is why I do it, of course. Yum, Evans cookies." She wedged herself next to the chef on the couch and took one. "We know who killed Lorenzo Puglia."

"Who?" Gia asked.

"Ralph Mastacciolo."

The others reacted with shock. "The deli guy?" Evans asked, perplexed.

"Oh my goodness," Gia said, upset. "That's why he was so upset at Lorenzo's funeral luncheon. I thought he was grieving but it was because he murdered him."

"It wasn't, because he didn't know he'd done it. He probably does by now, though. When I left the precinct, he was being brought in for questioning."

"Lorenzo's death was an accident," Mia mused. "That makes sense."

"*Mio Dio*." Elisabetta slapped her forehead. "Not to me. *È pazzesco*." She twirled her index fingers around her ears in the universal sign for crazy.

"How did the police even know to look at Ralph?" Gia asked.

Teri gestured to Mia with her cookie-free hand. "Mia, why don't you take this one."

"It truly was a joint effort," Mia said in an effort to be magnanimous. "I sent Teri a list of suspects to research because she's got the resources to do it. At the last minute, I threw another name on the list: Isabella Rispetto."

"Jamie's birth mother," Ravello said.

Mia nodded. "I was talking to Shane about everything—"

"Oh, you were talking to *Shane*," Cammie said, putting a teasing emphasis on the name.

"*Sta 'zitto*," Mia shot back at her friend. "That's Italian for 'shut up.'"

"I know. You've said it to me enough times."

Mia got back on track. "What Shane said was that Italian families will fight to the death for each other. There were Boldano, Puglia, and Esposito suspects. But what if someone who knew about Lorenzo's planned scam was related to Jamie's actual birth mother and angry about it? I gave Teri her name—Isabella Rispetto. Teri drilled down on a social media site and found a connection to Ralph. He's related to Isabella. They're second cousins or something. I thought about the bruises on Lorenzo and the bruises on Ralph's hands. His knuckles were raw in a way that looked familiar to me. It was how my brother Posi's knuckles looked after he got in a fistfight with someone."

"Posi did get into a lot of fights," Ravello acknowledged.

"Did he ever," Gia seconded.

The divorced couple shared a chuckle over the memory. Mia choked up, unable to remember the last time she'd seen her parents get along. She cleared her throat and continued. "Ralph seems like an old school guy, very traditional. Someone like him would be furious over a guy like Lorenzo turning a painful chapter in his family's history—Isabella's illegitimate baby—into a con."

"But how was it an accident?" Evans asked.

Teri stepped in. "Lag time between the fight and Puglia's death," she said through a mouthful of lace cookie. "Police served a warrant at Sorrento Deli. Security footage of the alley behind the shop shows Ralph going after Lorenzo. They fought, then Lorenzo fell

backward and hit his head on the corner of the deli dump-
ster, which caused the hemorrhage that eventually killed
him. But it took a couple of hours. As far as Ralph knew,
they both walked away with big owies, but that was it."

"What did the police do before security cameras?" Gia
wondered.

"All I can tell you is that them popping up everywhere
is one reason I knew it was time for me to get out of the
'business,'" Ravello said.

Cammie finished her espresso and held the cup up to
Elisabetta for a refill. "Pete says it makes it hard for him
to write his Steve Stianopolis detective novels. He always
has to come up with work-arounds for security cameras
that could solve a case by the second chapter."

The doorbell rang. "It's open," everyone chorused.

"Be right there," Philip called to them. "I need to hang
up my coat and take off my boots. It's coming down out
there."

A few moments later, he padded into the room in
stocking feet, carrying a strongbox. "Again, I'm so sorry
about blowing out the lights. And the contest."

"You've apologized a million times, *mio amico*," Elisabetta said. "The judges may have kicked us out of the
decorating contest, but we got a shot at winning for donations."

"And you still topped everyone when it comes to decorations. Didn't he, Nonna?"

Mia threw an impish grin at her grandmother. "*Si*,"
Elisabetta reluctantly admitted. For years, Nonna, her
friends, and frenemies had competed every holiday for
the most extravagant displays, boasting about effort and
expense. But no one would ever earn the bragging rights
Philip had by blacking out the entire neighborhood.

"About the donations." Philip sat down on the arm of the couch and opened the strongbox. "I got the figures from the other blocks that are competing, and we were a little behind." A defeated Elisabetta sighed. "I said *were*. I hadn't added in the donations from the Carina box. Which included . . ." He pulled a check out of the strongbox and waved it in the air. "*A check from Aurora Boldano for five thousand dollars*."

The room rang with cheers and applause. Ravello gazed at his daughter with pride. "Her way of saying thank you."

"*Yes!*" Elisabetta said with a triumphant fist pump. "In your face, Forty-third, Forty-fourth, and Forty-fifth Places!"

Mia woke up the next morning in a festive mood for the first time in weeks. She stretched, as did Doorstop. "Merry Christmas Eve, buddy." She stroked the cat's golden red fur, and he murmured a meow before rolling over and going back to sleep.

"Mia, I made my Christmas frittata," Elisabetta called from downstairs. "I'm getting in the shower but it's on top of the stove."

"*Grazie, Nonna*," Mia called back. She took her phone off the nightstand and checked for messages, tamping down a twinge of disappointment when she saw no text or email from Shane. Mia had hoped he might have heard about the danger she'd faced the night before and checked in to make sure she was all right. But either he hadn't heard or didn't care. She chose to go with the former.

She took a quick shower herself, slipped on leggings

decorated with colorful ornaments and a green oversized sweater, and headed downstairs to Elisabetta's kitchen. The room was redolent with the scent of Elisabetta's frittata and a fresh loaf of Italian bread sitting on the kitchen table. Mia was about to fix herself a hearty breakfast when she heard a tap at the kitchen back door. She glanced over and saw Gia standing outside, shivering. Mia found it odd her mother would use the back door, considering that Elisabetta, in gratitude for Gia's help saving Mia's life, had forgiven her ex-daughter-in-law all past transgressions the night before. Mia went to open the door.

"Mia—" Gia's teeth chattered so much she couldn't finish the sentence. She stumbled into the room. And Mia saw that her mother wasn't shaking from the cold, but from fear.

Behind Gia, holding a gun to her back, was her husband, fugitive Angelo Gabinetti.

CHAPTER 24

For a moment, Mia stood paralyzed. Finally, she spoke. "*Angelo?* What the f—"

Angelo favored her with a sneer. He hadn't completely lost his looks, but the last few years of heavy wine and pasta intake had added girth to his body and broken capillaries to his face. "Hey, Mia. How's my stepkid?"

"An—An—Angelo," she stuttered. "Wha—How—"

"Nice to see you too."

Mia recovered from the shock of seeing the fugitive. "How did you even get into the country? The TSA keeps the airports on a tight leash."

"Ever hear of a boat?" Angelo, loaded with braggadocio, gestured to himself with his free hand. "You're looking at Tomas DiVincenzo, Milanese businessman, who just crossed the sea on the Queen Mary *numero due*. You dummies forget that if anyone knows how to forge a passport and fake ID, it's me. Unfortunately, thanks to Lorenzo taking a dirt nap, my plan to connect with the Boldanos is also dead. My funds have dried up, so now I need the money you raised in your cute little donation boxes."

"I didn't tell him, I swear," Gia said. She looked at her husband with repulsion. "He's been snooping around the area for days and overheard your dad and me talking about the money when we left here last night."

"That is correct. So, if you would oblige me by handing over the funds, I'll get outta your hair." Angelo circled the room, eyeballing every corner of it, making sure Gia circled with him. "Where's your grandmother, by the way? I don't want any surprises."

"In the shower," Mia said. "Hear the water running? I'll give you the money, Angelo, but you gotta release Mom."

"I get the money; you get your mama."

"No deal."

"Mia, please." Gia spoke in a strained voice. "Give him the money. I'll find a way to make it up to Elisabetta."

"Fine." Mia said this through gritted teeth. "Nonna put everything in a cookie tin to disguise it, then hid it under the table." Mia bent down and reached under the kitchen table. She emerged holding a tin decorated with a cartoon bear holding a sign that read, *Have a Beary Nice Christmas!*

"Hand it over," Angelo said. Mia hesitated. "I said hand it—aghagh!"

A string of lights suddenly wrapped around the goon's neck. He stumbled, dropping his gun, and revealing Elisabetta behind him. She lost her hold on the lights but not before Mia grabbed the gun from the floor. She trained it on Angelo. "Freeze, you mother! My dad taught me how to shoot, so don't think I won't use this."

"Yeah, right," Angelo scoffed. "Like you'd actually fire that thing."

He lunged for Mia but before she could get off a shot, the large glass pan of frittata crashed down on his head. Chunks of frittata flew around the room. Angelo staggered, then collapsed.

"She won't have to," Gia said, clutching the pan. She closed her eyes, exhaled a relieved breath, then opened her eyes. "Is he dead?"

Mia checked and saw the unconscious criminal's chest rise and fall. "Nope."

"Forget him," Elisabetta said. "My poor frittata."

While Gia contacted the police, Mia used one light strand to tie Angelo's hands behind his back and another to immobilize his feet. In a matter of minutes, the police showed up. Mia noticed that Pete was wearing sleep sweats. "Let's make this quick. I wanna get back to Cammie."

Mia eyed his outfit. "Get back to her, huh?"

"Yeah." Pete sounded bashful. "She let me 'enjoy her company' last night. I wanna get there before her mood changes."

"I got nothing but time," his partner Ryan said. "Between my kid and my brother's and my sister's it's like a preschool zoo at our place." He addressed Gia. "Ma'am, let's go over what happened to you. Very slowly. With lots of details."

"Not here, Hinkle," Pete said with an eye roll. "We need to get this numbnut to the station. Mrs. Gabinetti—"

"Cornetta," Gia said. "I'm wiping my life clean of

anything to do with that *figlio di puttana*." Ryan yanked a dazed Angelo to his feet. "Do you think he'll go away for a while?"

"A long while," Pete said. Mia appreciated his sympathetic, gentle tone. Her mother still shook, traumatized by what she'd endured. "We got this what-you-called-him on attempted robbery and murder, on top of violating deportation."

"That's what I want to hear." Gia stood up. "I'll come with you to the station and give my statement."

"Call me when you're done, I'll come get you." Mia clutched her mother in a tight hug. "I love you so much."

"I love you more."

Mia felt Gia's tears on her cheek. She released her and Gia followed the detectives and their prisoner out the door. For the first time that morning, the house was quiet. "Well," Mia said. "I sure didn't need that to kick off my Christmas Eve day."

"Me neither," Elisabetta said with a nod. Her stomach growled. "*Ho fame.*"

"I'm hungry too," Mia responded. She cast a regretful look at the remnants of frittata. "RIP Christmas frittata."

"No worries." Elisabetta opened the refrigerator door and took out an ancient, taped-together to-go container. "I got leftover manicotti."

Mia cheered up. "Who says pasta isn't for breakfast? Not any Italian I know."

Humming a medley of holiday tunes, Mia set the dinette table for two as her grandmother heated up the breakfast manicotti.

* * *

That evening, the Bay Ballroom rang out with music and cheerful chatter as the Belle View Banquet Manor guests celebrated Christmas Eve, helping themselves to a true Feast of the Seven Fishes, laid out on two long tables covered with red-velvet tablecloths. A view of festive lights twinkling on boats in the Flushing Marina provided holiday decor. Snow that had blanketed New York with a six-inch accumulation in the course of the day, continued to fall in big, soft flakes. The occasional plane took off or landed at LaGuardia, bringing travelers to their loved ones for the holidays.

"This shrimp and crab cavatelli is outstanding." Pete held up his bowl. "I'm on my third serving."

"I know," Mia said. "Pauly really went all out for us." Since the event was akin to an office party for family, friends, and staff, she'd had it catered. Figuring that after the deaths of both Sorrento deliverymen and subsequent arrests of his girlfriend and co-owner, Pauly D'Annunzio could use good news, she'd given him the business. He'd shown his gratitude with selections far exceeding her original order. Mia planned on using the deli for many future events.

Pete cleaned his bowl with half a hard roll. "Once again, I gotta thank you. I needed a holiday-themed plot for next Stianopolis mystery. As usual, you delivered."

"Thanks, but I don't love being a constant source of murder mystery plots for Steve Stianopolis. It's physically and emotionally exhausting." She helped herself to a jumbo shrimp. "How's Ralph doing?"

"He feels terrible. Like you thought, he was outraged by Puglia's plot. Turns out he's close to his cousin Isabella, even though she's in Italy and he's here. He's charged with involuntary manslaughter, but he claims Puglia hit him first and it's backed up by the security tape. With that and the age difference between the two men, I think Mastacciolo's lawyer will get him off on self-defense."

"Did you ever figure out how Lorenzo ended up in Santa's workshop?"

"I got the story from Renata Esposito, who's hoping the more she talks, the less time she serves. She found Puglia dead on the kitchen floor with a doctored cookie next to him. Assuming she'd accidentally poisoned him, she panicked and got her brother to help her dispose of the body. Stashing him in a Christmas display somehow seemed logical to them. Do not ask me to make sense of the criminal mind. They'd driven on Forty-sixth Place a bunch of times on their way to Hot Bods and landed on Santa's workshop. They figured by the time anyone found the corpse, it'd be too late to connect him to them. What they didn't count on was the guy's body sliding down and his feet sticking out the door." Pete beamed. "It's little details like that which are gonna make this my best mystery ever."

Pete wandered over to the buffet to scrounge for more food. Mia scanned her guests as she had at least half a dozen times during the evening, with the same disappointing result: no Shane. Gia, who was talking to Jamie and Madison, caught her daughter's eye. She came to Mia. "I haven't had the chance to tell you how beautiful you look tonight."

Mia blushed, embarrassed. Madison had snuck her into a sample sale in the garment district, where she'd snagged a silver satin dress that flattered her lovely figure. She'd accessorized with rhinestone drop earrings in the shape of snowflakes. "Thanks, Mom." Mia was suddenly overcome with emotion. "I'm gonna miss you."

"Aww, *bambina*."

Gia embraced her daughter. She was returning to Italy for a position as assistant manager at the Boldano vineyard. Donny, operating under the mantra *keep your friends close and your enemies closer*, had offered her the job. He wasn't happy the gossip that kicked off the chain of recent events started at the vineyard. Plus, he had a feeling not all of his wine was making it to market.

"I may have to come back to New York to testify against Angelo," Gia said.

"I hope you come back for other reasons. You may not be needed for that one. Right, Nonna?"

Elisabetta pressed her lips together and squeezed her eyes shut. She sucked in a deep, theatrical breath. "*I ricordi.* The memories. I see them in my dreams. The gun. That awful man, threatening our lives. Ready to kill us for the donation money meant to save poor animals who might die without us." Elisabetta began weeping. "I will live with the horror for the rest of my life, which Angelo Gabinetti will have shortened with his brutal, terrible deed." The tears stopped, replaced with a devilish grin. "And . . . scene."

She took a bow to applause from Gia and Mia. "She's good," Gia said.

"Yup." Mia put her arm around Elizabetta and gave her grandmother an affectionate squeeze. "Angelo doesn't stand a chance."

"Ho ho, yo. Merry Christmas, peeps."

Mia looked toward the ballroom entrance and screamed. The greeting came from her brother Posi, who stood in the doorway to the ballroom, guard Henry Marcus behind him. She ran to her brother and threw her arms around him. Ravello, Elisabetta, and Gia joined her in a Posi pile-on dampened with joyful tears. "Posi, what the—? How the—?"

"My excellent new lawyer, a Mr. Philip Barnes-Webster, got me furloughed for a couple of hours," Posi said, grinning. "Henry here agreed to guard me."

"It was that or string popcorn and cranberries with the wife. *Bor-ing*." Henry saw the food buffet and his eyes lit up. "Nice spread."

"Help yourself to whatever you want," Mia said. "We'll send food home for your family. Anything to thank you for the best present in the world."

Mia allowed Posi to enjoy greetings from the other guests, then stole him back. "When you get out, this'll be your new work-home. What do you think?"

"I like it," Posi said, nodding approval. "I got ideas, of course, but we'll get to those. Where's my competition, the infamous Shane?"

"He's not your competition," Mia said. "And he's not here."

"Oh, sis," Posi said, compassionate. "I'm sorry."

Mia made a face. "Don't be. I think he's rude. I mean, to RSVP and not show up? That's like, Bad Event Behavior one-oh-one." She noticed a young woman peek her head into the ballroom. "I'll be right back. Eat, then mingle."

Mia strode over to the mysterious visitor, a beautiful girl around twenty with perfect features and lustrous blond hair that fell in curls below her shoulders. She held a tall, rectangular box. Mia thought she looked vaguely familiar. "Hello. Merry Christmas. Can I help you?"

"Yes. Shane told me to look for the Belle View staff party. Is this it?"

"Yes." Mia forced a smile. *Figures he'd date some model a decade younger than him. Jerk.*

Over the girl's shoulder, she saw Shane hurry in through Belle View's glass double doors. "Hey, sorry, took me a while to find a spot," he said, walking their way. "You met."

"Yes." Mia's tone couldn't have been colder.

"The coatrack's full," he said to the vision in front of Mia. "Give me your coat; I'll put it in my office."

"Okay." The girl held out her box to Mia. "Do you mind holding this?"

"Of course not," Mia replied, wondering if anyone would blame her for tossing the box into Flushing Bay.

The girl removed her coat and handed it to Shane. "Here."

"Thanks, sis."

Mia's mouth dropped open. Shane headed to his office with the coat. "Sis?" The word came out as a squeak. The girl nodded. "As in *sister*?" She nodded again.

Shane quickly returned. He'd shed his own coat and was clad in the perfect-fitting gray suit he'd worn the day Mia met him, but instead of a conservative tie, he wore a goofy one sporting the image of a polar bear carrying a Christmas tree. He whistled to get everyone's attention. "Hi, all. Merry Christmas." Guests responded in kind. "I want you all to meet my sister, Olivia Gambrazzo."

"Half-sister," she said with a shy smile.

"Whole sister in my heart," he corrected, placing a hand on his heart to illustrate. "Sorry we showed up so late. Olivia's present to me was a surprise visit. She just got back from a semester abroad in Paris. I picked her up at the airport last night."

That's why I didn't hear from him, Mia thought, elated. *He was picking up this lovely, non-girlfriend girl.*

"She wanted to bring something special to the party, so we stopped and got this crock—croquet—"

"Croquembouche," she said. "It's sort of the French version of *struffoli*."

"That's a college girl for you," Shane said with pride.

Posi stepped up to Shane. "I'm Positano Carina. It's an honor to meet both of you."

He extended his hand. Shane gave it a hearty shake, then turned to Mia and perplexed, mouthed, "Posi?"

She mouthed back, "I'll explain later."

"I'll take the croquembouche," Evans said. He removed the box from Olivia and walked it over to the dessert table, with Teri in tow. The reporter wore an elegant forest-green pantsuit and high heels. Her hair was styled in a low bun and she wore makeup, the transformation rendering her almost unrecognizable.

"I wanna do a general check on things," Shane told his sister.

"You don't have to," Mia said, "but if you want to, I'll keep Olivia company."

"Thanks."

Shane left. Mia walked Olivia to the buffet. "Are you hungry? We're pretty much up to dessert, but as you can see, there's tons of food."

"I'm okay," Olivia said with a smile. She had the same perfect teeth and peridot eyes of her brother. "But I wouldn't mind a sparkling water."

"You got it."

Mia fetched a sparkling water for Olivia. Feeling

giddy with what she insisted was the joy of the season, she poured a glass of champagne for herself, and returned to Shane's sister. "You were in Paris for a whole semester? Lucky. I always wanted to go there."

"Shane thought a semester abroad would be good for me and he was so right." Olivia sipped her drink. Her eyes gleamed as she talked about her brother. "He paid for everything. Shane's putting me through college. He didn't go and regrets it."

Something else we have in common, Mia thought.

"He's the best brother ever. He's more than that. Ever since our father died, he's been like a dad to me too."

"Is there anything he can't do?" Mia didn't mean this as a joke.

Olivia glanced at a corner of the room where guests had gathered around Aurora, who was playing Christmas carols at the piano. "Sing."

Shane joined the group. "*Glory to the newborn king,*" he sang so loudly and off-key that the people standing nearby threw horrified looks at him and backed away.

"Glory to the man upstairs," Mia said, laughing with relief. "Shane Gambrazzo is not perfect."

By ten p.m. most of the guests dispersed. Posi and Henry had left an hour earlier, Henry carrying bags laden with leftovers. Ravello and girlfriend Lin also took off early. Mia's father had found the perfect gift for his mate—a river cruise in her homeland of Vietnam. They'd be flying to Saigon Christmas night.

Jamie and then Madison hugged Mia. "Merry Christmas," Jamie said. Madison echoed the sentiment. "We need to get home and pack." The Boldanos would also be traveling the next day. Donny Senior was flying the whole family, plus Madison, to Italy for a reunion with Jamie's birth mother Isabella Rispetto and her family. Jamie and Madison left hand in hand and Mia sensed the trip might also include a marriage proposal.

"Hey, Mia . . ." Donny Junior lingered a minute. "I just wanna say I really appreciate what you did for us." She'd never seen Jamie's cocky older brother so serious. "This whole scene has been a real kick in the butt for me. I'm gonna be a different person. Settle down even." His eyes followed Olivia, who was snapping photos of Guadalupe holding her favorite butcher knife in front of the Christmas tree. "She's super hot."

"She's almost half your age, Donny. She's twenty."

"Awesome," Little Donny said. "She's legal."

Mia shook her head in frustration. "Donny, do yourself and the women of the world a favor. Crack open a dictionary and look up the definition of *different*."

The last of the partygoers trickled out, leaving behind only Olivia, Mia, Shane, and Elisabetta, who was napping in the upstairs bridal lounge until Mia was ready to go. "I had fun tonight," Olivia said. "Everyone was so nice." She yawned.

"I'm glad, honey," Mia said. "You must be really jet-lagged. Why don't you and Shane take off? I can finish up here."

"I won't let my brother leave you alone to handle all this."

Shane gave his sister an approving nod. "Thanks, Liv. If you hadn't said that, I would have."

"I guess I'm outnumbered." Mia smiled. "Tell you what. There's a daybed in the downstairs bridal lounge.

Why don't you nap until we're done, like my grand-mother?"

"Okay."

"I'll show you where it is," Shane said.

"I can find it myself. You stay here and clean up with Mia."

Olivia left to rest. Mia and Shane transferred dirty plates and glasses into rental company crates and tossed trash into heavy black garbage bags. "Great party tonight," Shane said.

"I thought it went really well. Between having my parents in the same room, along with my dad's new girl-friend, and a detective at a party with a capital-F Family, it could've been a train wreck."

"It's the holidays. Makes everyone magnanimous."

"Ooh, big word," Mia teased.

"Yeah, my college kid sister throws 'em at me some-times. For my edumacation."

He put a dumb spin on the fake word that made Mia laugh. She put down her garbage bag and stretched. "I'm pretty tired myself. Long day." She glanced above her. "Mistletoe. Darn. I totally forgot to tell everyone about it. Oh, well." She jumped up to pull it down but missed. "I can't reach."

"I'll get it."

Shane came over and reached above Mia's head. Their bodies touched. He dropped his arm and encircled her waist, pulling Mia close to him. A warmth coursed through her. Shane put a finger under Mia's chin, lifted her face to his, and gently kissed her. Mia responded and the two fell into each other's arms with a passion born of months spent fighting it back.

"I've been wanting to do this since we met," Shane managed to share.

"And I've been wanting you to."

They continued embracing, overwhelmed with attraction and desire. Finally—reluctantly—they separated, but Shane kept his arms around Mia's waist. Happy beyond words, Mia rested her head against his chest. He stroked her hair. "Merry Christmas, Mia."

"Merry Christmas, Shane." She sighed. "Best. Present. *Ever.*"

RECIPES

Three Cheese Baked Rigatoni

Ingredients:

1 lb. rigatoni, cooked according to instructions
2 T. olive oil, divided
½ cup chopped onion
2-3 tsp. minced garlic (depending on how much you like
    garlic. If you love it, feel free to add more)
½ cup chopped basil
1 large can (28 oz.) diced tomatoes
1 T Italian seasoning, plus 1 tsp. separated
1 can tomato sauce
1 T. tomato paste
2 cups part-skim mozzarella
¼ oz provolone, thinly sliced
¼ cup grated Parmesan Reggiano

Add a tablespoon of olive oil to a large, heavy pot, like a Dutch oven. Cook onion and garlic until the onion is translucent—a minute or two. Add the basil and cook for a minute. Then add the diced tomatoes, tomato sauce, Italian seasoning, and tomato paste. Bring to a boil, then reduce the heat to simmer. You can keep the sauce simmering while you make the pasta. Just make sure to stir it now and then.

While the rigatoni is cooking, preheat oven to 350 degrees.

Cook rigatoni according to package instructions for al

dente pasta. Drain and add to the sauce pot. Stir to combine the pasta and sauce.

Transfer pasta mixture to a 9 x 13 baking dish.

Combine mozzarella, Parmesan, and 1 tsp. seasoning in a bowl. Cover the pasta with a layer of provolone, then spoon the mozzarella mixture on top of the provolone, spreading it out so it covers all the pasta.

Bake for approx. ten or fifteen minutes, until the cheese has fully melted. Serve immediately with fresh Italian bread to sop up any leftover sauce.

Serves 6–8.

NOTE: Feel free to substitute your favorite type of pasta, like ziti or penne. Just make sure to cook whatever alternate you choose to its specific cooking time.

Shrimp, Crab, and Artichoke Cavatelli

NOTE: the mix of ingredients—minus the pasta—are made ahead of time and marinated from one hour to overnight.

Ingredients:

1 lb. cooked crabmeat, picked clean of shell and carti-
   lage
1 cup cooked shrimp, medium in size
4 canned artichokes
Liquid from canned artichokes
1 shallot
2 cloves garlic, peeled and minced
½ cup chopped parsley
1 cup chopped fresh basil
¼ cup extra virgin olive oil, plus 1 tsp. separated
Juice of two lemons
⅛ tsp. salt; more to taste if necessary
Ground pepper to taste
½ lb. cavatelli (or similar pasta)

Dice shallot. Add the teaspoon of oil to a skillet or sauté pan and sauté the shallot until it is soft. Set aside to cool.

In a medium-sized bowl, gently mix the crab, shrimp, garlic, lemon juice, parsley, cooled shallot, and basil. In a smaller bowl, whisk the olive oil, artichoke liquid, and salt together. Pour the liquid into the shellfish mixture and gently stir to combine. Cover the bowl and refrigerator for at least an hour but preferably overnight.

When you're ready to prepare the dish for dinner, re-move the shellfish mixture from the refrigerator and

bring to room temperature. Follow the directions that ac-
company your cavatelli or choice of pasta to cook it until
it's al dente. Drain the pasta and toss with the shellfish
mixture. Serve immediately. You can put out salt, pepper,
and lemon juice for any guest who wants to add a dash to
their meal, but no cheese. *Niente formaggio sul pesce*, as
the Italians say. No cheese on fish.

Serves 4–6.

Almond Florentine Lace Cookies

Ingredients:

$2/3$ cup unsalted butter
$1/2$ cup white sugar
$1/2$ cup brown sugar
$1/4$ cup heavy cream
1 tsp. almond extract
$2/3$ cup flour
$1/4$ tsp. salt
1 and $1/4$ cup sliced almonds
1 cup semisweet chocolate chips (optional)

Preheat the oven to 375 degrees.

Melt the butter in a large saucepan, making sure not to burn it. Remove the pan from the heat and one at a time, mix into the butter the white sugar, brown sugar, cream, almond extract, flour, salt, and almonds. I find a wooden spoon works best for mixing these ingredients.

Cover two cookie sheets with parchment paper. Drop the batter onto the paper by teaspoonfuls, leaving plenty of room—around six cookies to a sheet instead of the usual nine or twelve.

*IMPORTANT: At least some of the cookies **will melt together**. It's inevitable. Don't panic. Once the cookies cool and harden—and trust me, they will—you can use a knife to break them apart. Cookies that are cooked for around five minutes will have a pliable, chewy texture. Cookies cooked six to seven minutes will be crispy. Be careful not to burn them around the edges. This can happen when you begin to reach the seven-minute mark. To cool the cookies, I gently lift the parchment paper they're* *resting on and place it on our kitchen counter. I add another sheet of parchment to the cookie tray and continue baking the cookies until I've used up all the batter.*

If you want to add chocolate to your cookies, wait until they've cooled and then melt the cup of chocolate morsels either over a double boiler or in the microwave. (If you're using the microwave, nuke the drops for thirty seconds, then increments of fifteen seconds so you don't burn the chocolate.) Dip a fork in the melted chocolate and drizzle or pull it across each cookie.

Makes 24—36 cookies, depending on size.

Rummy Tiramisu

I am that rare person who is not a fan of coffee. To put it mildly. Tiramisu is about the only thing coffee-flavored I'll even take a bite of. Since coffee is such an important ingredient in this delicious dessert, my personal attempt not to let it overwhelm the favor is to increase the amount of rum in this recipe. If you prefer, you can use more coffee and less rum.

Important recipe notes: Many tiramisu recipes, including this one, utilize uncooked eggs. According to author and Cinnamon Sugar and a Little Bit of Murder blogger Kim Davis, if you can't find pasteurized eggs, you can pasteurize them at home using this method: place eggs in a saucepan and fill with water to cover completely. Over medium-low heat, bring the water to 140 degrees F. A digital thermometer is most accurate. Maintain the water temperature at 140 degrees for 3 minutes, reducing heat on the stove if necessary. Immediately remove eggs from hot water and submerge in ice water. Store in refrigerater if not using immediately. This recipe also calls for the tiramisu to be chilled overnight or for at least six hours.

Ingredients:

6 eggs, separated into yolks and whites
½ cup white sugar, divided into two ¼ cups
1 lb. mascarpone cheese
1 cup black coffee
¾ cup rum
48 ladyfinger cookies, sturdier ones if possible

¼ cup heavy cream
4 T. cocoa powder
½ cup ground or shaved semi-sweet chocolate

Beat the egg yolks and a ¼ cup sugar together on medium-high speed until they are creamy. Add the mascarpone cheese and beat on medium-high speed until so well-combined the mixture is smooth. Transfer to a large bowl and wash out the first bowl.

In the clean bowl, beat the whipped cream on heavy speed until soft peaks form. Gently fold the whipped cream into the mascarpone-yolk mixture. Wash out the bowl again.

In the clean bowl, whisk the egg whites with an electric mixer on medium-high speed until stiff peaks form, then whisk in the second ¼ cup of sugar. Gently fold the whipped egg whites into the other mixture until all the ingredients are well-combined.

Combine the coffee and rum in a wide, shallow bowl. Quickly dip the ladyfingers in the liquid one at time— quickly, because you do not want to soak them. They'll disintegrate, especially if they're the small, light kind. Line the ladyfingers in a single layer at the bottom of a 13"x 9" baking dish. Spread half the mascarpone mixture evenly over the ladyfingers. Sprinkle half the cocoa powder and ground chocolate over this layer, and then repeat: another layer of dipped ladyfingers, evenly covered with the remaining mascarpone mixture, and sprinkled with the rest of the cocoa powder and chocolate.

Cover the dish and refrigerate overnight or for at least six hours.

Serves 8–12. Or even 16! It's rich.

Christmas Frittata

Ingredients:

2 T. chopped pepperoncini salad peppers
1 (2¼ oz.) can sliced black olives, drained
1 cup chopped fresh spinach (you can also use frozen
 spinach, but it must be defrosted and drained)
½ red bell pepper, finely chopped
1 cup shredded mozzarella
4 oz. Provolone cheese, diced
¼ cup grated Parmesan cheese
1 cup diced hard salami (optional)
½ cup chopped fresh basil
¼ cup chopped green onions
½ cup chopped mushrooms

1 T. olive oil
2 T. cooking sherry
1 T. red wine vinegar
1 tsp. Italian seasoning
1 tsp. minced garlic

6 eggs
1½ cups egg whites
¼ tsp. salt
¼ tsp. pepper

Mix the first eleven ingredients (through the mushrooms) in a large mixing bowl. In a separate bowl, whisk
together the olive oil, sherry, red wine vinegar, garlic, and
Italian seasoning. Pour onto the vegetable and cheese
mixture and toss to combine well. Cover and chill anywhere from one to twenty-four hours.

When ready to prepare the dish, preheat the oven to 375 degrees. Grease a 9"x13" pan with olive oil. In a medium-size mixing bowl beat the eggs, egg whites, salt, and pepper. Pour the egg mixture into the chilled ingredients and stir them together until well combined. Pour the mixture into the greased pan, making sure the ingredients are evenly distributed.

Bake for 15–25 minutes, until the eggs are firm. If they're not firm, keep cooking until they are.

Serves 6–8.

Mushroom Pasta alla Carbonara

This vegetarian take on a delicious iconic dish was inspired by Rachael Ray's recipe for traditional pasta carbonara. Meat eaters, feel free to substitute ⅓ cup pancetta for the mushrooms. Or include both.

Ingredients:

1 lb. uncooked fettucine or another long pasta, like linguini or spaghetti
3 T. olive oil
2 tsp. minced garlic
¼ tsp. salt
¼ tsp. black pepper
½ cup dry white wine
3 large egg yolks
10 oz. cremini or white mushrooms, coarsely chopped
1 cup grated Parmigiano Reggiano cheese
1 cup grated Pecorino Romano cheese
¼ cup Italian parsley, finely chopped
1 and ½ cup saved pasta water, separated

Follow the instructions to cook your pasta in a large pot of boiling water, but cook it one minute less than instructed so that it's al dente. Save 1 and ½ cups of the cooking water when you drain the pasta and set it aside.

Heat the olive oil in a large, deep skillet or Dutch oven. Add the garlic and mushrooms and cook over medium heat for several minutes, stirring so they don't stick to the bottom of the pan. Add the wine and stir to incorporate. Cook for a few more minutes, then reduce the heat to low.

In a medium bowl, whisk together the three egg yolks. Whisk in one cup of the reserved pasta water.

Add the pasta to the mushroom mixture and toss to combine the ingredients. Remove the pan or pot from the heat and add the yolk liquid. Toss well to combine. Add the cheese and parsley and toss all the ingredients well to make sure the pasta is coated. If you need additional liquid, you can add some or all of the ½ cup of pasta water.

Serve immediately. This dish goes great with garlic bread and a side salad.

Servings: 4–6.

Christmas *Tarrali*

Recipe by Lucia DiRico Tenaglia

My cousin Lauren Testa follows her late grandmother Lucia's recipe to make these tasty cookies that our family's Italian hometown of Orsogna is famous for. "These are the traditional Christmas *tarrali* that were made in Orsogna every year," Lauren says. "As I understand it, the filling was made with the crushed grapes left over from making wine."

Lauren substitutes grape preserves for those leftover wine grapes, but the end result couldn't be more delicious. The recipe that follows is in Lauren's own words.

Ingredients for Tarrali *Filling:*

4 jars (2 lbs. each) grape preserves
1 lb. black raisins (optional)
½ lb. semisweet chocolate chips
2 lbs. walnuts, chopped
1 lb. roasted almonds, finely chopped
2 pkgs. (7 oz. each) Stella D'oro Egg Biscotti (ground
   very fine, like powder)
Rind of 1 large orange
1 T. cinnamon

In a large pot, add grape preserves, raisins, and cinnamon. Bring to a boil, stirring constantly to prevent burning (approx. ½ hour). Add chocolate, walnuts, almonds, and orange rind. Stir and let everything boil for five minutes, then stir in the Stella D'oro biscuits. Lower the heat and cook for another ½ hour, stirring to prevent burning.

Ingredients for Tarrali *Dough:*

5 lbs. flour (plus extra flour to add as needed)
2 dozen jumbo eggs
2 T. vanilla
2 T. lemon juice
4 cups vegetable oil
4 T. baking powder
Rind of 1 lemon

Beat eggs, lemon juice, grated lemon rind, vanilla, sugar, oil, and baking powder. Slowly add flour until you can work the dough on a table or work board. The dough should be the consistency of a rolled cookie dough that you can roll without it sticking. (Sprinkle flour on the work area and rolling pin if the dough does get sticky.)

Assembly instructions:

To make the *tarrali,* we use a pasta machine to roll out the dough. A rolling pin will work just as well. Roll the dough to the thickness of a nickel. I make a long strip with the pasta machine that is between 5–6 inches wide and 24 inches long. I use a 3-inch round doughnut cutter to make the circles, or the lid from a wide mouth ball jar. Each *tarrali* is filled with about a teaspoon of filling. I use a small ice cream scoop to keep them uniform. Place the filling in the middle of the circle and fold the dough circle in half to make a half-moon shape. Crimp the edges with a fork or ravioli crimper to seal the cookie. To make the rounded *tarrali* shape gently join the two end points of the folded cookie. The shape looks like a tortellini with the small hole in the middle of the cookie. Poke a small air hole in the top of the bulky side of the cookie so the filling doesn't explode out.

Baking instructions:

Preheat your oven to 350 degrees for gas; 300 for electric. Bake tarrali for thirty minutes or until lightly brown. Check them once or twice to prevent burning. After the tarrali have cooled, brush lightly with white wine and sprinkle with sugar.

Servings: makes 120 tarrali cookies.

Note: the recipe for honey phyllo cookies appears in *Long Island Iced Tina* as honey phyllo rollups.

EVENT TIPS

When you're hosting an event at a banquet hall, or any rental facility, skip the decorative confetti. It clogs the facility's vacuum cleaners and if a vacuum cleaner breaks, you might end up being charged for it. You might also incur extra cleanup costs for the time it takes to remove the confetti from the premises.

Throwing a holiday party? White poinsettias make an elegant, nondenominational favor. They're widely available in December and usually quite affordable. But think twice before using them as table centerpieces. The large size that makes these lovely plants an impressive favor blocks the view of guests seated across from each other. This is something to keep in mind for any event. Think horizontal, not vertical, for all centerpieces.

ACKNOWLEDGMENTS

I'm grateful to my terrific agent, Doug Grad, who found the perfect home for the Catering Hall Mysteries, as well as the perfect editor, John Scognamiglio. *Mille grazie* to both of you, and to Larissa Ackerman, Lou Malcangi, Lauren Jernigan, and everyone at Kensington. You are all absolutely wonderful to work with, offering energy and enthusiasm that inspire me.

A shout-out to my fabulous partners in crime (writing) at chicksonthecase.com: Lisa Q. Mathews, Leslie Karst, Vickie Fee, Cynthia Kuhn, Becky Clark, Kathy Valenti, and Jennifer Chow, as well as awesome emeritus Mariella Krause and Kellye Garrett. Vickie gets a special shout-out for fact-checking my Catholicism! More love to my fellow eleven members of Cozy Mystery Crew, especially fearless leader and fellow Kensington author Libby Klein. And even more love to the booksellers, bloggers, and reviewers who toil away to support us, in many cases their only payment being our undying gratitude. I'm talking to you, Dru Ann Love, Mark Baker, Lesa Holstine, Lisa Kelly, Sandra Murphy, Kristopher Zgorski, Lori Lewis Ham and Kings River Life, Anne Saller, Debbie Mitsch, John McDougall, Liz Donatelli, and Debra Jo Burnette—profuse apologies but much love to whoever I missed. Not only have you rewarded me with kind words, some of you have also rewarded me with treasured friendships.

As always, I have to thank husband Jer and daughter Eliza for their endless patience. And a special thank you goes to Astoria, Queens. *Grazie di tutto*, Astoria. I miss you.

Connect with U(s)

Visit us online at
KensingtonBooks.com
to read more from your favorite authors, see books
by series, view reading group guides, and more.

Join us on social media

for sneak peeks, chances to win books and prize packs,
and to share your thoughts with other readers.

Tell us what you think!